EDGAR RICE BURROUGHS

Perhaps the most famous character this extraordinary writer ever created is "Tarzan"—Tarzan of the Apes—so familiar and beloved a figure in the hearts of young and old the world over that he needs no introduction.

While thunder crashes and lightning spikes the gloom of a passing storm, The Ape Man, sheltering under a forest giant, hears the drone of an aircraft passing overhead, circling, searching for a place to land, and he pities the unknown pilot. For Tarzan knows the land lies all about him in miles of unbroken jungle, protecting the country of the Kuvuru—a mysterious tribe said to have the secret of eternal youth.

For years the Kuvuru have been stealing young women from many different tribes. Holding the Kuvuru in superstitious dread, the bereaved families have been unwilling to do anything—until one of the daughters of the Waziri is taken and Tarzan hears about it! Now, with the storm over, Tarzan sets out to find the *kraal* of the Kuvuru— while only a few miles away, Jane and her companions are fighting for their lives where they have crash landed in the dense and teeming jungle . . .

The Novels of Edgar Rice Burroughs

(Published in Book Form)

* Available in 50¢ Authorized Editions from Dept. CS, Ballantine Books, Inc., 101 Fifth Ave., New York 3, N. Y. (Please add 5¢ per book postage on orders for less than 4 books.)

† Available in permanent, clothbound, illustrated editions from Dept. BB, Canaveral Press, 63 Fourth Avenue, New York 3, N. Y. For full particulars, please contact Canaveral Press.

Tarzan's Quest

EDGAR RICE BURROUGHS

Ballantine Books
New York

Publishing History: First published serially in *The Blue
Book Magazine* from October, 1935, to March, 1936,
under title of "Tarzan and the Immortal Men."
First published in book form under title of "Tarzan's Quest," 1936.
Edgar Rice Burroughs, Inc. Authorized Edition published by
Ballantine Books, Inc.

FIRST PRINTING: MARCH 1964

Cover Painting: Dick Powers

Ballantine Books are distributed in the U.S.A. by
Affiliated Publishers, a division of Pocket Books,
Inc., 630 Fifth Avenue, New York 20, N. Y.

Printed in the United States of America

BALLANTINE BOOKS, INC.
101 Fifth Avenue, New York 3, N. Y.

CONTENTS

1

The Princess Sborov

"MY DEAR Jane, you know everyone."

"Not quite, Hazel; but one sees everyone in the Savoy."

"Who is that woman at the second table to our right?—the one who spoke so cordially. There is something very familiar about her—I'm sure I've seen her before."

"You probably have. Don't you remember Kitty Krause?"

"O-oh, yes; now I recall her. But she went with an older crowd."

"Yes, she's a full generation ahead of us; but Kitty'd like to forget that and have everyone else forget it."

"Let's see—she married Peters, the cotton king, didn't she?"

"Yes, and when he died he left her so many millions she didn't have enough fingers to count 'em on; so the poor woman will never know how rich she is."

"Is that her son with her?"

"Son, my dear! That's her new husband."

"Husband? Why, she's old enough to——"

"Yes, of course; but you see he's a prince, and Kitty always was—er—well, ambitious."

"Yes, I recall now—something of a climber; but she climbed pretty high, even in aristocratic old Baltimore, with those Peters millions."

"But she's an awfully good soul, Hazel. I'm really very fond of her. There isn't anything she wouldn't do for a friend, and underneath that one silly complex of hers is a heart of gold."

"And kind to her mother! If anyone ever says *I'm* good-hearted, I'll——"

"S-sh, Hazel; she's coming over."

The older woman, followed by her husband, swooped down upon them. "My darling Jane," she cried, "I'm so glad to see you."

"And I'm glad to see you, Kitty. You remember Hazel Strong, don't you?"

"Oh, not of *the* Strongs of Baltimore! Oh, my dear! I mean I'm just—how perfectly wonder—I must present my husband, Prince Sborov. Alexis, my very, very dearest friends, Lady Greystoke and Miss Strong."

"Lady Tennington now, Kitty," corrected Jane.

"Oh, my dear, how perfectly wonderful! Lady Greystoke and Lady Tennington, Alexis, dear."

"Charmed," murmured the young man. His lips smiled; but the murky light in his deep eyes was appraising, questioning, as they brooded upon the lovely face of Jane, Lady Greystoke.

"Won't you join us?" invited the latter. "Please sit down. You know it's been ages, Kitty, since we had a good visit."

"Oh, how perfectly won—oh, I'd love to—I mean it seems—thank you, Alexis dear—now you sit over there."

"Why, Kitty, it must be a year since I have heard anything of you, except what I have read in the newspapers," said Jane.

"At that, you might be very well informed as to our goings and comings," remarked Sborov, a little ironically.

"Yes, indeed—I mean—we have a whole book filled with newspaper clippings—some of them were horrid."

"But you kept them all," remarked the prince.

"Oh, well," cried Princess Sborov, "I mean—I suppose one must pay for fame and position; but these newspaper people can be so terribly horrid."

"But what have you been doing?" inquired Jane. "Have you been back home again? I'm sure you haven't been in London for a year."

"No, we spent the whole year on the continent. We had a perfectly wonderful time, didn't we, Alexis dear? You see it was last Spring in Paris that we met; and dear, dear Alexis just swept me off my feet. He wouldn't take no for an answer, would you, darling?"

"How could I, my sweet?"

"There, you see, isn't he won—and then we were married, and we've been traveling ever since."

"And now, I suppose, you are going to settle down?" asked Jane.

"Oh, my dear, no. You never could guess what we're planning on now—we are going to Africa!"

"Africa! How interesting," commented Hazel. "Africa! What memories it conjures."

"You have been to Africa, Lady Tennington?" inquired the prince.

8

"Right in the heart of it—cannibals, lions, elephants—everything."

"Oh, how perfectly wonder—I mean how thrilling—and I know that Jane knows all there is to know about Africa."

"Not quite all, Kitty.'"

"But enough," interposed Hazel.

"I'm going down myself, shortly," said Jane. "You see," she added, turning to Prince Sborov, "Lord Greystoke spends a great deal of time in Africa. I am planning on joining him there. I have already booked my passage."

"Oh, how perfectly wonderful," exclaimed the princess. "I mean, we can all go together."

"That is a splendid idea, my dear," said the prince, his face brightening.

"It would be lovely," said Jane, "but you see, I am going into the interior, and I am sure that you——"

"Oh, my dear, so are we."

"But, Kitty, you don't know what you're talking about. You wouldn't like it at all. No comforts, no luxuries; dirt, insects, smelly natives, and all kinds of wild beasts."

"Oh, but my dear, we are—I mean, we really are. Shall I tell Lady Greystoke our secret, darling?"

The prince shrugged. "Why not? She could have little more than a passing interest."

"Well, maybe some day she will. We all grow old, you know, my dear."

"It seems incredible to think——" murmured Alexis half to himself.

"What did you say, darling?" interrupted his wife.

"I was just going to say that Lady Greystoke might think the story incredible."

"Now you must tell me," said Jane. "You have my curiosity aroused."

"Yes, indeed, do tell us," urged Hazel.

"Well, my dears, you see it was like this. We have been doing a great deal of flying the past year, and it's perfectly wonderful. We just love it, and so I bought an aeroplane in Paris last week. We flew to London in it; but what I was going to tell you is about our pilot. He is an American, and he has had the most amazing experiences."

"I think he is what you call a rackster in America," said Alexis.

"You mean a gangster, my dear," corrected the princess.

"Or a racketeer," suggested Hazel.

"Whatever he is, I do not like him," said Alexis.

"But, my dear, you have to admit that he is a good pilot. I mean that he is perfectly wonder—and he has been to Africa and had the most frightful experiences.

"The last time he was there, he got track of a witch-doctor who possesses the secret of an amazing formula for renewing youth and inducing longevity. He met a man who knows where the old fellow lives way in the interior; but neither of them had money enough to organize an expedition to go in search of him. He says that this will make people as young as they wish to be and keep them that way forever. Oh, isn't it wonderful?"

"I think the fellow is a scoundrel," said Alexis. "He has induced my wife to finance this expedition; and when he gets us down there in the interior, he will probably slit our throats and steal our jewelry."

"Oh, my darling, I am sure you are quite wrong. Brown is the last word in loyalty."

"He may be all of that, but still I don't see why you want to drag me to Africa—the bugs, the dirt; and I do not like lions."

Jane laughed. "Really, you might spend a year in Africa without seeing a lion; and you will get used to the bugs and the dirt."

Prince Sborov grimaced. "I prefer the Savoy," he said.

"You will go with us, dear, won't you?" insisted Kitty.

"Well," hesitated Jane, "I really don't know. In the first place, I don't know where you are going."

"We are going to fly direct to Nairobi and outfit there; and, my dear, to get any place in Africa, you *have* to go to Nairobi first."

Jane smiled. "Well, it happens that that is where I intend going anyway. Lord Greystoke is to meet me there."

"Then it's all settled. Oh, isn't it wonderful?"

"You almost make me want to go," said Hazel.

"Well, my dear, we would be delighted to have you," exclaimed Princess Sborov. "You see, I have a six-passenger cabin plane. There are four of us, and the pilot and my maid will make six."

"How about my man?" asked the prince.

"Oh, my dear, you won't need a man in Africa. You will have a little colored boy who will do your washing and cooking and carry your gun. I read about it time and time again in African stories."

"Of course," said Hazel, "it's awfully sweet of you; but I really couldn't go. It's out of the question. Bunny and I are sailing for America Saturday."

"But *you'll* come with us, Jane dear?"

"Why, I'd like to, Kitty, if I can get ready in time. When do you start?"

"We were planning on going next week; but, of course, I mean—if——"

"Why, yes, I think I can make it all right."

"Then it's settled, my dear. How perfectly won—we'll take off from the Croydon Airdrome next Wednesday."

"I'll cable Lord Greystoke today; and Friday I am giving a farewell dinner for Lord and Lady Tennington, and you and Prince Sborov must be there."

2

Sound Above the Storm

THE LORD of the Jungle rose from a crude, leaf-covered platform constructed in the crotch of two branches of a mighty patriarch of the jungle. He stretched luxuriously. The slanting rays of the morning sun mottled his bronze body through the leafy canopy that stretched interminably above him.

Little Nkima stirred and awoke. With a scream, he leaped to the shoulder of the ape-man and encircled his neck with his hairy arms.

"Sheeta!" screamed the monkey. "He was about to spring on little Nkima."

The ape-man smiled. "Nkima has been seeing things in his sleep," he said.

The monkey looked about him among the branches of the trees and down at the ground below. Then, seeing that no danger threatened, he commenced to dance and chatter; but presently the ape-man silenced him and listened.

"Sheeta comes," he said. "He is coming up wind toward us. We cannot smell him but if Manu had the ears of Tarzan, he could hear him."

The monkey cocked an ear down wind and listened. "Little Nkima hears him," he said. "He comes slowly." Presently the sinuous, tawny body of the panther forced its way through the brush and came into view below them.

"Sheeta is not hunting," said Tarzan. "He has fed and he is not hungry." And thus reassured, Nkima commenced to hurl invectives at the savage beast below them. The great cat paused and looked up, and when he saw Tarzan and Nkima he bared his fangs in an angry snarl. But he started on again, for he had no business with them.

Feeling secure in the protection of Tarzan, little Nkima

11

waxed belligerent, as he always did under similar circumstances when the possibility of danger seemed remote. He hurled at his hereditary enemy every jungle epithet that he could put his tongue to, but as these seemed to make no impression upon Sheeta he leaped from Tarzan's shoulder to a trailing vine that bore a soft, ill-smelling fruit, and gathering one of these he hurled it at the panther.

By accident, his aim proved true; and the missile struck Sheeta on the back of the head.

With an angry snarl, the beast wheeled about and started toward the tree that harbored his annoyer. Screaming with terror, little Nkima fled upwards to the safety of the smaller branches that would not bear the weight of the great cat.

The ape-man grinned up after the fleeing monkey and then glanced down at the angry panther. A low, growling "Kreegah" rumbled from his throat, and the other beast below returned an answering growl. Then it turned and slunk away into the jungle, rumbling in its throat.

The ape-man was returning leisurely from an excursion into a remote district of the great forest, far from his own haunts.

He had heard strange rumors, and he had gone to investigate them. From deep in the interior, on the borders of a tractless waste that few men had entered and from which some had never returned alive, had come a strange and mysterious story since so long before the memory of living man that the facts had become interwoven with the legends and the folklore of the tribes inhabiting this borderland to such an extent that they had come to be accepted as something inevitable and inescapable; but recently the disappearance of young girls had increased to an alarming extent and had occurred in tribes far removed from the mysterious country.

But when Tarzan investigated and sought to solve the mystery, he was balked by the fear and superstition of the natives. So fearful were they of the malign, mysterious power that snatched their young girls from them, that they would give Tarzan no information or assist him in any way to aid them; and so, disgusted, he had left them to their fate.

After all, why should the ape-man concern himself? Life to the jungle-bred is a commodity of little value. It is given and taken casually as a matter of course. One loves or kills as naturally as one sleeps or dreams. Yet the mystery of the thing intrigued him.

Young girls, always between the ages of fourteen and twenty, vanished as in thin air. No trace of them ever was seen again. Their fate remained an unsolved mystery.

But by now Tarzan had relegated the matter to the background of his thoughts, for his active mind could not long

12

concern itself with a problem that did not closely concern him and which at any event seemed impossible of solution.

He swung easily through the trees, his alert senses conscious of all that transpired within their range. Since Sheeta had passed up wind, he had known by the decreasing volume of the great cat's spoor that the distance between them was constantly increasing—proof that Sheeta was not stalking him. From far away, muted by the distance, sounded the roar of Numa, the lion; and deeper in the forest Tantor, the elephant, trumpeted.

The morning air, the sounds and smells of his beloved jungle, filled the ape-man with exhilaration. Had he been the creature of another environment, he might have whistled or sung or whooped aloud like a cowboy in sheer exuberance of spirit; but the jungle-bred are not thus. They veil their emotions; and they move noiselessly always, for thus do they extend the span of their precarious lives.

Scampering sometimes at his side, sometimes far above him, little Nkima travelled many times the distance of his master, wasting much energy; as, safe in the protection of his benefactor, he insulted all living things that came his way.

But presently he saw his master stop and sniff the air and listen, and then little Nkima dropped silently to a great bronzed shoulder.

"Men," said Tarzan.

The little monkey sniffed the air. "Nkima smells nothing," he said.

"Neither does Tarzan," replied the ape-man, "but he hears them. What is wrong with the ears of little Nkima? Are they growing old?"

"Now Nkima hears them. Tarmangani?" he asked.

"No," replied Tarzan, "Tarmangani make different sounds —the squeeking of leather, the rattle of too much equipment. These are Gomangani; they move softly."

"We shall kill them," said Nkima.

The ape-man smiled. "It is well for the peace of the jungle that you have not the strength of Bolgani, the gorilla; but perhaps if you had, you would not be so blood-thirsty."

"Ugh, Bolgani," sneered Nkima, contemptuously. "He hides in the thickets and runs away at the first sound that he hears."

The ape-man changed his direction to the right and made a great circle through the trees until presently he reached a point where Usha, the wind, could carry the scent spoor of the strangers to him.

"Gomangani," he said.

"Many Gomangani," exclaimed Nkima, excitedly. "They

13

are as the leaves upon the trees. Let us go away. They will kill little Nkima and eat him."

"There are not so many," replied Tarzan, "no more than the fingers upon my two hands, a hunting party, perhaps. We will go closer."

Moving up on the blacks from behind, the ape-man rapidly closed up the distance between them. The scent spoor grew stronger in his nostrils.

"They are friends," he said. "They are Waziri."

The two jungle creatures moved on in silence then, until they overhauled a file of black warriors who moved silently along the jungle trail. Then Tarzan spoke to them in their own tongue.

"Muviro," he said, "what brings my children so far from their own country?"

The blacks halted and wheeled about, gazing up into the trees from which the voice had seemed to come. They saw nothing, but they knew the voice.

"Oh, Bwana, it is well that you have come," said Muviro. "Your children need you."

Tarzan dropped to the trail among them. "Has harm befallen any of my people?" he asked, as the blacks clustered about him.

"Buira, my daughter, has disappeared," said Muviro. "She went alone toward the river, and that is the last that was ever seen of her."

"Perhaps Gimla, the crocodile—" Tarzan commenced to suggest.

"No, it was not Gimla. There were other women at the river. Buira never reached the river. We have heard stories, Bwana, that fill us with terror for our girls. There is evil, there is mystery in it, Bwana. We have heard of the Kavuru. Perhaps it is they; we go to search for them."

"Their country lies far away," said Tarzan. "I have just come from a place that is supposed to be near it, but the people there are all cowards. They were afraid to tell me where I might find the Kavuru, even though their girls have been stolen by these people for so long that no man can remember when it began."

"Muviro will find them," said the black, doggedly. "Buira was a good daughter. She was not as other girls. I will find those who stole her, and kill them."

"And Tarzan of the Apes will help you," said the ape-man. "Have you found the trail of the thieves?"

"There is no trail," replied Muviro. "That is why we know it was the Kavuru; they leave no trail."

"Many of us think that they are demons," said another warrior.

"Men or demons, I shall find them and kill them," replied Muviro.

"From all that I could learn," said Tarzan, "these Bukena live nearest to the Kavuru. They have lost the most girls. That is the reason it is thought that they live nearest to the Kavuru, but they would not help me. They were afraid. However, we will go first to the kraals of the Bukena. I can travel faster; so I will go ahead. In four marches, perhaps three if nothing detains you, you should be there. In the meantime, it may be that Tarzan will have learned more."

"Now that the big Bwana is with me, my mind is happy again," said Muviro, "for I know that Buira will be found and returned to me, and that those who took her will be punished."

Tarzan glanced up at the skies and sniffed the air. "A bad storm is coming, Muviro," he said. "It is coming from where Kudu, the sun, beds down at night; you will have to trek directly into it, and it will hold you back."

"But it will not stop us, Bwana."

"No," replied Tarzan. "It takes more than Usha, the wind, and Ara, the lightning, to stop the Waziri.

"Already Usha is drawing his veil of clouds across the face of Kudu, hiding him from his people."

Torn and ragged clouds scudded across the sky; and in the distance, far to the West, thunder reverberated. The ape-man remained with his head thrown back, watching the impressive spectacle of the gathering storm.

"It will be a bad storm," he said, musingly. "See how frightened the clouds are. Like a great herd of buffaloes, they stampede in terror, fearful of the roars of the thunder god that pursues them."

The wind now was whipping the topmost branches of the trees. The thunder grew nearer and increased in violence. As the clouds sank thicker across the sky, gloomy darkness settled upon the jungle. Lightning flashed. Thunder crashed terrifically, and then the rain fell. It came in solid sheets, bending the trees beneath its weight; and over all Usha screamed like a lost soul.

The eleven men squatted with shoulders hunched against the beating rain, waiting for the first fury of the storm to spend itself.

For half an hour they sat there, and still the storm raged unabated. Suddenly the ape-man cocked an attentive ear upward, and a moment later several of the blacks raised their eyes to the heavens.

"What is it, Bwana?" asked one, fearfully. "What is it in the sky that moans and whines?"

"It sounds very much like an aeroplane," replied Tarzan,

"but what an aeroplane would be doing here, I cannot understand."

3

Out of Gas

PRINCE ALEXIS poked his head into the pilot's compartment. His face, overcast with a greenish pallor, reflected apprehension, if not actual fright. "Are we in any danger, Brown?" he shouted above the roar of the exhaust and the blast of the propeller. "Do you think you can get us out of here?"

"For God's sake, shut up," snapped the pilot. "Ain't I got troubles enough without you asking fool questions every five minutes?"

The man in the seat beside the pilot looked horrified. "S-s-sh," he cautioned. "You shouldn't speak to his 'ighness like that, my man. It's most disrespectful."

"Nuts," snapped Brown.

The prince staggered back to his seat in the cabin. He almost succeeded in registering offended dignity when a current of air tossed the ship at the moment and threw him off his balance, so that it was a very angry prince who lurched awkwardly into his seat.

"Fasten your safety belt, darling," admonished his princess. "We are apt to turn over at any minute. I mean, really, did you ever see anything so terribly rough? Oh, I wish we had never come."

"So do I," growled Alexis. "I didn't want to come in the first place; and if I ever get my feet on the ground again, the first thing I am going to do is fire that impudent boor."

"I think, under the circumstances," said Jane, "that we really ought to overlook any idiosyncrasy of manner that he may manifest. He's got all the responsibility. He must be under a terrific nervous strain; and, regardless of everything else, I think you will have to admit that so far he has proved himself a splendid pilot."

"Annette, my smelling salts, please," cried Princess Sborov, in a weak voice; "I am sure I'm going to faint. I certainly am."

"Sapristi, what a trip!" exclaimed Sborov. "If it were not

for you, dear lady, I should go crazy. You seem to be the only one in the party with any poise. Are you not afraid?"

"Yes, of course I am afraid. We have been flying around in this storm for what seems an eternity, but getting excited about it won't do us any good."

"But how can you help being excited? How could anyone help being excited?"

"Look at Tibbs," said Jane. "He's not excited. He's as cool as a cucumber."

"Bah!" exclaimed Sborov. "Tibbs is not human. I do not like these English valets—no heart, no feeling."

"Really, my dear," expostulated the princess, "I think he is perfect—a regular gentleman's gentleman."

A vivid flash of lightning shot the dark clouds that enveloped them. Thunder roared and crashed. The ship lurched drunkenly onto one wing and nosed suddenly down. Annette screamed; the Princess Sborov swooned. The plane spun once before Brown could pull her out of it. He righted her with an effort.

"Wh-ew!" he exclaimed.

"My word," said Tibbs.

Princess Sborov was slumped in her chair. Her smelling salts had fallen to the floor. Her hat was over one eye; her hair dishevelled. Alexis made no move to come to her aid.

"You had better look after the princess, Annette," said Jane. "I think she needs attention."

There was no answer. Jane turned to see why the girl had not responded. Annette had fainted.

Jane shook her head. "Tibbs," she called. "Come back here and look after the princess and Annette. I'm coming up to sit with Brown."

Gingerly Tibbs made his way into the cabin, and Jane took the seat beside the pilot.

"That last was a bad one," she said. "I really thought we were through. You handled the ship marvellously, Brown."

"Thanks," he said. "It would be easier if they were all like you. The rest of them get in my hair. Although," he added, "Tibbs ain't so bad. I guess he's too dumb to be scared."

"You are having real trouble with the ship, aren't you, Brown?" she asked.

"Yes," he said. "I didn't want to tell the others. They'd have gone nutty. We've got too much of a load. I told the old lady so before we took off; but she was set on bringing everything but the kitchen sink, and now I can't get no elevation. That's the reason I can't get up above this storm, just wallowing around here in this muck without any idea where we are or which way we're going; and there's mountains in Africa, Miss, some damned high mountains."

"Yes, I know that," replied Jane. "But you must have some idea where we are; you have a compass, and you know your air speed."

"Yes," he said, "I got a compass; and I know my air speed; but there's another thing that the rest of 'em better not know. The compass has gone haywire."

"You mean——?"

"I mean we're just flying blind in this pea soup without a compass."

"Not so good; is it, Brown?"

"I'll say it's not."

"What are we going to do about it?"

"If we could get at the baggage compartment, we could throw all the junk out," he replied; "but we can't, and there you are."

"And in the meantime we may crash into a mountain at any moment, is that it?"

"Yes, Miss," he replied, "or run out of gas and have to come down, which will probably be just as bad as hitting a mountain."

"There's no other way out?" she asked. Her voice was level, her eyes unafraid.

"Well, I've got a little plan I'd like to work," he said, and turned to her with a grin.

"What is it, Brown?"

"Well, we can't get at the junk to throw it overboard; but the prince must weigh about a hundred and fifty pounds. That would help some."

Jane turned her head away to hide a smile, but evidently he saw it.

"I thought you'd like the idea," he said.

"We shouldn't joke about such a thing, Brown," she reprimanded.

"I guess we can't help it," he said. "We both got that American sense of humor."

"Is the petrol—gas really very low, Brown?" she asked.

"Look," he indicated the gauge on the dash. "We're good for about an hour at the outside."

"And no parachutes."

"Nary a chute. Most people don't bother with them on a cabin job."

She shook her head. "It does look bad, doesn't it? But we'd better not tell the others how really bad it is. There is nothing they can do to help themselves."

"Not a thing," he said, with a wry smile, "unless they want to pray."

"I think they've been doing that already."

"What are you going to do—just cruise around until the gas is gone?"

"No, of course not. If I don't find a hole in this mess in half an hour, I'm going to nose down easy and try to get under it. There'll be nothing to it, if we ain't over mountains. That's all I'm afraid of. Then I may find a place where I can get her down, but I'm hoping for a hole. I'd like to look down first."

"Jane! Jane!" It was a plaintive wail from the cabin. "Oh, my dear, where are we? I mean are we all dead?"

Jane looked back. Tibbs had recovered the lost smelling salts and had successfully applied first-aid to the princess. Annette had come to and was sobbing hysterically. The prince sat tense and ashen-faced, beads of perspiration standing upon his forehead. He was quite evidently in a blue funk. He caught Jane's eye.

"Is there any hope?" he asked. "Has Brown said anything?"

"We'll be all right if he can find an opening in the clouds," she replied. "That is what he is looking for."

"If we'd had a decent pilot, we'd never have gotten into this," grumbled the prince. "As I told you, Kitty, you should have hired a good French pilot. These Americans don't know anything about flying; and into the bargain you don't know anything about this fellow, Brown."

"I guess that guy never heard of the Wright Brothers or Lindbergh," grumbled Brown.

"Don't mind what he says," said Jane. "We are all under a terrific nervous strain, and not exactly accountable for what we say or do."

"It doesn't seem to be bothering you much, Miss," said Brown.

"Well, it's just the way we happen to be," she said, "and we can't help that either. Just because I succeed in hiding it, doesn't mean that I am not frightened to death."

"You're sure a good sport," said Brown. "You've got guts, and so I don't mind telling you that I don't feel like no little school girl going to her first picnic. I can think of lots of things I'd rather do than crash in the middle of Africa."

"What did he say?" demanded Sborov. "We are going to crash? Look what you have gotten me into, you old fool," he cried, angrily, turning upon his wife, "you and your rejuvenation and your perpetual youth. Sapristi! You've had your face lifted so many times now that you could be arrested for indecent exposure."

The Princess Sborov gasped. "Why, Alexis!" she exclaimed. Then she burst into tears.

"Oh, why did I ever come?" wailed Annette. "I did not wish to come. I am afraid. I do not want to die. Oh, mon Dieu, save me! Save me!"

"Here, madam, try the smelling salts again," said Tibbs.

"Nice party," remarked Brown. "Perhaps they think I'm enjoying it."

"In great danger, we think mostly of ourselves," said Jane.

"I suppose so. I'm thinking mostly of myself right now; but I'm thinking of you and Annette and Tibbs, too. You're worth saving. As far as the other two are concerned, I'd like to chuck 'em overboard; but I think I read somewhere that there was a law against that."

"Yes, I believe there is," smiled Jane. "But, really, Brown, do you know I have an idea that you are going to get us out of this all right?"

"That's the first encouragement I've had," he replied. "And I'm sure going to try to get us out of this. It all depends upon what's underneath this mess. If there's any ceiling at all, we'll have a chance; and that's what I'm hoping for."

"I'm praying for it."

"I'm going to start down now, Miss. I'll just ease her down slowly."

"At a hundred and fifty miles an hour."

"Well, we won't lose elevation that fast."

The ship struck a down current and dropped a hundred feet, careening wildly. The screams of the Princess Sborov and Annette, the maid, mingled with the curses of Alexis.

Jane gasped. "Well, we went down pretty fast that time," she said.

"But when she drops like that, you can be sure you're not on the ground, anyway. The air has to have some place to go. It can't get through the earth; so they never carry you all the way down."

For tense minutes the two sat in silence. Then suddenly Jane voiced a quick exclamation. "Look, Brown," she cried, "trees! We're below it."

"Yes," he said, "and with five hundred feet to spare but——"

She looked at him questioningly. "We're not much better off, are we? How much gas have you left?"

"Oh, maybe fifteen or twenty minutes, and I don't need to tell you—well, it doesn't look so hot."

"Nothing but forest," she said; "there's not a place to land anywhere."

"We may find an opening, and believe me it won't have to be a Croydon either."

"And if you don't find an opening?"

He shrugged. "We'll just have to set down in the tree tops," he said. "The chances are pretty fair that we won't all be killed, Miss." He turned and looked back in the cabin. "Tibbs, get into a seat and fasten your safety belt. Put your wraps and pillows in front of your faces. I am going to make a forced landing in a few minutes. I will tell you when. If you pad your faces, you may not get hurt at all."

Nobody made any reply. The princess moaned, and Annette sobbed.

"There's a terrific wind, isn't there?" said Jane. "Look at those tree tops bend."

"Yes," he said, "and in a way that may help us. The wind will cut down our ground speed a lot; and if I can hook the tail skid into those trees, we may land on them easy-like and hang there."

"You know those tree tops may be a couple of hundred feet from the ground, or even more?"

"Yes," he said, "I suppose they may, but I don't think we'll go through them; they look too dense. And if I set her down easy, the wings and fuselage will catch and hold her. I think we've got a chance."

The ship skimmed on a few hundred feet above the swaying forest top for several minutes. There was no sign of a clearing; no break in those wildly tossing waves of green.

"We're out of gas now, Miss," said Brown, and mechanically he cut the switch. Then he turned back once more to the cabin. "Hold everything," he said; "I'm going to bring her down."

4

In the Kraal of Udalo

THE SHIP settled toward the madly tossing sea of green foliage below. Blinding rain drove in sheets against the windows of the cabin. Vivid lightning shot the gloom beneath the dark, glowering clouds. Thunder crashed. Straight into the teeth of the gale, Brown nosed down. The force of the wind held the ship until it seemed to hover above the tree tops as the pilot leveled off just above them; and as the ship settled, he brought the tail down sharply. There was a crash of splintering wood, the ripping of torn fabric as the ship nosed down into the swaying, slashing branches. And above the noise of the storm and the crashing of the ship were the screams and curses of the terrified passengers in the cabin.

But at last it was over. With a final ripping, tearing jolt, the ship came to rest.

Then, for a tense and terrible moment, silence.

Brown turned to the girl at his side. "Are you hurt, Miss?" he asked.

"I don't think so," she said; "just dazed. It was terrible, wasn't it?"

He turned then and glanced back into the cabin. The four passengers were hanging in their safety belts in various stages of collapse. "All right back there?" he demanded. "How about you, Annette?" There was a note of greater concern in Brown's voice.

"Oh, mon Dieu!" moaned the French girl. "I am already dead."

The Princess Sborov groaned. "Oh, how horrible! Why doesn't someone do something for me? Why doesn't someone help me? Annette! Alexis! Where are you? I am dying. Where are my smelling salts?"

"It would serve you right," growled Alexis, "dragging me off on a crazy adventure like this. It's a wonder we weren't all killed. If we'd had a French pilot, this would never have happened."

"Don't be so stupid," snapped Jane. "Brown handled the ship magnificently."

Alexis turned upon Tibbs. "Why don't you do something, you idiot? You English and Americans are all alike—stupid, dumb. I wanted a French valet in the first place."

"Yes, sir," said Tibbs. "I am very sorry that you didn't get one, sir."

"Well, shut up and do something."

"What shall I do, sir?"

"Sapristi! How should I know? But do something."

"I am sorry, sir, but I am not a mountain goat nor a monkey. If I unfasten this seat belt, I shall simply land on your head, sir."

"Wait a minute," called Jane. "I'll see what can be done." And she unfastened her belt and climbed up into the cabin.

The ship had come to rest at an angle of about 45 degrees with the nose down, but Jane easily made her way into the cabin; and Brown followed close behind her. She went first to the Princess Sborov.

"Are you really seriously hurt, Kitty?" she asked.

"I am torn in two; I know that all my ribs are broken."

"You got us into this, Brown," snapped Alexis. "Now get us out of it."

"Listen," said the American, "you may be better off in than out, for when we get on the ground I ain't pilot no more. I ain't responsible then, and I won't be taking any of your lip."

"Did you hear that, Kitty?" demanded Alexis. "Would you sit there and let a servant talk to me like that? If you don't discharge him, I will."

Brown snorted. "Don't make me laugh. You didn't hire me, you little runt; and you ain't going to fire me."

"Don't be impudent, my man," cried Alexis, his voice trembling. "You forget who I am."

"No, I don't forget who you are; you ain't nothing. In the country you come from, half the cab drivers are princes."

"Come, come," snapped Jane. "Stop bickering. We must find out if anyone is really injured."

"Get me out of here," wailed Princess Sborov. "I can't stand it any longer."

"It would be foolish to try to get out now," said Jane. "Just look at that storm. We shall be safer and much more comfortable here in the ship while the storm lasts."

"Oh, we'll never get down from here. We are way up in the tops of the trees," wailed Annette.

"Don't worry none, sister," said Brown, reassuringly. "We'll find a way to get down from here when the storm lets up. The ship's lodged tight; she won't fall no farther; so we might as well sit tight like Lady Greystoke says and wait for it to quit raining and blowing."

Tibbs strained his eyes upwards through the window at his side. "It doesn't seem to be clearing any, if I may say so," he remarked.

"These equatorial storms oftentimes end as suddenly as they commence," said Jane. "It may be all over, and the sun out, within half an hour. I've seen it happen a hundred times."

"Oh, it won't ever stop raining; I know it won't," wailed the princess, "and I don't see how we are ever going to get down from here if it does. This is terrible. I mean I wish I'd never come."

"Crying about it now, Kitty, won't do any good," said Jane. "The thing to do is try to make ourselves comfortable and then make the best of it until the storm lets up and we can get down. Here, Brown, get a couple of those seat cushions and put them down here on the floor in front of the princess' chair. Then we'll unfasten her seat belt and she can turn around and sit on the floor with her back against the pilot's compartment."

23

"Let me help, milady," said Tibbs, as he unfastened his belt and slid forward.

"The rest of you had better do the same thing," said Brown. "Unfasten your belts and sit on the floor with your backs against the seat in front of you."

With some difficulty and much sobbing on her part, the Princess Sborov was finally arranged in a more comfortable position; and the others, following Brown's suggestion, disposed themselves as best they could for the wait, long or short, until the storm should subside.

Tarzan and the Waziri hunched in what meager protection they could find until the storm should abate; for, in its fury, it was a force against which it were foolish for man to pit himself unless the need were great.

For awhile Tarzan had heard the roar of the ship's motor, even above the storm. It had been evident to him that the ship was circling, and then gradually the sound had diminished and quickly faded into nothingness.

"Bwana," said Muviro, "were there men up there above the storm?"

"Yes, at least one," replied the ape-man, "above it or in it. In either event, I should not care to be in his place. The forest stretches many marches in all directions. If he were looking for a place to land, I do not know where he would find it."

"It is well to be on the ground," said Muviro. "I do not think that the gods intended that men should fly like birds. If they had, they would have given them wings."

Little Nkima cuddled close to his master. He was drenched and cold and miserable. The world looked very black to Nkima, and there was no future. He was quite sure that it would always be dark, but he was not resigned to his fate. He was merely too crushed and unhappy to complain. But presently it commenced to get lighter. The wind passed on with a last, dismal wail. The sun burst forth, and the crushed jungle arose once more to its full life.

The ape-man arose and shook himself, like a great lion. "I shall start now for Ukena," he said, "and talk with the Bukena. This time, perhaps, they will tell me where the Kavuru dwell."

"There are ways of making them talk," said Muviro.

"Yes," said Tarzan, "there are ways."

"And we will follow on to Ukena," said Muviro.

"If you do not find me there, you will know that I am searching for the Kavuru and Buira. If I need you, I will send Nkima back to guide you to me."

Without further words, without useless good-byes and Godspeeds, Tarzan swung into the dripping trees and disappeared toward the West.

Strange stories had come from the Bukena, and filtered by word of mouth through a hundred tribes to Uziri, the land of the Waziri. They were tales of the Kavuru, tales of a savage, mysterious people, whom no man saw, or seeing, lived to tell. They were demons with horns and tails. Or again, they were a race of men without heads. But the most common report was that they were a race of savage whites, who had reverted to barbarism and went naked in their hidden fastness. One story had it that they were all women, and another that they were all men. But Tarzan knew the distortion that was the fruit of many tongues, and gave little heed to things he heard; only the things that he had seen with his own eyes was he sure of.

He knew that many tribes stole women, but oftentimes these women were seen again. Yet the women that the Kavuru stole were not, and so he was willing to admit that there was some tribe dwelling in a remote fastness that specialized in the stealing of young girls. But many of the other stories he heard, he did not believe.

For instance, there was the fable of the longevity and perpetual youth of the Kavuru. That, Tarzan did not believe, although he knew that there were many strange and unbelievable happenings in the depths of the Dark Continent.

It was a long trek, even for Tarzan, back to the country of the Bukena. The forest was soggy and dripping; the jungle steamed. But of such things and their attendant discomfort, the ape-man took small note. From birth he had become inured to discomfort, for the jungle is not a comfortable place. Cold, heat, danger were as natural to him as warmth and comfort and safety are to you. As you take the one, he took the other, as a matter of course. Even in infancy, he had never whined because he was uncomfortable, nor did he ever complain. If he could better conditions, he did so; if he could not, he ignored them.

Just before dark, Tarzan made a kill; and the fresh meat warmed him and gave him new life, but that night he slept cold and uncomfortable in the dank and soggy forest.

Before dawn he was astir again, eating once more of his kill. Then he swung off swiftly upon his journey, until the good red blood flowed hot through his veins, bringing warmth and a sense of well-being.

But Nkima was miserable. He had wanted to go home, and now he was going back into a strange country that he did not like. He scolded and fretted a great deal; but when the sun came out and warmed him, he felt better; and then he

25

scampered through the trees, looking for whom he might insult.

On the morning of the third day, Tarzan came to the kraal of Udalo, chief of the Bukena.

The sight of the tall, bronzed white, with the little monkey perched upon his shoulder, striding through the gate into the village, brought a horde of blacks jabbering and chattering about him. He was no stranger to them, for he had been there a short time before; and so they were not afraid of him. They were a little awed, however, for tales of the mighty ape-man had reached them even over the great distance that separated Ukena from the land of the Waziri.

Paying no more attention to them than he would have to a herd of wildebeest, Tarzan strode straight to the hut of Udalo, the chief, where he found the old man squatting beneath the shade of a tree, talking with some of the elders of the tribe.

Udalo had been watching the approach of the ape-man along the village street. He did not seem overly pleased to see him.

"We thought the big Bwana had gone away, and that he would not return," said the chief; "but now he is back. Why?"

"He has come to make talk with Udalo."

"He has made talk with Udalo before. Udalo has told him all that he knows."

"This time Udalo is going to tell him more. He is going to tell him where lies the country of the Kavuru."

The old man fidgeted. "Udalo does not know."

"Udalo does not talk true words. He has lived here all his life. The young girls of his tribe have been stolen by the Kavuru. Everyone knows that. Udalo is not such a fool that he does not know where these young girls are taken. He is afraid of what the Kavuru will do to him, if he leads people to their kraal. But he need not be afraid; the Kavuru need not know how Tarzan finds them."

"Why do you want to go to the kraal of the Kavuru? They are bad people."

"I will tell you," said Tarzan. "Buira, the daughter of Muviro, the hereditary chief of the Waziri, has disappeared. Muviro thinks that the Kavuru took her; that is why Tarzan, who is war chief of the Waziri, must find the kraal of the Kavuru."

"I do not know where it is," insisted Udalo, sullenly.

As they talked, warriors had been approaching from all parts of the village, until now Tarzan and the chief had been surrounded by scowling, silent spear-men.

Udalo appeared ill at ease; his eyes shifted restlessly. The whole atmosphere seemed surcharged with suspicion and danger. Even little Nkima sensed it; he trembled as he clung tightly to Tarzan.

"What is the meaning of this, Udalo?" demanded the ape-man, indicating the surrounding warriors, with a nod. "I came in peace, to talk to you as a brother."

Udalo cleared his throat nervously. "Since you were here and went away, there has been much talk. Our people remembered the stories they had heard about the Kavuru. It is said that they are white men who go naked, even as you. We do not know anything about you; you are a stranger. Many of my people think that you are a Kavuru, that you have come to spy upon us and select young girls to steal from us."

"That is foolish talk, Udalo," said Tarzan.

"My people do not think it is foolish talk," growled the chief. "You have come to the kraal of Udalo once too often." He rose slowly to his feet. "You shall not steal any more of our young girls." And with that, he slapped his palms sharply together; and instantly the surrounding warriors leaped upon the ape-man.

5

"The Lion Is Coming!"

I CAN'T stand it any longer," said the princess. "I mean this cramped position is killing me, and it is cold in here; I am nearly frozen."

"What right have you got to whine?" growled Alexis. "You got us into this, you and your aviator." He spat the last word out contemptuously.

"Listen, Prince," said Jane, "you and the rest of us can thank Brown's cool head and efficiency for the fact that we are alive and uninjured. It is little short of a miracle that none of us is hurt. I'll venture to say that there's not one pilot in a thousand who could set this ship down as he did."

"I beg your pardon," said Tibbs, "if I may say so, it has stopped raining."

"And there's the sun," cried Annette, excitedly.

Making her way to the door, Jane opened it and looked down. "We are only fifty feet from the ground," she said, "but we may have a little difficulty getting down—that is, some of us may."

"What in the world are you doing, my dear?" demanded the princess, as Jane commenced to take off her shoes and stockings.

"I am going to have a look around. I want to see if I can get at the baggage compartment. We are going to need some of the stuff in there. I'm afraid we are going to find it mighty uncomfortable on the ground; it may be cold in here, but it will be cold and wet both, down there."

"We might make a fire, madam, if I might be so bold as to suggest it," offered Tibbs.

"Everything is rather wet and soggy, but perhaps we can manage it. It's too bad we haven't gasoline left. That would help a lot."

"There'll be some in the sump in the bottom of the tank," said Brown.

"But why are you taking off your shoes and stockings?" asked the princess.

"It's the only safe way to climb around in trees, Kitty."

"But my dear, I mean—after all, you don't intend to climb around in that tree?"

"Precisely, and that is what you will have to do, too, if you ever want to get down from here."

"Oh, but my dear, I couldn't. I positively couldn't do it."

"We'll help you when the time comes, and see that you don't fall; and while I am looking around, Brown, I wish you and Tibbs would remove all the safety belts and fasten them together into one long strap. It may be necessary to lower the princess to the ground, and a strap will come in handy in getting the luggage down safely."

"You better let me go out and look around, Miss," said Brown; "you might fall."

Jane smiled. "I am used to it, Brown," she said. "You'd probably be in far more danger than I." And then she stepped out onto the crumpled wing and leaped lightly to a nearby branch.

"Great scott, look out, Miss, you'll fall!" shouted Brown.

"Be careful, madam! You'll kill yourself." Tibbs almost showed emotion.

"My dear, I mean, come back," wailed the princess.

Annette screamed and covered her eyes with her palms.

"My dear lady, come back! For my sake, come back!" begged Alexis.

But Jane paid no attention to them, as she took two short steps along the branch that brought her within reach of the baggage compartment. It was not locked, and she quickly opened the door.

"Wh-ew!" she exclaimed. "What a mess. There's a broken

28

branch rammed right up through here. It's a good thing for us it didn't come through the cabin."

"Is everything ruined?" asked Alexis.

"Oh, my no, some of the things must be damaged, but I imagine we can salvage nearly everything; and one of the first things I want to salvage is a pair of shorts. Skirts are bad enough at any time, but in a treetop they are a calamity. What luck! Here is my bag right in front. I won't be but a jiffy, and after I've changed I'll be able to accomplish something."

She opened her bag and selected two or three garments. Then she swung lightly to a lower branch and disappeared from their view beneath the ship.

"Say!" exclaimed Brown, admiringly. "She's as much at home in the trees as a monkey. I never say anything like it."

Alexis clambered to a point from which he could look out of the door. Brown and Tibbs were removing the safety belts and fastening them together.

Alexis looked down and shuddered. "It must be a hundred feet to the ground," he said. "I don't see how we are ever going to make it; and those branches are wet and slippery."

"Take off your shoes and stockings like she did," advised Brown.

"I'm no monkey."

"No?"

"If I might venture to suggest it, sir, we could fasten the strap around you and lower you."

"It will hold a thousand pounds," said Brown; "it's tested for that. It'll sure hold you, but you'd better leave your title behind; that's the heaviest part of you."

"I've stood about enough of your impertinence, fellow," snapped Alexis. "Another word like that from you and I'll—I'll——"

"You'll what?" demanded Brown. "—you and who else?"

"I wish you two would quit quarrelling," said the princess. "I mean, aren't things bad enough as they are without that?"

"My dear, I do not quarrel with servants," said Alexis, haughtily.

"In the first place," said Brown, "I ain't no servant; and in the second place, you'd better not quarrel if you know what's good for you. There's nothing I'd like better than an excuse to smack you on the beezer."

"If you ever dare lay hands on me, I'll——"

"What? Fire me again?" exclaimed Brown. "Now I'll just naturally have to paste you one to learn you your place; then maybe you'll remember that you ain't nothing but a worm,

29

and that if you had a title a block long you'd still be a worm."

"Don't you dare strike me," cried the prince, shrinking back.

"What is the meaning of all this?" Jane stepped lightly into the doorway of the cabin. "I thought I told you two to stop quarrelling. Now before we go any further, I want to tell you something. We're stranded here, the Lord only knows where; there may not be a white man within hundreds of miles; we shall have to depend solely upon our own resources. Quarrelling and bickering among ourselves won't get us anywhere; it will just make our plight all the worse. One of us has got to take charge. It should be a man, and the only man here having any jungle experience, insofar as I know, or who is capable of commanding, is Brown. But there's too much friction between him and the prince; so Brown is out of the question."

"I will take full charge," said Alexis.

"The heck you will!" exclaimed Brown.

"My rank entitles me to the post," insisted Alexis, haughtily.

"You said it," jibed Brown. "You're rank all right."

"No, Alexis, you're out, too," said Jane. "We've got to have someone whom all will obey."

"That just leaves Tibbs, then," said Brown. "Tibbs will suit me all right."

"Oh, dear me, no," cried Tibbs. "Really, if you'll permit me, I couldn't think of assuming so much authority. I—I—well, you know, I haven't been accustomed to it, madam." He turned piteously to Jane. "But you, madam, I am sure that we would all be extraordinarily proud to have you for our leader."

"That is what I was going to suggest," said Jane. "I know the jungle better than any of you, and I am sure there isn't anyone else we could all agree on."

"But it's our expedition," objected Alexis. "We paid for everything; we own the ship and all the supplies; I am the one who should command. Isn't that right, my dear?" He turned to his wife.

"Oh, really, my dear, I mean. I don't know. Since you said those horrid things to me, I am crushed. My world has collapsed around my ears."

"Well," said Brown, "there's no use chewing the fat any more about that. Lady Greystoke is boss from now on, and if there's anybody that don't like it, I'll attend to them."

The Princess Sborov was slumped dejectedly on the floor of the ship, her handkerchief pressed to her eyes. "It doesn't make any difference to me," she said; "I don't care what happens now. I don't care if I die; I hope I do." As she finished, she glanced up, presumably to note the effect of her words upon her listeners, and for the first time since Jane had returned to the ship she saw her. "Oh, my dear," she exclaimed, "what a cute outfit. I mean, it's perfectly ducky."

"Thanks," said Jane, "I'm glad you like it; it's practical, at least." She was wearing shorts, and a leather jacket. Her legs and feet were bare. A figured red scarf, wrapped once around her head, confined her hair and served the purposes of a hat.

"But, my dear, won't you freeze to death?" demanded the princess.

"Well," laughed Jane, "I won't exactly freeze to death, but I shall probably be cold lots of times—one gets used to being either too hot or too cold in the jungle. Now I am going down to look around for a suitable camping place, and you'd all better pray that there's one close by. While I am gone, Brown, you and Tibbs lower the luggage to the ground. Alexis, you go below and receive it; there's got to be someone there to unfasten the strap each time."

"Let Annette do it," growled Alexis. "What do you suppose we've got servants for?"

"Each of us has got to do his share, Alexis," said Jane, quietly, "and there are certain things, the heavier and more dangerous work, that will naturally fall to the men. There are no servants and no masters among us now. The sooner we all realize that, the better off and the happier we are going to be."

Alexis approached the door of the ship gingerly and looked down. "Let Brown go down," he said; "I'll help Tibbs lower the baggage to him." Then he glanced in the direction of the baggage compartment. "How could anyone get out there on that branch," he said, "and do anything? He'd fall and break his neck."

"Ah, can the chatter and go on down, as Lady Greystoke told you to," said Brown. "Say the word, Miss, and I'll toss him down."

"No you won't; you don't dare touch me."

"Then get on over the edge and start down."

"I can't; I'd fall."

"Put the strap around him, Brown," said Jane, "and you and Tibbs lower him to the ground. I'm going along now." And with that, she jumped lightly to a nearby branch and swung down through the leafy foliage toward the ground below.

She breathed the odors of the steaming jungle with a keen delight. The restrictions of ordered society, the veneer of

31

civilization, fell away, leaving her free; and she sensed this new freedom with a joy that she had not felt since she had left the jungle to return to London.

Everything about her reminded her of Tarzan. She looked about her, listening intently. It seemed inevitable that at the next moment she would see a bronzed giant swing down through the foliage to clasp her in his arms; and then, with a sigh and a rueful smile, she shook her head, knowing full well that Tarzan was probably hundreds of miles away, ignorant both of her whereabouts and her plight. It was possible that he might not even yet have received her cable, telling him that she was flying to Nairobi. When he did receive it and she did not come, how would he know where to search for her? They had flown blind for so long that even Brown had no idea how far off their course they had been, nor even the approximate location of their landing place. It seemed quite hopeless that they should expect outside help. Their only hope lay within themselves.

Whatever their situation, she and Brown she felt might reasonably expect to pull through; that is, if they had been alone. But how about the others? Tibbs, she thought, might have possibilities of resourcefulness and endurance. She had her doubts about Alexis. Men of his stamp were oftentimes almost as helpless as women. Annette was young and strong, but temperamentally unfitted for the grim realities of the jungle against which they would have to pit themselves. Her efficiency and even her strength would be lessened by the constant terror in which she would exist. As for Kitty, Jane mentally threw up her hands—hopeless, absolutely hopeless, in the face of any hardship, emergency, or danger. Yes, she felt that she and Brown could pull through; but could they pull the others through? It went without saying that they would not desert them.

Her mind partially occupied with these thoughts, she moved through the lower terrace of the jungle, for so thickly was the ground overgrown with underbrush that she had kept to the lower branches of the trees to make her progress easier.

She did not go far in one direction, because she realized the difficulty of transporting their supplies for any great distance through the heavy undergrowth.

Circling, she sought for an open space, however small, in which they might build a temporary camp; but the jungle appeared to become wilder and less penetrable.

She had completed half the circle, and was on the side of the ship opposite that from which she had descended, when she came unexpectedly upon a game trail.

Immediately her spirits rose, for now they were assured of comparatively easy going and the certainty, almost, that eventually they would find natives.

Before returning to the ship, she followed the trail a short distance, when suddenly she came upon a small stream and, beside it, an opening in the underbrush, perhaps an acre in extent.

Elated, she turned back toward the ship, following the trail to ascertain how close it ran to the point from which the baggage must be transported.

As she turned, she heard a slight rustling in the undergrowth behind her, a sound which her trained ears detected quickly and almost identified. Yet she was not sure.

Nevertheless, she increased her gait, taking quick glances ahead and upward that she might always have an avenue of escape located in the event of sudden necessity.

The sound continued, a little behind her and paralleling the trail along which she moved.

She could hear Brown and Alexis quarrelling with one another and bickering over the handling of the baggage. Alexis was on the ground, and he seemed very close. Of course, she might be mistaken. The thing that she heard might not be what she feared it was; but perhaps it would be as well to warn Alexis before it was too late, and so she called to him.

"What is it?" he demanded, sullenly.

"You had better climb a tree, Alexis. I think a lion is following me. He is very close."

"I can't climb a tree," shouted Alexis. "I can't move through this undergrowth. Help! Brown, help! Do something, somebody!"

"Lower the strap to him and pull him up," shouted Jane. "It may not be a lion; and he may not bother us if it is, but we'd better be on the safe side."

"Hurry up with that strap, you fool," shrieked Alexis.

"There ain't no hurry," Brown replied, tantalizingly; "at least, I ain't in no hurry."

"If you let that lion get me, it'll be murder."

"Oh, I guess he can stand it," replied Brown.

"Hurry up and lower that strap, you murderer."

"Ain't I lowering it, as fast as I can?"

"Oh, I can hear him now; he's right on top of me; he'll get me."

"That is me you hear, Alexis," said Jane, reassuringly.

"Well, what if he does get you?" demanded Brown. "Ain't a lion got to eat? In California they feed them animals that ain't no good; so what are you crabbing about?"

"Hurry now, Brown," cried Jane. "The lion is coming, and he's coming fast."

6

The Ballot of Death

As the Bukena warriors closed in upon him, Tarzan stood with folded arms, ignoring them. He was surrounded by many spears; and he knew that at this instant, if he sought to escape or give battle, a dozen spearpoints would transfix him instantly.

His one hope lay in gaining time, and he felt that he could accomplish this best by feigning indifference.

"Kill the Kavuru!" shouted a woman in rear of the warriors. "They stole my daughter."

"And mine," screamed another.

"Kill him! Kill him!" urged others of the savage throng.

A very old man, who had been squatting beside Udalo, leaped to his feet. "No! No!" he screamed. "Do not kill him. If he be a Kavuru, his people will come and punish us. They will kill many of us and take all of our girls."

Instantly the blacks commenced arguing among themselves. Some insisted upon killing him, others wanted to take him prisoner, while others thought that he should be released to mollify the Kavuru.

As they jabbered, the spearmen in the front rank relaxed their vigilance. Some of them turned around and sought to expound their views to those behind them, and in this circumstance Tarzan thought he saw his chance to escape. With the speed of Ara, the lightning, and the strength of Gorgo, the buffalo, he leaped upon a nearby warrior and holding him as a shield in front of him, charged through the human ring that surrounded him, turning constantly so that no weapon could be directed against him without endangering the life of the black.

So quickly had he acted that the blacks were taken entirely off their guard; and he had won almost to the clear, where he might have made a quick run for the village gate, when something struck him heavily on the back of the head.

When he regained consciousness, he found himself in the dark interior of an evil-smelling hut, his wrists and ankles securely bound.

With the return of consciousness came recollection of what had transpired; and the ape-man could not restrain a slow smile, for it was evident to him that the faction that had been afraid to kill him was more powerful than that which would have taken his life. Once again luck was with him.

For the time being, therefore, he was safe; and so he was certain of escape; for he was so constituted that while life remained in him, he could not conceive a permanent captivity; nor could anything for long shake his confidence in his ability to extricate himself from any predicament that might overtake him; for was he not Tarzan of the Apes, Lord of the Jungle?

Presently he commenced to test the bonds that secured his wrists and ankles. They were very strong and there were a great many strands, and soon he saw that it would be hopeless to attempt to liberate himself. There was nothing to do, therefore, but wait.

Unlike an ordinary man, he did not waste time wondering what his fate would be. Instead, he composed himself as comfortably as he could and fell asleep.

And while he slept, a council of warriors plotted in the council house with Udalo, the chief. It was they who were wondering what Tarzan's fate should be.

The old man who had first warned them against killing their prisoner was still his staunchest defender. He was Gupingu, the witch-doctor. He prophesied that dire calamity would befall them if they harmed this man who, he assured them, was a Kavuru. But there were others who spoke quite as insistently for death.

"If he is a Kavuru," said one of these, "his people will come and punish us as soon as they find that we have attacked him and made him prisoner. If we kill him, he cannot go back to them and tell them; and the chances are that they will never know what became of him."

"Those are true words," said another; "a dead Kavuru is better than a live one."

Then Udalo spoke. "It is not for one man to decide," he said. "The talk of many men is better than the talk of one."

On the ground beside him were two bowls. One contained kernels of corn and the other small, round pebbles. He passed one of these bowls to the warrior upon his right and one to him upon his left. "Let each warrior take a kernel of corn and a pebble—just one of each, not more," he said.

They passed the bowls from hand to hand about the circle; and each warrior took a kernel of corn and a pebble; and when the bowls were returned to Udalo, he set them down beside him and picked up a gourd with a small neck.

"We will pass this gourd around the circle," he said, "and each man shall speak either with a kernel of corn or with a pebble for the life or the death of the stranger. If you wish him to live, put a kernel of corn in the gourd; if you wish him to die, put a pebble."

In silence, the gourd was passed around the grim circle as savage eyes followed it from the tense, painted faces of the warriors.

The dropping of the fateful ballots into the hollow gourd sounded distinctly in every part of the large council-house. At last the gourd completed the circle and came back to Udalo.

There were fully a hundred warriors in the circle; and Udalo could not count to a hundred, but he had an equally certain way of determining the outcome of the voting even though he was unable to determine how many votes were cast upon each side.

He emptied the contents of the gourd upon the ground in front of him. Then with one hand, he picked up a grain of corn and, simultaneously, with the other, a pebble, and placed each in its respective bowl; and this he continued to do as long as there were kernels of corn and pebbles to match one another. But this was not for long, for he soon ran out of corn; and even then there were seventy-five or eighty pebbles left, showing that only a few had voted to spare the life of the ape-man.

Udalo looked up and around the table. "The stranger dies," he said. A savage, sinister shout rose from the assembled warriors.

"Let us go and kill him now," said one, "before the Kavuru can come and find him among us."

"No," said Udalo, "tomorrow night he dies. Thus will the women have time to prepare a feast. Tomorrow night we shall eat and drink and dance, while we torture the Kavuru. Let him suffer as he has made us suffer when he stole our children."

A roar of approval and satisfaction greeted this suggestion.

The council was over. The warriors had returned to their huts. Fires were banked. Silence had fallen upon the village of the Bukena. Even the usually yapping curs were silent. The kraal was wrapped in slumber.

From a hut near the chief's, a figure crept silently into the night. It paused in the shadow of the hut from which it had emerged and looked fearfully about.

Nothing stirred, and silently as a ghostly shadow the figure crept along the village streets.

Tarzan had been awakened by the savage cries from the council-house; and he had lain sleepless for some time because of the discomfort of his bonds, but presently he dozed again.

He was not yet fully asleep when something awakened him —a sound that you or I, with our dull ears, might not have

36

heard—the sound of naked feet creeping slowly and stealthily toward the hut where he lay.

Tarzan rolled over so that he could see the entrance to the
hut, and presently it was filled by a shadowy form. Someone
was entering. Was it the executioner coming to destroy him?

7

The Merry Company

THE LION broke through the underbrush into the trail a
short distance behind Jane. It was then that she called
her warning to Alexis.

At sight of Jane, the lion bared his fangs and growled.
Then he came toward her at a trot, and as he did so the girl
leaped for an overhanging branch. As she caught it, the lion
charged. He leaped for her, and his raking talons barely
missed her bare foot as she drew herself safely out of his
reach. With a hideous growl, he turned and leaped again.

The prince was only a short distance away, but he was hidden by the dense underbrush beneath the ship. The angry
growl sounded very close; the man was paralyzed with terror.

From her position on the branch of the tree, Jane could
see him. "You'd better get out of there, Alexis," she said,
"but don't make any noise. If he hears you, he'll come for
you; he's terribly sore about something—must have missed his
kill last night."

Alexis tried to speak, but no sound came from his throat.
He just stood there trembling, an ashen pallor on his face.

Jane could not see Brown, but she knew that he was directly
above Alexis. "Brown," she called, "drop the end of the strap
to the prince. Fasten it around your body underneath your
arms, Alexis; and Brown and Tibbs will pull you up. I'll try
and keep Numa's attention riveted on me."

The lion was pacing back and forth beneath the tree, glaring hungrily up at the girl.

Jane broke off a small, dead branch and threw it at the
beast. It struck him in the face; and, with a roar, he leaped
again for the branch on which Jane stood.

In the meantime, Brown lowered the end of the strap quickly to Alexis. "Hurry up; fasten it around you," he said. "For
Pete's sake, what's the matter with you? Get a move on."

37

But Alexis just stood there trembling, his teeth chattering, and his knees knocking together.

"Alexis, snap out of it," cried Jane. "You've got to get that belt fastened around you before the lion discovers you. Don't you understand? It's a matter of life and death with you."

"You poor sap," yelled Brown. "Get a move on."

With trembling hands, Alexis reached for the belt, and at the same time he seemed to find his voice and commenced to scream lustily for help.

"Keep still," warned Jane. "The lion hears you; he is looking in your direction now."

"Hurry up, you dumb cluck," shouted Brown.

The lion was tearing through the underbrush, searching for the author of these new sounds. Jane threw another branch at him, but it did not distract his attention. He only growled and started cautiously into the brush.

With fumbling fingers, Alexis was tying the belt about his body.

"Hoist away, Brown," cried Jane; "the lion is coming!"

Brown and Tibbs pulled away lustily, and Alexis rose out of the underbrush.

The lion came steadily on. At last he was directly beneath the terrified man. Alexis, looking down straight into the cruel eyes of the carnivore, voiced a scream of horror.

Slowly, a few inches at a time, Brown and Tibbs were raising Alexis out of harm's way; but still he was perilously close to the great beast. Then the lion rared up to its full height and struck at him. A raking talon touched the heel of the man's shoe; and, with a final scream, Alexis fainted.

Brown and Tibbs redoubled their efforts. The lion dropped back to the ground, gathered himself and sprang. Again he missed, but only by inches; and before he could spring again, Alexis was safely out of his reach.

The two men hoisted the limp body of Sborov to the ship, and with considerable difficulty dragged him into the cabin.

At sight of him, the princess commenced to scream. "He's dead! he's dead! Oh, my darling, and your Kitty was so cross to her Allie."

"For Pete's sake, shut up," snapped Brown. "My nerves are about shot, and anyway the sap isn't dead; he's just scared stiff."

"Brown, how dare you speak to me like that!" cried the princess. "Oh, it's terrible; nobody knows what I'm suffering. I mean, no one understands me; everyone is against me."

"Lord," cried Brown, "a little more of this and we'll all be nuts."

"Excuse me, madam, but he seems to be coming to," said Tibbs; "I think he'll be all right in a minute, mam."

"Do something, Annette," cried the princess. "What are you sitting there for—just like a bump on a log? I mean, where are the smelling salts? Get some water. Oh, isn't it terrible? Oh, darling, Allie, speak to your Kitty."

Alexis opened his eyes and looked about him. Then he closed them and shuddered. "I thought he had me," he said, in a trembling whisper.

"No such luck," said Brown.

"It was a very close call, sir, if I may make so bold as to say so, sir," said Tibbs.

Jane stepped into the cabin doorway. "All right?" she asked. "From the noise you were making, Kitty, I thought something dreadful had happened."

"The Lord only knows what would happen if something really should happen," said Brown, disgustedly. "I'm getting fed up on all this screaming and bellyaching. I never had no royalty in my hair before, but I sure got 'em now."

Jane shook her head. "Be patient, Brown," she said. "Remember this is all new to them, and naturally anyway their nerves are on edge after all that we have passed through."

"Well, ain't the rest of us got nerves, Miss? Ain't we got a right to be upset, too? But you don't hear none of us bawling around like them. I suppose being royal gives 'em the right to be nuisances."

"Never mind, now," said Jane; "you're getting as bad as the others, Brown. The thing that I am interested in just now is what we are going to do about that lion. He may hang around here for hours; and as long as he does, we're just blocked. He's in a nasty mood, and it won't be safe to go down there until we know that he has cleared out. The best thing for us to do is to kill him, as he may hang around this neighborhood waiting for a chance to get some of us. He's an old fellow; and because of that, he may be a man-eater. They get that way when they are too old to bag their regular prey."

"A man-eater!" The Princess Sborov shuddered. "How horrible. I mean, how terribly horrible."

"I think we can get rid of him," said Jane. "You brought rifles, of course, Alexis?"

"Oh, yes, indeed, two of them—high-powered rifles—they'd stop an elephant."

"Good," said Jane, "where are they?"

"They're in the baggage compartment, Miss; I'll get them," said Brown.

"And bring some ammunition, too," said Jane.

"Who's going down there to shoot the horrid thing?" demanded the princess.

"I, of course," said Jane.

"But, my dear," cried the princess, "I mean, you just couldn't."

Brown returned with a rifle. "I couldn't find no ammunition, Miss," he said. "Where is it packed, Sborov?"

"Eh, what?" demanded the prince.

"The ammunition," snapped Brown.

"Oh, ammunition?"

"Yes, ammunition, you——"

The prince cleared his throat. "Well, you see, I—ah"

"You mean you didn't bring any ammunition?" demanded Brown. "Well, of all the——"

"Never mind," said Jane. "If there's no ammunition, there's no ammunition, and grousing about it isn't going to get us any."

"If I may be permitted, I think I can be of assistance, Milady," said Tibbs, not without some show of pride.

"How is that, Tibbs?" asked Jane.

"I have a firearm in my bag, Milady. I will kill the beast."

"That's fine, Tibbs," said Jane; "please go and get it."

As Tibbs was moving toward the doorway, he suddenly stopped. A flush slowly mantled his face; he appeared most uncomfortable.

"What's the matter, Tibbs?" asked Jane.

"I—I had forgotten, Milady," he stammered, "but my bag has already been lowered down there with the bloomin' lion."

Jane could not repress a laugh. "This is becoming a comedy of errors," she cried, "—rifles without ammunition, and our only firearm in possession of the enemy."

"Oh, my dear, what are we going to do?" demanded the princess.

"There's nothing to do until that brute goes away. It's almost too late now anyway to try to make camp; we'll simply have to make the best of it up here for the night."

And so it was that a most unhappy and uncomfortable party shivered and grumbled through the long, dark night—a night made hideous by the roars of hunting lions and the shrill screams of stricken beasts. But at last day broke with that uncanny suddenness that is a phenomenon of equatorial regions.

The moment that it was light enough Jane was out reconnoitering. The lion was gone; and a survey of the surrounding country in the immediate vicinity of the ship, from the lower branches of the trees, revealed no sign of him or any other danger.

"I think we can go down now and start making camp," she said, after she had returned to the ship. "Is most of the baggage down, Brown?"

"All but a few pieces, Miss," he replied.

"Well, get it down as rapidly as possible; and then we'll cut an opening to the trail; it is only a few yards."

"All right, Miss," said Brown. "Come on, your majesty, we'll lower you down to unhook the stuff at the other end."

"You won't lower me down," said Alexis. "I wouldn't go down there alone again for all the baggage in the world."

Brown looked at the man with disgust that he made no effort to conceal. "All right," he said, "you stay up here and help Tibbs; I'll go down and unfasten the stuff when you lower it to me."

"If you think I'm going to balance out there on that limb and unload the baggage compartment, you're mistaken," said the prince. "It's absolutely out of the question; I get very dizzy in high places, and I should most certainly fall."

"Well, what are you going to do?" demanded Brown; "sit around here while the rest of us wait on you?"

"That's what you servants were hired for," said Alexis.

"Oh, yeah? Well——"

"I'll go down below," said Jane. "Brown, you and Tibbs lower the stuff to me. Now let's get busy," and with that she turned and dropped down through the trees to the ground below.

With a grunt of disgust, Brown climbed out on the limb that led to the baggage compartment, followed by Tibbs; and the two soon lowered away the remainder of the luggage.

"Now lower your passengers," called Jane, after Brown had told her that there was no more baggage. "Alexis, you come first."

"Come on, your majesty," said Brown; "you're going first."

"I told you that I wouldn't go down there alone," said the prince. "Lower the others."

"All right, your majesty, but if you don't go now, you'll either climb down yourself or stay here till Hell freezes over, for all I care. Come ahead, Annette; I guess you're the one to go first, and then we'll lower the old lady."

"Brown, how dare you refer to me so disrespectfully?" It was the voice of the Princess Sborov coming from the interior of the cabin.

"There's nothing wrong with her ears," said Brown, with a grin.

"I'm terribly afraid, Mr. Brown," said Annette.

"You needn't be, little one," he replied; "we'll see that nothing happens to you. Come on, sit down in the doorway and I'll put this belt around you."

"You won't drop me?"

"Not a chance, my dear. I might drop royalty, but not you."

She flashed him a quick smile. "You are so very nice, Mr. Brown," she said.

41

"You just finding that out? Well, come on, sister; climb out on this branch here. I'll help you. Steady—now sit down. Ready, Tibbs?"

"Ready, sir," replied Tibbs.

"All right. Now down you go."

Annette clutched her rosary, closed her eyes, and started praying, but before she realized it she had touched the ground and Jane was helping to remove the belt from about her.

"Now, princess," called Brown.

"Oh, I can't move," cried the princess. "I'm paralyzed. I mean, I really am."

Brown turned to Sborov. "Go in there, mister, and fork your old lady out," he snapped. "We ain't got no time to fool around. Tell her if she don't come pronto, we'll leave you both up here."

"You unspeakable ruffian," sputtered the prince.

"Shut up, and go on and do what I tell you to," growled the pilot.

Sborov turned back to his wife and helped her to the door of the cabin, but one glance down was enough for her. She screamed and shrank back.

"Hurry up, hurry up, hurry up," said Brown.

"I can't. I mean, I just can't, Brown."

Brown made his way to the cabin. He carried the end of a long strap with him. "Come on," he said, "let me get this around you."

"But I can't do it, I tell you. I mean, I shall die of fright."

"You won't die of nothing; half-witted people live forever."

"That will be enough out of you, Brown. I have endured all of your insults that I am going to." The princess bridled and attempted to look very dignified, in which, in her dishevelled condition, she failed miserably.

Brown had stooped and fastened the belt about her.

"Ready, Tibbs?" he asked.

"Yes, sir. All ready, sir," replied the valet.

"Come on then, princess. Here, you, give me a lift. Shove on her from behind."

Brown pulled from in front, and Alexis pushed from behind, and the Princess Sborov shrieked and clawed at everything in sight in an attempt to get a hold that they could not break.

"What's the matter up there?" demanded Jane. "Is anyone hurt?"

"No," replied Brown. "We're just moving the better half of the royal family. Now listen, princess, we're doing this for your own good. If you stays up here alone, you starves to death."

"Yes, go on, Kitty. You're delaying things," said Alexis.

"A lot you'd care if I were killed, Alexis. I suppose you'd be glad if I were dead—it's all that will you got me to make. I was a big fool to do it; but, believe me, I mean, just as soon as I find writing materials, I'm going to change it, after what you said to me and what you called me. I'll cut you off without a cent, Alexis, without a cent."

The eyes of Prince Sborov closed to two ugly slits. His brow contracted in a frown, but he made no reply.

Brown took the princess' hands and held them away from the chair to which she had been clinging. "There ain't no use, princess," he said, a little less harshly this time, for he saw that the woman was genuinely terrified. "Tibbs and I'll see that you don't get hurt none. We'll lower you easy, and Lady Greystoke and Annette are down there to help you. Just get hold of yourself and show a little spunk for a minute and it will be over."

"Oh, I shall die, I know I shall die."

Brown and Alexis lifted her out of the cabin onto the branch that passed close to the doorway. Slowly they eased her off it and then lowered her carefully to the ground.

"Well, Tibbs," said Brown, "I guess you're next. Do you want to be lowered, or will you climb down?"

"I shall climb down," replied Tibbs. "You and I can go together and perhaps help one another."

"Hey, how about me?" demanded Sborov.

"You climb, too, you louse, or you can stay up here," replied Brown, "and I don't mean maybe!"

8

Ydeni, the Kavuru

FRAMED in the small doorway of the hut and silhouetted against the lesser darkness beyond, Tarzan saw the figure of his stealthy nocturnal visitor and knew that it was a man.

Helpless in his bonds, the Lord of the Jungle could only wait, for he could not defend himself. And though he chafed at the thought of giving up his life without an opportunity to defend it, he was still unmoved and unafraid.

The figure crept closer, groping in the darkness, when suddenly Tarzan spoke. "Who are you?" he demanded.

The creature sought to silence him with a sibilant hiss. "Not so loud," he cautioned. "I am Gupingu, the witch-doctor."

"What do you want?"

"I have come to set you free. Go back to your people, Kavuru, and tell them that Gupingu saved you from death. Tell them that because of this, they must not harm Gupingu or take his daughters from him."

Darkness hid the faint smile with which Tarzan received this charge. "You are a wise man, Gupingu," he said; "now cut my bonds."

"One thing more," said Gupingu.

"What is that?"

"You must promise never to tell Udalo, or any of my people, that I freed you."

"They will never know from me," replied the ape-man, "if you will tell me where your people think we Kavuru live."

"You live to the north, beyond a barren country, by a high mountain that stands alone in the center of a plain," explained Gupingu.

"Do your people know the trail to the Kavuru country?"

"I know it," replied the witch-doctor, "but I promise not to lead anyone there."

"That is well—if you know."

"I do know," insisted Gupingu.

"Tell me how you would reach this trail; then I shall know whether you know or not."

"To the north of our kraal, leading to the north, is an old elephant trail. It winds much, but it leads always toward the country of the Kavuru. Much bamboo grows on the slopes of the mountain beside your village, and there the elephants have gone for years to feed on the young shoots."

The witch-doctor came closer and felt for the bonds around Tarzan's ankles. "After I have freed you," he said, "wait here until I have had time to return to my hut; then go silently to the gates of the village; there you will find a platform just inside the palisade from which the warriors shoot their arrows over the top when enemies attack us. From there you can easily climb over the top of the palisade, and drop to the ground on the outside."

"Where are my weapons?" demanded Tarzan.

"They are in the hut of Udalo, but you cannot get them. A warrior sleeps just inside the doorway; you would awaken him if you tried to enter."

"Cut my bonds," said the ape-man.

With his knife, Gupingu severed the thongs about the prisoner's ankles and wrists. "Wait now, until I have reached my hut," he said, and turning, crawled silently through the doorway.

The ape-man stood up and shook himself. He rubbed his wrists and then his ankles to restore circulation. As he waited for Gupingu to reach his hut, he considered the possibility of regaining his weapons.

Presently, dropping to his knees, he crawled from the hut; and when he stood erect again upon the outside, he drew a deep breath. It was good to be free. On silent feet he moved down the village street. Other than in silence, he sought no concealment for he knew that even if he were discovered they could not take him again before he could reach the palisade and scale it.

As he approached the chief's hut, he paused. The temptation was very great; for it takes time and labor to produce weapons, and there were his own only a few paces from him.

He saw a faint light illuminating the interior of the hut— a very faint light from the embers of a dying fire. He approached the entrance, which was much larger than those of the other huts, and just inside and across the threshold he saw the figure of a sleeping warrior.

Tarzan stooped and looked into the interior. His quick, keen eyes, accustomed to darkness, discovered much more than might yours or mine; and one of the first things that they discovered were his weapons lying near the fire beyond the body of the warrior.

The throat of the sleeping man lay bare and fully exposed. It would have been the work of but a moment for the steel-thewed fingers of the ape-man to have throttled life from that unconscious figure. Tarzan considered the possibilities of this plan, but he discarded it for two reasons. One was that he never chose to kill wantonly; and the other, and probably the dominating reason, was that he was sure that the man would struggle even if he could not cry out and that his struggles would awaken the sleepers inside the hut, an event which would preclude the possibility of Tarzan retrieving his weapons. So he decided upon another and even more dangerous plan.

Stooping and moving cautiously, he stepped over the body of the warrior. He made no sound, and the two steps took him to his weapons.

First of all, he retrieved his precious knife, which he slipped into the sheath at his hip; then he adjusted the quiver of arrows behind his right shoulder and looped his rope across his left. Gathering his short spear and bow in one hand, he turned again toward the entrance, after a hasty glance around the interior of the hut to assure himself that its occupants were all asleep.

At that instant, the warrior rolled over and opened his eyes. At the sight of a man standing between himself and the fire, he sat up. In the gloom of the interior, it was impossible for him to know that this was an enemy, and the natural assumption was that one of the inmates of the hut was moving about in the night. Yet the figure did not seem familiar, and the warrior was puzzled.

"Who's that?" he demanded. "What's the matter?"

Tarzan took a step nearer the man. "Silence," he whispered. "One sound and you die; I am the Kavuru."

The black's lower jaw dropped; his eyes went wide. Even in the semi-darkness, Tarzan could see him tremble.

"Go outside," directed the ape-man, "and I will not harm you; and go quietly."

Shaking like a leaf, the warrior did as he was bid; and Tarzan followed him. He made the warrior accompany him to the gates and open them; then he passed out of the village of Udalo into the black jungle night. A moment later he heard the shouts of the warrior as he aroused the village, but Tarzan knew that there would be no pursuit. They would not dare follow a Kavuru into the night.

For an hour Tarzan followed the trail toward the north in accordance with Gupingu's directions. All about him were the noises of the jungle night—stealthy movements in the underbrush, the sound of padded feet, the coughing grunts of a nearby lion, the roar of a distant one; but his sensitive ears and nostrils told him where danger lurked; so that he was always alert to avoid it.

He was moving up wind, and presently he caught the scent of a lion that had not fed—a hunting lion, a hungry lion; and Tarzan took to the trees. A short search revealed a comfortable resting place, and here he lay up for the remainder of the night. Wondering what had become of Nkima, whom he had not seen since he was captured, he fell asleep, soothed by the familiar jungle sounds.

With the coming of dawn, he moved on again toward the north; and back in the village of Udalo, little Nkima cowered among the branches of the tree above the chief's hut.

He was a most unhappy little monkey, a very frightened little monkey. During the night the blacks had run from their huts shouting and jabbering. That had awakened Nkima, but he had not known the cause of it; he did not know that it meant that his master had escaped from the village. He thought he was still lying in the hut where he had seen the Bukena take him.

When Nkima awoke again, dawn was dispelling the darkness. Below him, the village streets were deserted. He heard no sound of life from any hut. He looked down upon that one to which they had dragged his master; and, summoning all his courage, he dropped quickly to the ground and scampered along the village street to the entrance to this hut.

A woman, coming from her hut to start her cooking fire, saw the little monkey and tried to catch him; but he escaped her and, racing across the village, scaled the palisade.

Not daring to enter the village again, and terrified at the thought of being alone in this strange country, Nkima fled through the jungle in the direction of home. And so Nkima went his way not knowing that his master had escaped.

All day Tarzan made his way north along the winding elephant trail. It was not until late in the afternoon that he was able to make a kill; and then after feeding he lay up once more for the night.

In the afternoon of the second day the nature of the country changed. The jungle became more open and there were park-like places where there was little or no underbrush and the trees grew farther apart. It was a country entirely new to Tarzan, and as such whetted his imagination and aroused within him the instinct of exploration which had always been a powerful factor in affecting his destiny; for he had that intelligent inquisitiveness which set him above the other beasts of the jungle.

As he moved silently along his way, constantly on the alert, a vagrant breeze carried to his nostrils a strange scent that brought him to a halt. For a moment he stood in statuesque pose, every faculty alert.

Tarzan was puzzled. The scent was that of a tarmangani, and yet there was a difference. It was an odor entirely new to him; and then, mingling with it, but fainter, came the familiar scent spoor of Numa, the lion.

Those two in proximity often meant trouble, and while Tarzan was not particularly interested in saving the man from the lion, or the lion from the man, whichever was hunting the other, natural curiosity prompted him to investigate.

The trees ahead of him grew sufficiently close together so that he could move through their branches; and this he elected to do, since always it gave him an advantage to come from above upon those he sought, especially where, in the case of men, they would not be expecting him.

The perception of the eyes of man is normally in a horizontal plane, while those of the cat family, with their vertical pupils, detect things above them far more quickly than would a man. Perhaps this is because for ages the cat family has hunted its prey in trees, and even though the lion no longer does so, he still has the eyes of his smaller progenitors.

As Tarzan swung in the direction of the strange scent

47

spoor, he was aware that the odor of the lion was becoming stronger much more rapidly than the other scent, a fact which convinced him that the lion was approaching the man, though whether by accident or intent he could not of course determine; but the fact that the lion scent was that of a hungry lion, led him to believe that the beast was stalking the man.

Any beast with a full belly gives off a different odor from one that is empty; and as an empty stomach is always a hungry one, and as hungry lions are hunting lions, to Tarzan's mind it was a foregone conclusion that the man was the quarry and the lion the hunter.

Tarzan came in sight of the man first, and the initial glimpse brought the Lord of the Jungle to a sudden stop.

Here, indeed, was a white man, but how different from any white man that Tarzan had seen before! The fellow was clothed only in a loin cloth that appeared to be made of gorilla hide. His ankles and wrists and arms were loaded with bracelets; a many-stranded necklace of human teeth fell across his breast. A slender cylinder of bone or ivory ran transversely through the pierced septum of his nose; his ears were ornamented with heavy rings. Except for a mane of hair from his forehead to the nape of his neck, his skull was shaved; and in this mane were fastened gay feathers which floated above a face hideously painted; and yet, with all these earmarks of the savage Negro, the man was undoubtedly white, even though his skin was bronzed by much exposure to the weather.

He was sitting on the ground with his back against a tree, eating something from a skin bag fastened to the string that supported his loin cloth, and it was apparent that he was absolutely unaware of the proximity of the lion.

Cautiously, silently, Tarzan moved nearer until he was in the tree directly above the unconscious man. As he examined him more closely, he recalled the many fables concerning the Kavuru, and especially the one which described them as white savages.

This stranger then, might be a Kavuru. It seemed reasonable to assume that he was, but further speculation on this subject was interrupted by a low snarl a short distance away.

Instantly the savage white was on his feet. In one hand he grasped a heavy spear, in the other a crude knife.

The lion burst from the underbrush at full charge. He was so close that the man had no chance to seek safety in the tree above him. All that he could do, he did. Swiftly his spear hand flew back, and in the next lightning move he launched the heavy weapon.

Perhaps the suddenness of this unexpected attack had

momentarily unnerved him, for he made a clean miss; and simultaneously Tarzan leaped for the carnivore from a branch above the two.

He struck the lion at the shoulder diagonally from above just as he reared upon his hind legs to seize his victim. The impact of the ape-man's body toppled the lion upon its side. With a frightful roar, it regained its feet but not before the ape-man had locked his powerful legs around the small of its body and encircled its massive throat with one great arm.

As the two beasts fought, the white savage stood an awe-struck witness to the strange duel. He heard the growls and roars of the man mingle with those of the lion. He saw them roll upon the ground together as lashing talons sought to reach the bronzed hide of the man-thing; and then he saw the knife hand rise and fall; and each time he drove the blade deep into the side of the king of beasts, until at last the roaring ceased and the tawny body collapsed in the final spasm of death.

The ape-man leaped erect. He placed a foot upon the carcass of his foe and raising his face to the sky voiced the kill-cry of the victorious bull ape.

At that weird and hideous call, the white savage shrank back and clutched the hilt of his knife more tightly.

As the last weird note died away in the distance, Tarzan turned and faced the creature whose life he had saved.

The two stood appraising each other in silence for a moment; then the savage spoke. "Who are you?" he demanded, in the same dialect that the Bukena used.

"I am Tarzan of the Apes," replied the ape-man. "And you?"

"I am Ydeni, the Kavuru."

Tarzan experienced that sense of satisfaction which one feels when events bear out his judgment. This was, indeed, a bit of good fortune, for now he would at least know what sort of people the Kavuru were. Perhaps this fellow would even guide him to the country he sought.

"But why did you kill the lion?" asked Ydeni.

"If I had not, he would have killed you."

"Why should you care if he killed me? Am I not a stranger?"

The ape-man shrugged. "Perhaps it was because you are a white man," he said.

Ydeni shook his head. "I do not understand you. I've never seen anyone like you before. You are not a black; you are not a Kavuru. What are you?"

"I am Tarzan," replied the ape-man. "I am looking for

the village of the Kavuru; now you can take me there. I wish to speak with your chief."

Ydeni scowled and shook his head. "No one comes to the village of the Kavuru," he said, "other than those who come there to die. Because you have saved my life, I will not take you there, nor will I kill you now, as I should. Go your way, Tarzan, and see that it does not lead you to the village of the Kavuru."

9

Sheeta, the Leopard

WITH THE aeroplane party safely deposited on the ground, Brown cut a narrow path to the trail, using a small hand axe that fortunately had been included in the heterogeneous and generally quite useless impedimenta that the Prince and Princess Sborov had thought essential to the success of their expedition.

Tibbs had offered to help cut trail, but a lifetime of valeting had not fitted him for anything so practical as wielding a hand axe. He meant well, but he could hit nothing that he aimed at; and for fear that he might commit mayhem or suicide, Brown took the implement from him.

Sborov did not offer to help; and Brown ignored him entirely, knowing that he would prove less efficient, if possible, than Tibbs. But when it came to transporting the baggage, the pilot insisted that the prince do his share.

"You may be the scion of a long line of cab drivers," he said, "but you are going to work or get a punch on the nose."

Sborov grumbled, but he worked.

After the luggage had been transported to the little clearing beside the stream that Jane had found, she directed the building of a boma and some rude shelters.

In this, the brunt of the work fell on Brown and Jane, though Annette and Tibbs assisted to the best of their ability. No one expected Kitty Sborov to do anything but moan, and she didn't. Alexis was assigned to the building of the boma after someone else had cut the brush—a job that was far beyond either his physical or mental attainments.

"I can't see how guys like him ever live to grow up,"

grumbled Brown, "nor what good they are after they do grow up. I never seen such a total loss before in my life."

Jane laughed. "He dances divinely, Brown," she said.

"I'll bet he does," replied the pilot. "Damned gigolo, bringing along just a dinky little hand axe and rifles without any ammunition." He spat the words out disgustedly. "And look at all this here junk. Maybe there's something in it; we ought to take an inventory and see what we got."

"That's not a bad idea," said Jane. "Oh, by the way, Tibbs, where's that gun of yours? We really should have it handy."

"Yes, Milady, right away," said Tibbs. "I never travel without it; one can never tell when one is going to need it, and especially in Africa with all these lions and things."

He located his bag, rummaged through it, and finally located his weapon, which he withdrew gingerly and exhibited not without considerable pride, holding it up where all might see it.

"There she is, Milady," he said, "and rather a beauty I fancy, too."

Jane's heart sank as she looked at the little single shot .22 short pistol that Tibbs dangled before her so proudly.

Brown burst into a loud laugh. "Say," he said, "if the Germans had known you had that, there wouldn't have been no World War."

"Beg pardon, Mr. Brown," said Tibbs, stiffly; "it is really a very fine weapon. The man I got it from said so himself. It stood me back seven bob, sir."

"Let me see it," said Brown. Taking the pistol he opened the breech. " 'Tain't loaded," he said, "and it wouldn't be no good if it was."

"Bless me, no!" exclaimed Tibbs; "I wouldn't think of carrying a loaded weapon, sir; it's too dangerous. One never knows when it might go off."

"Well," said Jane, "it may come in handy shooting small game. Got plenty of ammunition for it?"

"Well—er—Milady," stammered Tibbs, "you see I've always been intending to buy ammunition for it, but I never got around to it."

Brown looked at the Englishman in pitying astonishment. "Well, I'll be——"

Jane sat down on an upended suitcase and burst into laughter. "Forgive me, Tibbs, but really it's too funny," she cried.

"I'll tell you what we'll do," said Brown. "We'll put Tibbs on guard tonight and if he sees a lion he can throw that thing at him. It ain't any good for nothing else."

"I don't see how you can laugh, Jane," said Kitty. "'Suppose a lion should come. Tibbs, you should have brought ammunition. It is very careless of you."

"It doesn't make any difference, Kitty, for as far as a lion is concerned, that pistol is just as effective empty as it would be loaded."

"I know we are all going to be killed," moaned Kitty. "I wish I were back in the ship; it's much safer there."

"Don't worry," said Jane; "the boma will be some protection, and we will keep a fire going all night. Most beasts are afraid of a fire; they won't come near one."

Late in the afternoon, a shelter had been completed with two compartments, one for the women and one for the men. It was a very crude affair, but it provided some shelter from the elements and it induced a feeling of security far greater than it warranted, for it is a fact that if we can hide in something, however flimsy, we feel much safer than we do in the open.

While the shelters and boma were being built, Jane busied herself with another activity. Kitty had been watching her for some time, and finally her curiosity got the best of her.

"What in the world are you doing, dear?" she asked, as she watched Jane shaping a small branch with the hand axe.

"I am making weapons—a bow and arrows, and a spear."

"Oh, how perfectly wonder—I mean, isn't it ducky? It's just like you, my dear, to think of archery; it will help us to pass the time away."

"What I am making will help us obtain food and defend ourselves," replied Jane.

"Oh, of course!" exclaimed Kitty; "how perfectly silly of me, but when I think of archery I always think of little arrows sticking in the straw target. They are so colorful, my dear—I mean, the way they are painted. I recall such beautiful pictures of young people in sport clothes, of green turfs, and sunshine against a background of lovely trees. But who do you suppose ever thought of using bows and arrows to hunt game? I'm sure it must be original with you, my dear; but it's very clever of you, if you can hit anything."

Toward the middle of the afternoon Jane had completed a very crude bow and half a dozen arrows, the tips of which she had fire-hardened.

Her work completed, she stood up and surveyed the camp. "You are getting along splendidly," she said. "I'm going out to see what I can rustle for supper. Have you a knife, Brown? I may need one."

"But, my dear, I mean you're not going out there alone?" cried Kitty.

"Sure she's not," said Brown. "I'll go along with you, Miss."

"I'm afraid," said Jane, with a smile, "that where I am

52

going, you couldn't follow. Here, let me have your knife."

"I reckon I can go anywhere you can go, Miss," said Brown, grinning.

"Let me have the knife," said Jane. "Why it's a nice big one! I always did like to see a man carrying a man-sized knife."

"Well, if we are ready," said Brown, "let's start."

Jane shook her head. "I told you, you couldn't follow me," she said.

"Want to lay a little bet on that?"

"Sure," said Jane. "I'll bet you a pound sterling against this knife that you can't keep up with me for a hundred yards."

"I'll just take you up on that, Miss," said Brown; "let's get going."

"Come ahead, then," said Jane. And with that, she ran lightly across the clearing, leaped for a low hanging branch and swinging herself into the trees was out of sight in an instant.

Brown ran after her, seeking to catch a glimpse of her from the ground, but he was soon floundering in heavy undergrowth.

It didn't take him long to realize that he was beaten, and rather crestfallen he returned to the camp.

"Gracious!" exclaimed the princess. "Did you ever see anything like it? It was perfectly wonderful. I mean, it really was; but I am so afraid something will happen to her out there alone. Alexis, you should not have permitted it."

"I thought Brown was going with her," said Alexis. "If I had known that he was afraid, I would have gone myself."

Brown eyed Alexis with contempt too deep for words as he returned to his work on the shelter.

"I should think anyone would be afraid to go out there," said Annette, who was helping Brown thatch the roof with large leaves. "Lady Greystoke must be so very brave."

"She's sure got guts," said Brown; "and did you see the way she took to them trees? Just like a monkey."

"Just as though she had lived in them all her life," said Annette.

"Do you really think she can kill anything with her bow and arrows?" asked Tibbs; "they look so—er—ah inadequate, if I may make so bold as to say so."

"Say," said Brown, "she's not the kind that would go out there if she didn't know what she was doing. I thought all the time, until just before we crashed, that she was another one of them silly society dames that had never had anything in her noodle heavier than champagne bubbles; but believe me I take my hat off to her now; and you can believe me, when I take orders from a dame she's got to be some dame."

"Lady Greystoke is a very remarkable woman," said Alexis, "and a very beautiful one. Kindly remember also, Brown, that she is a lady, a member of the English nobility, my man; I resent the lack of deference you show by referring to her as a dame, and saying that she has guts. I know you Americans are notoriously ill-bred, but there is a limit to what I can stand from you."

"Yeah?" inquired Brown; "and what are you going to do about it, you damned pansy?"

"Alexis, you forget yourself," said the princess. "You should not stoop to quarrel with an employee."

"You're darned tootin', lady," said Brown. "He better not stoop to quarrel with this bozo; I'm just laying for an excuse to push in his mush."

Annette laid a hand upon Brown's arm. "Please, Mr. Brown," she said, "do not quarrel. Is it not bad enough as it is, that we should make it worse by always quarreling among ourselves?"

Brown turned and looked at her quizzically; then he covered her little hand with his. "I guess you're right, girlie, at that. I'll lay off him, if he'll lay off me." He closed his hand on hers. "I guess you and me's going to hit it off O.K. kid."

"Hit what off, Mr. Brown?"

"I mean, we're going to be pals!" he exclaimed.

"Pals? What are they?"

"Buddies—friends. I thought you savvied English."

"Oh, friends; yes, I understand that. I should like to be friends with Mr. Brown. Annette likes to be friends with everyone."

"That's all right, baby, but don't be too promiscuous, for I have a feeling that I'm going to like you a lot."

The French girl cast her eyes down coquettishly. "I think, Mr. Brown, we had better get along with our work, or we shall have only half a roof over our heads tonight."

"O.K. kiddo, but we'll talk about this friendship business later—there ought to be a full moon tonight."

After she left the camp, Jane moved rapidly and silently through the trees paralleling the little stream which she tried to keep in view while she searched for a place where the signs indicated the beasts were accustomed to come to drink.

A light breeze was blowing in her face, bringing faintly various scent spoors to her nostrils, which, while not as sensitive as those of her mate, were nevertheless far more sensitive than those of an ordinary civilized person. Jane had learned long ago that senses may be developed by training, and she had let no opportunity pass to train hers to the fullest of her ability.

Now, very faintly, she caught the suggestion of a scent that set her nerves to tingling with that thrill which only the huntsman knows. Quarry lay ahead.

The girl moved even more cautiously than before; scarcely a leaf stirred to her passage, and presently she saw ahead that which she sought—a small, harnessed antelope, a bush buck, which was moving daintily along the trail just ahead of her.

Jane increased her speed; but now more than ever it was imperative that she move silently, for the little animal below her was nervous and constantly alert. At the slightest unusual sound, it would be gone like a flash.

Presently she came within range, but there was always intervening foliage that might deflect her arrow.

Patience is the most important asset of the jungle hunter, and patience she had learned from Tarzan and from her own experiences.

Now the antelope halted suddenly in its tracks and turned its head to the left; at the same instant Jane was aware of a movement in the underbrush in that direction. She saw that she could wait no longer; already something had startled her quarry. There was a small opening in the foliage between her and the antelope. Like lightning, she drew her bow; the string snapped with a whang and the shaft buried itself deep in the body of the antelope behind its left shoulder. It leaped high into the air and fell dead.

Jane had reason to suspect that something else was stalking the antelope; but she could see nothing of it, and the turn in the trail had resulted in a cross-wind that would carry the scent of the creature away from her.

She knew that it was a risky thing to do; but she was hungry, and she was aware that all her companions were hungry; they must have food, for a cursory examination of the baggage had revealed the fact that besides some sandwiches which had already been eaten, their stock of provisions consisted of a few chocolate bars, six bottles of cognac and two of cointreau.

Trusting to luck and pinning her faith in her speed, Jane dropped lightly to the trail and ran quickly to the fallen animal.

She worked rapidly, as Tarzan had taught her to work. Slitting its throat to let it bleed, she quickly eviscerated it to reduce the weight; and as she worked, she heard again those stealthy sounds in the underbrush not far distant along the back trail.

Her work completed, she closed the knife and slipped it

into her pocket; then she raised the carcass of the little antelope to her shoulder. As she did so, an angry growl shattered
the silence of the jungle; and Sheeta, the leopard, stepped into the trail twenty paces from her.

Instantly Jane saw that it would be impossible to escape
with her kill, and resentment flared high in her bosom at the
thought of relinquishing her prey to the savage cat.

She felt reasonably sure that she could save herself by taking to the trees and leaving the carcass of the antelope to
Sheeta, but a sudden anger against the injustice of this con-
tretemps impelled her to stand her ground and caused her to
do a very foolish thing.

Dropping the antelope, she strung her bow and pulling it
back to the full limit of her strength she drove an arrow
straight at the breast of Sheeta.

As it struck, the beast voiced a horrifying scream of pain
and rage; then it charged.

To those in the camp, the cry sounded almost human.

"Sapristi! What was that?" cried Alexis.

"Mon Dieu, it was a woman's scream!" exclaimed Annette.

"Lady Greystoke!" said Brown, horrified.

"Oh, Alexis, Alexis! Annette!" cried the princess; "My
smelling salts, quick; I am going to faint."

Brown seized the puny hand axe and started in the direction of the sound.

"Oh, where are you going?" cried Kitty. "Don't leave me,
don't leave me."

"Shut up, you old fool," snapped Brown. "Lady Greystoke must be in trouble. I am going to find out."

Tibbs pulled his empty pistol from his pocket. "I'll go
with you, Mr. Brown," he said; "we can't let anything happen
to Milady."

10

Abduction

WHEN Ydeni refused to lead him to the village of the
Kavuru, Tarzan was neither surprised nor disappointed. He knew men and especially savage men
and the numerous taboos that govern their individual and
tribal lives. He would have preferred to have gone to the

chief of the Kavuru with one of his own people whom Tarzan had befriended; but if this were impossible, he was at least no worse off than he had been before he had met Ydeni. And he was confident that no matter how brutal or savage the man might be, he was probably not without a spark of gratitude for the service Tarzan had rendered him.

"If I came as a friend," said Tarzan, "surely there could be no harm in that."

"The Kavuru have no friends," replied Ydeni. "You must not come."

The ape-man shrugged. "Then I shall come as an enemy."

"You will be killed. You saved my life; I do not wish you to be killed, but I could not prevent it; it is the law of the Kavuru."

"Then you kill the girls that you steal?" demanded the ape-man.

"Who says that the Kavuru steal girls?"

"It is well known among all people. Why do you do it? Have you not enough women of your own?"

"There are no Kavuru women," replied Ydeni. "The rains have come and gone as many times as there are fingers and toes upon four men since there was a Kavuru woman—since the last one gave her life that the men of the Kavuru might live."

"Eighty years since there have been women among you?" demanded the ape-man. "That is impossible, Ydeni, for you are still a young man, and you must have had a mother; but perhaps she was not a Kavuru?"

"My mother was a Kavuru, but she died long before the last woman. But I have told you too much already, stranger. The ways of the Kavuru are not as the ways of lesser people, and they are not for the ears of lesser people. To speak of them is taboo. Go your way now, and I will go mine."

Convinced that he could get no more information from Ydeni, Tarzan took to the trees; and a moment later was lost to the sight of the Kavuru. Purposely he had gone toward the west so that Ydeni would be deceived into thinking that he was not on the right trail toward the Kavuru country. However, he did not go far in that direction; but quickly doubled back toward the spot where he had left the white savage; for he was determined that if Ydeni would not lead him willingly to his village, he should do so unknowingly.

When Tarzan had returned to the spot where he killed the lion, the Kavuru was no longer there; and assuming that he had gone toward the north, his pursuer set off in that direction.

After pursuing a northerly course for a short time, Tarzan realized that there were no indications that his quarry had come this way.

Quickly he started a great circle in order to pick up the scent spoor.

For an hour he ranged through forest and open glade before, at last, Usha, the wind, carried to his nostrils the scent spoor of Ydeni; and when at last he came upon the object of his search Tarzan was perplexed, for the Kavuru was moving due south.

Tarzan reasoned that Ydeni might be doing this to throw him off the trail, or perchance he had misinformed him as to the location of the Kavuru village; but he was sure now that if he clung tenaciously to the trail, Ydeni would eventually lead him to his goal.

Back over the long trail he had come since he had escaped from the village of Udalo, the chief, Tarzan dogged the footsteps of his quarry; yet never once was Ydeni aware that he was being followed, though oftentimes he was plainly visible to the ape-man.

Tarzan found it interesting to study this strange creature whose very existence was tinged with mystery. He noted the weapons and the ornaments of Ydeni and saw that they differed from any that he had ever seen before. He was particularly interested in the slender fibre rope that was wrapped many times around the Kavuru's waist; for of all the savages in the jungle, as far as Tarzan knew, he alone used a rope as a weapon. He wondered just how Ydeni would use it.

Late one afternoon, when Tarzan knew they must be approaching the village of the Bukena, he was surprised to see Ydeni take to the trees, through which he moved with considerable agility and speed, though in no respect to compare with those of the Lord of the Jungle.

He moved with the utmost wariness, stopping often to listen intently. Presently he uncoiled the rope from about his waist, and Tarzan saw there was a running noose in one end of it.

Now Tarzan heard voices ahead of them; they came faintly as from a great distance. It was evident that the Kavuru heard them, too, for he slightly changed his direction to bear more in that from which the voices came.

Tarzan was keenly interested. The attitude of the man in front of him was that of the keen hunter, stalking his prey. He felt that one mystery was about to be cleared up.

In a short time, the Kavuru came to the edge of a clearing and halted. Below him, working in the small fields, were a number of women. Ydeni looked them over; presently he espied a girl of about fifteen and made his way to another tree nearer her.

Tarzan followed, watching intently every move of the Kavuru. He heard him voice a strange call, so low that it must barely have reached the ears of the girl. For a moment she paid no attention to it; and then presently she turned and looked with dull, uncomprehending eyes toward the jungle. The sharpened stick with which she had been cultivating the maize dropped from her limp hand.

Ydeni continued to voice that weird, insistent call. The girl took a few steps in the direction of the jungle; then she paused; and Tarzan could almost sense the struggle that was going on within her breast to overcome the mysterious urge that was drawing her away from the other women; but Ydeni's voice was insistent and compelling, and at last she again moved listlessly toward him. She moved as one in a trance, with staring eyes fixed on Ydeni.

Now the Kavuru retreated slowly deeper into the forest, calling, always calling to the helpless girl that followed.

Tarzan watched; nor did he make any effort to interfere. To him, the life of the black girl was no more than the life of an antelope or that of any other beast of the jungle. To Tarzan, all were beasts, including himself, and none with any rights greater than another, except that which he might win by strength or cunning or ferocity.

Much more important than the life of the black girl was the possibility of fathoming the mystery that had always surrounded the disappearance of girls supposed to have been taken by the Kavuru.

Ydeni lured the girl deeper into the forest, halting at last upon a broad limb.

Slowly the girl approached. It was evident that she was not the master of her own will. The weird, monotonous droning chant of the Kavuru seemed to have numbed all her faculties.

At last, she came directly beneath the tree and the branch where Ydeni crouched. Then the man dropped his noose about her.

She made no outcry, no protest, as he tightened it and drew her slowly up toward him; nor ever once did the chant cease.

Removing the rope from about her, he threw her limp body across one of his broad shoulders and turning, started back in the direction from which he had come.

Tarzan had watched the abduction of the girl with keen interest, for it explained the seeming mystery of the disappearance of so many other young girls during past times.

59

He could readily understand the effect that these mysterious disappearances would have upon the superstitious minds of the natives; yet it was all very simple except the strange, hypnotic power of the Kavuru. That was not at all clear to him.

He wondered how the natives had come to connect these disappearances with the Kavuru, and the only reasonable explanation seemed to be that in times past some exceptionally tenacious relatives had prosecuted their search until they had come by accident upon the abductor and his prey and so learned the identity of the former without ascertaining the method he had used to achieve his ends.

Feeling no responsibility in the matter, Tarzan was not moved by any impulse to rescue the girl, his only concern now being to follow Ydeni back to the village of the Kavuru, where he was confident he would find Muviro's daughter, Buira, if she still lived.

Ydeni kept to the trees for hours, until he must have been reasonably certain that he had passed beyond the point where possible pursuers would be likely to search, since they had no trail to follow. Then he came to the ground; but he still carried the girl, who lay across his shoulder as one dead.

On and on he plodded, apparently tireless; and in the trees just behind him followed Tarzan of the Apes.

It was very late in the afternoon when the Kavuru halted. He carried the girl into a tree then, and tied her securely to a branch with the same rope that had snared her. Leaving her, he departed; and Tarzan followed him.

Ydeni was merely searching for food; and when he found some edible fruits and nuts, he returned with them to the girl.

The hypnosis which had held her in its spell for so long was now relinquishing its hold upon her, and as Ydeni approached her she looked at him with startled eyes and shrank away when he touched her.

Releasing her bonds, he carried her to the ground and offered her food.

By this time, full consciousness had returned; and it was evident that the girl was aware of her plight and the identity of her abductor, for an expression of utter horror distorted her features; and then she burst into tears.

"Shut up," snapped Ydeni. "I have not hurt you. If you give me no trouble, I shall not hurt you."

"You are a Kavuru," she gasped in horror-laden tones. "Take me back to my father; you promised him that you would not harm any member of his family."

Ydeni looked at the girl in surprise. "I promised your father?" he demanded. "I never saw your father; I have never spoken to one of your men."

"You did. You promised him when he liberated you from the hut in which Udalo had you bound. Udalo would have killed you; my father, Gupingu, the witch-doctor, saved you. Because of that you made the promise."

This recital made no impression upon Ydeni, but it did upon the grim and silent watcher in the trees above. So this was the daughter of Gupingu. Apparently Fate was a capricious wench with a strange sense of humor.

Knowledge of the identity of the girl gave a new complexion to the affair. Tarzan felt that by accepting his freedom at the hands of Gupingu he had given the witch-doctor passive assurance that his daughters would be safe from the Kavuru. It was a moral obligation that the Lord of the Jungle could not ignore; but if he took the girl from Ydeni and returned her to her people, he would be unable to follow the Kavuru to his village. However, with a shrug he accepted the responsibility that honor seemed to lay upon him.

Now he devoted himself to a consideration of ways and means. He could, of course, go down and take the girl by force, for it never occurred to him that any creature, least of all man, might be able to prevent him from having his way; but this plan he scarcely considered before discarding it. He did not wish Ydeni to know that it was he who took the girl from him, since he realized the possibility of Ydeni being useful to him in the event that he reached the village of the Kavuru, for after all he had saved the man's life; and that was something that only the lowest of beasts might forget.

He waited therefore to see what disposal Ydeni would make of the girl for the night, for he had it in mind now to take her by stealth; and if that failed, the likelihood of Ydeni recognizing him would be greatly lessened after dark; and so he waited, patient as any other beast of prey that watches for the propitious moment to attack.

Seeing that she would be unable to move the Kavuru by her pleas, the girl had lapsed into silence. Her brooding eyes glowered sullenly at her captor. Fear and hate were reflected in them.

Darkness was approaching rapidly when the Kavuru seized the girl and threw her roughly to the ground. She fought like a young lioness, but Ydeni was powerful and soon overcame her. Then he deftly bound her hands behind her back and trussed her legs so tightly that she could scarcely move them. Terrified, she lay trembling.

"Now," he said, when he had finished, "you cannot run away. Ydeni can sleep; you had better sleep; we have a long march tomorrow, and Ydeni will not carry you."

The girl made no reply. The man threw himself upon the ground near her. A silent figure moved stealthily closer in the trees above them. It was very dark and very quiet. Only the roar of a distant lion, coming faintly to their ears, gave evidence of life in the jungle.

Tarzan waited patiently. By the man's regular breathing, he knew that Ydeni slept; but his slumber was not yet deep enough to satisfy the ape-man.

A half hour passed, and then an hour. Ydeni was sleeping very soundly now, but the girl had not yet slept. That was well; it was what Tarzan wished for.

He bent low from the branch where he lay and spoke to the girl in a low whisper. "Do not cry out," he said. "I am coming down to take you back to your people."

Very gently he lowered himself to the ground. Even the girl beside whom he stood did not know that he had descended from the trees. He stooped over her with a sibilant caution on his lips.

The girl was afraid; but she was more afraid of the Kavuru, and so she made no outcry as Tarzan raised her to his shoulder and carried her silently along the jungle trail until he could take to the trees with less likelihood of arousing Ydeni.

At a safe distance from the sleeping man he paused and cut the girl's bonds.

"Who are you?" she whispered.

"I am the man that Udalo would have killed and that your father set free," replied the ape-man.

She shrank back. "Then you are a Kavuru, too," she said.

"I am no Kavuru. I told them that, but they would not believe me. I am Tarzan of the Apes, chief of the Waziri whose country lies many marches toward the rising sun."

"You are a Kavuru," she insisted; "my father said so."

"I am not, but what difference does it make if I take you back to your father?"

"How do I know that you will take me back?" she demanded. "Perhaps you are lying to me."

"If you'd rather," said the ape-man, "I will set you free now; but what will you do here alone in the jungle? A lion or a leopard will surely find you; and even if one did not you might never find your way back to your village, because you do not know in what direction the Kavuru carried you while you were unconscious."

"I will go with you," said the girl.

11

"Seventy Million Dollars"

B ROWN and Tibbs followed the game trail in the direction of the uncanny scream that had startled the camp.

"Milady!" shouted Tibbs. "Milady, where are you? What has happened?"

Brown quickly forged ahead of Tibbs who had not run a hundred feet in ten years. "Yes, Miss!" he bellowed, "where are you?"

"Here, follow the trail," came back the answer in clear, unshaken tones. "I'm all right; don't get excited."

Presently Brown came in sight of her. She was withdrawing the last of three arrows from the carcass of a leopard, and just beyond her lay the eviscerated carcass of an antelope.

"What the—what's all this?" demanded Brown.

"I just killed this bush-buck," explained Jane, "and Sheeta here tried to take it away from me."

"You killed him?" demanded Brown. "You killed him with your arrows?"

"Well, I didn't bite him to death, Brown," laughed the girl. "Was it him or you that let out that yell?"

"That was Sheeta. He was charging; and when my first arrow struck him, he didn't seem to like it at all."

"And one arrow settled him?" asked the pilot.

"I let him have two more. I don't know which one stopped him. All three went into his heart."

Brown wiped the perspiration from his forehead. "By golly," he said, "I've got to take my hat off to you, Miss."

"Well, you can put it back on, Brown, and pack that antelope back to camp. I'll like that a whole lot better."

Tibbs had come up and was standing in wide-eyed astonishment gazing at the dead leopard. "If I may make so bold, Milady, I might say that it's most extraordinary. I would never have believed it, Milady, upon my honor, I wouldn't. I never thought those little arrows would kill anything bigger than a bird."

"You'd be surprised, Hibbs," said Jane.

"I am, Milady."

"Do we take the cat back to camp, too?" asked Brown.

"No," replied Jane. "Saving the pelt is too much of a job; and, besides that, Princess Sborov would probably collapse with fright at sight of it."

The pilot picked up the carcass of the antelope, and together the three returned to camp.

Annette was standing wide-eyed, awaiting them. She breathed a sigh of relief when she saw that all three had returned safely.

"Oh," she cried, "you really got something to eat. I am so hungry."

"Where are the prince and princess?" demanded Jane.

Annette snickered, and pointed toward the shelter. "As soon as Brown and Tibbs left, they ran in there and hid," she whispered.

Almost immediately the prince appeared. He was very white, and he was also very angry. "You men had no right running off and leaving this camp unguarded," he snapped. "There's no telling what might have happened. Hereafter, see that both of you are never absent at the same time."

"Oh, Lord, give me strength," groaned Brown. "I am long suffering, but I can't stand much more of this bozo."

"What's that?" demanded Alexis.

"I was just going to say that if you ever shoot off your yap in that tone of voice to me again, I'm going to make a king out of you."

"What?" demanded Alexis, suspiciously.

"I'm going to crown you."

"I suppose that is another weird Americanism," sneered the prince; "but whatever it is, coming from you, I know it is insulting."

"And how!" exclaimed Brown.

"Instead of standing around here quarreling," said Jane, "let's get busy. Brown, will you and Tibbs build a fire, please. Alexis, you can cut up the antelope. Cut five or six good-sized steaks, and then Annette can cook them. Do you know how to grill them over an open fire, Annette?"

"No, Madame, but I can learn, if you'll just show me once."

The princess emerged from the shelter. "Oh, my dear, whatever have you there?" she demanded. "Oh, take it away; it's all covered with blood."

"That's your supper, Kitty," said Jane.

"Eat that thing? Oh, don't; I shall be ill. Take it away and bury it."

"Well, here's your chance to reduce, lady," said Brown, "because if you don't eat that, you ain't going to eat nothing."

"How dare you, Brown, intimate that you would even think of keeping food away from me?" demanded the princess.

"I ain't going to keep no food away from you. I'm just trying to tell you that there ain't no food except this. If you won't eat this, you don't eat, that's all."

"Oh, I never could bring myself—really, my dear, how it smells."

Less than an hour later, the princess was tearing away at an antelope steak like a famished wolf. "How perfectly thrilling," she took time out to remark. "I mean, isn't it just like camping out?"

"Quite similar," said Jane, drily.

"Terrible," said Alexis; "this steak is much too rare. Hereafter, Annette, see that mine are quite well done."

"You take what you get, playboy, and like it," said Brown. "And hereafter don't use that tone of voice in speaking to Annette or anyone else in this bunch."

Tibbs was very much embarrassed. He always was when what he considered a member of the lower classes showed lack of proper deference to one of what he liked to call the aristocracy. "If I may make so bold as to inquire, Milady," he said, addressing Jane in an effort to divert the conversation into another channel, "might I ask how we are going to get out of here and back to civilization?"

"I've been thinking a lot about that myself, Tibbs," replied Jane. "You see, if we were all in good physical condition, we might follow this stream down to a larger river when eventually we would be sure to come to a native village where we could get food and employ guides and carriers to take us on to some settlement where there are Europeans; or, failing in that, we could at least hire runners to carry a message out for us."

"I think that is a splendid idea, Milady; I 'ope we start soon."

"I doubt that we could all stand the hardships of a long trek," said Jane.

"I suppose you mean me, my dear," said the princess, "but really I am very fond of walking. I remember I used to walk a mile every morning. That was before dear Mr. Peters passed on. He insisted upon my doing it; he was such an athletic man himself. He played golf every Wednesday afternoon. But after he went, I gave it up; it hurt my feet so."

"We could build a litter," suggested Alexis. "I have seen pictures of them in the cinema. Brown and Tibbs could carry the princess."

"Yeah?" demanded Brown, "and who'd carry you?"

"Oh, I think that would be just wonderful, I mean, I think that would solve every problem!" exclaimed Kitty. "We could build the litter large enough for two and then we could both ride."

"Why not a four-passenger job?" demanded Brown; "and then Tibbs and I could carry you all."

"Oh, no," exclaimed the princess. "I'm afraid that would be much too heavy a load for you."

"The fellow is attempting to be facetious, my dear," said Alexis; "but certainly there is no reason why they could not carry you."

"Except only one," said Brown.

"And pray, what is that?" asked Kitty. "I mean, I see no reason why you and Tibbs should not carry me."

"It's absolutely out of the question, Kitty," said Jane, with some asperity. "You simply don't know what you're talking about. Two men could not carry anyone through this jungle; and no matter what you may think, you wouldn't last an hour if you tried to walk."

"Oh, but my dear Jane, what am I going to do—stay here forever?"

"One or two of us will have to go out and look for help; the others will remain here in camp. That is the only way."

"Who's going?" asked Brown, "me and Tibbs?"

Jane shook her head. "I'm afraid Tibbs couldn't make the grade," she said; "he's never had any experience in anything of this sort, and anyway he'd be very much more useful in camp. I thought you and I should go. We know something about Africa, and how to take care of ourselves in the jungle."

"I don't know about that," said Brown. "I don't see how both of us can go and leave these people. They are the most helpless bunch of yaps I've ever seen."

The Sborovs showed their resentment of Brown's blunt appraisal, but they said nothing. Tibbs appeared shocked, but Annette turned away to hide a smile.

"I'll tell you what we'll do," continued the pilot. "You stay here and take care of these people and run the camp. I'll go out and look for help."

"I wouldn't trust him, Jane," said Alexis. "If he once got away, he'd never come back; he'd leave us here to die."

"Nonsense," snapped Jane. "Brown is perfectly right in saying that both of us should not leave you. None of you is experienced; you couldn't find food; you couldn't protect yourselves. No; one of us will have to stay; and as I can travel faster through the jungle than any of you, I shall go out and look for help."

There were several protesting voices raised against this program. Alexis sat regarding the girl through half-closed lids; he seemed to be appraising her; the expression in his eyes was not pleasant. Presently he spoke.

"You shouldn't go alone, Jane," he said. "You're right in

saying that I couldn't be of much help around the camp. I'll go with you; you should have someone to protect you."

Brown laughed, a very rude and annoying laugh. The princess looked shocked and startled.

"Why, Alexis," she cried, "I am surprised that you would even suggest such an impossible thing. Think of Jane's reputation."

It was now Jane's turn to laugh. "My dear Kitty," she cried, "don't be ridiculous. Of course, I don't intend to let Alexis go with me, but not for the reason that you suggest. When one's life is at stake, one may ride rough-shod over conventions."

"Naturally," agreed the prince.

"Well," said the princess, definitely, "Alexis may go; but if he goes, I go with him."

"That's right," said Alexis, "you got us into this mess; and now you're trying to put obstacles in the way of our getting ourselves out of it. If it were not for you, we could all leave together; and as for that, if it hadn't been for you and your American pilot, we wouldn't be in this fix now."

"Oh, Alexis," sobbed the princess, "how can you be so cruel to me? You don't love me any more."

He shot a contemptuous glance at her, and turned and walked away. There was an uncomfortable silence that was finally broken by Jane.

"I shall leave in the morning," she said, "very early. Do you think, Brown, that you could provide food for these people while I am away?"

"I reckon I can if they're light eaters and ain't particular what they eat," he replied, with a grin.

"Do you know which plants and fruits are edible and which are unsafe?" she asked.

"I know enough of the safe ones to get by on," he said, "and I'll leave the others alone."

"That's right; be very careful about what you eat and drink."

Brown grinned. "We won't have much to be careful about."

In the growing coolness of the jungle night, the warmth of the beast-fire was pleasant; and most of the party remained around it, only Alexis, moody and sullen, holding aloof. He stood in the opening of the men's shelter, glowering at the figures illuminated by the fire. His dark eyes rested upon his wife, who sat with her back toward him; and his expression at this time that he was free from observation was marked with loathing. The thoughts that were passing through his petty brain were not lovely thoughts. In the outer rim of the light from the fire, he looked what he was, a small, cheap grafter who had suddenly become sinister and dangerous.

And then his eyes moved on to Jane and his expression changed. He licked his full, weak lips—lips that were flabby and repulsive.

His gaze wandered again to his wife. "If it were not for you," he thought—"seventy million dollars—I wish I were out of here—that fellow, Brown; I'd like to kill him—Annette's not so bad looking—seventy million dollars—Paris, Nice, Monte Carlo—the old fool—Jane is beautiful—I suppose the old fool will live forever—dead, dead, dead—seventy million dollars."

Over by the fire, Jane was arranging for the guarding of the camp by night. "I think three four-hour shifts will be long enough," she said. "It's just a matter of keeping the fire going. If any animals come around, you'll be able to see their eyes shining in the dark. If they come too close, light a brand and throw at them. They are all afraid of fire."

"Oh, my dear, do I have to do that?" cried Kitty. "I never could, really, I mean, do I have to sit out here alone at night?"

"No, my dear," said Jane, "you'll be excused from guard duty. How about you, Annette? Do you think you could do it?"

"I can do my share, Madame," said the girl, "whatever the others do."

"Atta girl," said Brown.

"If I may make so bold as to suggest it, Milady," said Tibbs, deferentially, "I rather think the three men should stand guard. It's no job for a lady."

"I think Tibbs is perfectly right," said the princess. "And I really think that Alexis should not stand guard; he's a very susceptible person to colds; and night air always affects him; and now I think that I shall go to bed. Annette, come and help me."

"You'd better turn in, too, Miss," said Brown. "If you're going to start out early in the morning, you'll need all the sleep you can get."

Jane rose. "Perhaps you're right," she said. "Good night."

When she had gone, Brown glanced at his watch. "It's nine o'clock now, Tibbs. Suppose you stand guard until midnight, then wake me, and I'll take it until three. After that, his nibs, the grand duke, can watch until morning."

"Really, Mr. Brown, if you mean the prince, I rather fawncy he won't be caring to stand guard."

"Well, he's going to," said Brown, "and he's going to like it."

Tibbs sighed. "If it weren't for the princess," he said, "we wouldn't have to stay here at all. I don't fawncy staying here and just waiting. I'm sure something terrible will happen to us if Lady Greystoke leaves us. She's the only one that can do anything."

"Yes," said Brown, "the old girl is a damned nuisance. You might bump her off, Tibbs." Brown grinned, rose, and stretched. "I'll be turning in, Tibbsy. Wake me at midnight."

Sborov was sitting in the entrance of the shelter which was only a few steps from the fire and as Brown entered, he spoke to him. "I couldn't help but overhear your conversation with Tibbs," he said. "I am perfectly willing to do my share. Call me at three, and I will stand guard. I'm going to bed now. I am a very sound sleeper, and you may have difficulty in waking me."

The change in the man's tone and attitude so surprised Brown that for once he had no reply to make. He merely grunted as he passed on into the shelter. Sborov followed and lay down, and in a few moments Brown was fast asleep.

It seemed to him when Tibbs woke him at midnight that he had not slept at all.

He had been on guard but a few minutes when Annette joined him. She came and sat down beside him.

"What the dickens are you doing up this time of the morning, girlie?" he demanded.

"Something awoke me about half an hour ago," she said, "and I haven't been able to get back to sleep. I don't know what it could have been, but I awoke with a start; and I had a feeling that there was someone crawling around inside the hut. You know, it's really very dark in there after the curtain is hung up in front of the door."

12

Murder In the Night

MAYBE it was Lady Greystoke you heard moving around in the hut," suggested Brown.

"No," said Annette, "I could hear her breathing. She was sound asleep."

"Then it must have been the old girl."

"It was not she, either. After I woke up, I heard her sort of groaning in her sleep and snoring I guess it was, but she stopped right away."

"Then I guess you must have been dreaming, girlie," said Brown.

"Perhaps I was," said the girl; "but some unusual sound must have awakened me, for I sleep very soundly; and I was sure that I heard someone afterward."

"Perhaps you had better go back and go to sleep again now," he suggested.

"Really, Mr. Brown, I couldn't. I am so wide awake; and then I—I felt funny in there, as though—oh, I don't know." She lowered her voice to a whisper. "It was as though there were something terrible in there, something that frightened me. You don't mind my staying out here with you, do you, Mr. Brown?"

"I'll say I don't, girlie. You and Lady Greystoke are about the only human beings in the bunch. The rest of 'em are nuts."

"You do not like them, Mr. Brown?"

"Oh, the old girl's harmless; she's just a nuisance; and Tibbsy means well, I guess; but when it comes to doing anything more than pressing somebody's pants, he just ain't all there."

"And the other one?" inquired Annette. "I think you do not like him so much."

"Him? He's the last zero after the decimal point."

"No, I do not like him, either, Mr. Brown. I am afraid of him."

"Afraid of him? What you got to be afraid of him about?"

"In London he say things to me a man should not say to a nice girl."

"Well, the dirty so and so," growled Brown. "If he ever makes any cracks at you again, honey, let me know. Say, I'd spill him all over the ground and then wipe him up with himself."

"You would protect me, Mr. Brown?" She raised her dark eyes to his, questioningly.

"And how!"

The girl sighed. "You are so beeg and strong."

"You know," said Brown, "I like you a lot, girlie."

"I am glad. I think I like you, too."

Brown was silent for a moment. "If we ever get out of here," he said, presently, and then stopped.

"Yes?" she inquired. "If we ever get out of here, what?"

He fidgeted uneasily, and threw another piece of wood on the fire. "I was just thinking," he said, lamely.

"What were you thinking?"

"I was just thinking that maybe you and me—that maybe——"

"Yes?" she breathed, encouragingly.

70

"Say, you don't have to call me Mr. Brown."

"What shall I call you?"

"My best friends call me Chi."

"What a funny name; I never hear a name like that before. What does it mean? It is not really your name?"

"It's short for the name of the town where I come from—Chicago," he explained.

"Oh," she laughed, "then you spell it C-h-i and not S-h-y. I think maybe you should spell it the last way."

"I ain't never been accused of being shy before," he said, "but I guess you're right. When I try to say things to you, my tongue runs out on me."

"What funny expressions you use. You Americans are all so funny."

"Oh, I don't know," he said; "it's the foreigners that seem funny to me."

"Am I funny?"

"Well, you got some funny little ways with you, but when you pull them, they're cute."

"You think so? I am glad that you do, Mr. Brown."

"Chi."

"Chi. Have you another name? Maybe that would be easier to say."

"Yep. My real name's Neal."

"That's a nice name."

"So's Annette. I'm crazy about Annette."

"You like the name?"

"Yes, and the girl, too—I like the girl a lot." He reached over and took her hand and drew her toward him.

"No, you must not do that," she said sharply, and pulled away; and then suddenly she cried out, "oh, look, look," and pointed.

Brown looked up in the direction that she indicated. Blazing against the dark background of the forest were two yellow-green points of flame.

Annette moved quickly toward him and pressed against his side. "What is it?" she whispered in a frightened voice.

"Don't be scared, honey; it's only looking at us. That won't hurt us none."

"What is it?" she demanded.

"I've seen cow's eyes shine like that in the dark," he said; "it might be a cow."

"But you know it's not a cow. There are no cows in the jungle. You just say that so that I will not be frightened."

"Well, now that you mention it, maybe there ain't no cows in the jungle; but whatever it is, I'm going to frighten it away." He stooped over and gathered a stick from the fire;

71

one end of it was blazing. Then he stood up and hurled it at the burning eyes.

There was a shower of sparks, an angry growl, and the eyes disappeared.

"That fixed him," he said. "See how easy it was?"

"Oh, you are so very brave, Neal."

He sat down beside her; and this time, he boldly put an arm about her.

She sighed and snuggled closer to him. "A nice girl should not do this," she said, "but it make me feel so safe."

"You never was less safe in your life, girlie," said Brown.

"You think the eyes will come back?" she asked, with a shudder.

"I was not thinking about eyes, girlie."

"Oh."

It was long after three o'clock before Brown thought to awaken Sborov. When the prince came into the firelight, he was nervous and ill at ease.

"Did you see or hear anything during the night?" he asked.

"Something came up and looked at us," said Brown; "but I threw some fire at it, and it beat it."

"Everything all right in camp?" he asked.

"Sure," said Brown, "everything's O.K."

"I slept so soundly that anything might have happened," said the prince. "I never knew a thing from the time I lay down until you awakened me."

"Well, I guess I'll go tear off a few yards myself," said the pilot, "and you better go back in and try to get some sleep, girlie."

They walked together the few paces to the shelter. She shuddered a little. "I hate to go back in there," she said. "I do not understand why, but I just dread it."

"Don't be silly," he said. "There ain't nothing going to hurt you. That dream got your nanny."

"I do not know what is my nanny," she replied, "and I am not so certain it was a dream."

"Well, you run along like a good girl; and I'll sleep with one eye open. If you hear anything, call me."

It was daylight when Brown was awakened by a piercing scream from the adjoining shelter.

"My word!" exclaimed Tibbs. "What was that?" But Brown was already on his feet and running to the women's quarters. He saw Sborov standing by the fire, ashen-grey in the morning light. His lower jaw drooped loosely; his eyes were staring, fixed upon the hut in which the women slept.

Brown collided with Annette, who was running from the hut as he started to enter.

"Oh, Neal," she cried, "it was no dream. Something horrible happened in there last night."

He brushed past her and went into the hut. Jane was standing in horrified silence, gazing down at the Princess Sborov.

"God!" exclaimed Brown.

Kitty Sborov was dead, her skull split wide.

"How horrible," breathed Jane. "Who could have done this thing?"

Tibbs joined them. He remained silent and unmoved in the face of this gruesome discovery, always the perfect servant.

"Where is the prince?" asked Jane.

"He was on guard," said Brown. "He was standing there by the fire when I came in."

"Somebody will have to tell him," she said.

"I reckon it won't be no news to him," said Brown.

Jane looked up at him quickly. "Oh, he couldn't!" she cried.

"Well, who could, then?" demanded the pilot.

"If you wish, Milady," suggested Tibbs, "I will inform his 'ighness."

"Very well, Tibbs."

The man stepped out into the open. The prince was still standing gazing at the hut; but when he saw Tibbs coming toward him, he gathered himself together.

"What's the matter in there?" he asked. "What was Annette screaming about?"

"Something has happened to her 'ighness—she's—she's dead."

"What?—Who?—It can't be possible. She was quite all right when she went to bed last night."

"She has been murdered, your 'ighness," said Tibbs, "oh, so 'orribly!"

"Murdered!" He still stood where he was, making no move to approach the hut. He watched Jane and Brown emerge and come toward him.

"It is horrible, Alexis," said Jane. "I can't imagine who could have done it, nor why."

"I know who did it," he said, excitedly. "I know who did it and I know why."

"What do you mean?" demanded Jane.

Alexis pointed a trembling finger at Brown. "Last night I heard that man tell Tibbs to kill her. One of them must have done it, and I don't believe that it was Tibbs."

"Prince Sborov, I don't believe that it was either one of them," said Jane.

"Ask Tibbs if he didn't tell him to kill her," cried Sborov.

Jane looked questioningly at Tibbs.

"Well, Milady, Mr. Brown did suggest that I 'bump her off'; but it was only by way of being a joke, Milady."

"How was she killed?" asked the prince.

Jane looked puzzled. "Why—why, it must have been with the hatchet. Where is the hatchet?"

"Find the hatchet, and you'll have the murderer," said Sborov.

"But suppose he threw it away?" asked Jane.

"He couldn't have thrown it away. I've been on guard here since three o'clock, and nobody entered your part of the shelter after Annette went in after I came on guard. Whoever did it, probably hid it."

"It happened before you went on guard," said Annette. "It happened before Mr. Brown went on guard. It was that that awakened me; I know it now; and when I thought she was moaning in her sleep and snoring, she was really dying —it was the death rattle. Oh, how horrible!"

"Just when was that, Annette?" asked Jane.

"It was while Tibbs was on guard and about half an hour before Mr. Brown went on. I couldn't get back to sleep, and I went out and joined him. I sat up with him until he awoke the prince."

Jane turned to Tibbs. "Was Mr. Brown asleep when you went in to wake him at midnight?" she asked.

"Yes, Milady," replied Tibbs.

"How do you know?"

"Well, I could tell by his breathing for one thing; and then I had difficulty in arousing him."

"He might have feigned that," said Sborov.

"Was the prince asleep when you went in there, Tibbs, to awaken Brown?"

"He seemed to be sound asleep, Milady. I carried a burning brand in for a torch. I could see them quite distinctly."

"He was asleep, and I was pretendin' to be, I suppose," said Brown.

"Find the hatchet," said Sborov.

"Well, suppose *you* find it," retorted Brown. "I don't know where it is."

"Tibbs says that both of you were asleep. That leaves Tibbs and Annette and me under suspicion," said Jane.

"There ain't no sense to that way of figuring," said Brown. "We all know that you and Annette didn't have nothin' to do with it; so you two are out. I know damned well that I didn't do it, and I'm just about as sure that Tibbs didn't; so that puts it up to the only one in the bunch that would profit by the old woman's death."

"You'd profit as much as any of us," pointed out Sborov,

sullenly. "You knew that your life was at stake, that if you didn't get out of here very soon you might never get out. You knew and you said that my wife was all that made it impossible for us to start together tomorrow. I can see your whole line of reasoning, my man. You felt that the princess could never get out of here, anyway; and so you just hurried matters along by killing her yourself."

"All right, Sherlock Holmes, you've got it all figured out, haven't you? But what are you going to do about it?"

"Find the hatchet," repeated Sborov.

"All right," said Jane. "You men go in the women's part of the shelter and search, and Annette and I will search your part."

Sborov followed Jane to the door of the men's hut. "I cannot go in there where she is," he said, "I want to remember her as she was when I last saw her—alive."

Jane nodded. "Help us search here, then," she said.

There was really no place to search except among the litter of grasses that the men had used as beds.

Jane searched the pile upon which Alexis had slept, while Alexis took Tibbs' and Annette poked around in those belonging to Brown. Presently the girl's hand came into contact with something cold and hard. She stiffened as her fingers touched it, as though by intuition she knew what it was. With a shudder she withdrew her hand. For a moment she remained very quiet and tense. She was thinking rapidly. Then she arose to her feet. "There is nothing here," she said.

Sborov glanced up at her quickly. "There is nothing here, either," said Jane.

"I can find nothing in Tibbs' bed," said Alexis; "but perhaps, Annette, you did not search Brown's bed carefully enough. Let me see."

She took a step toward him as though to prevent the search. "What is the use?" she said. "It is not there; it's just a waste of time to look again."

"Nevertheless, I shall look," said Alexis.

Sborov stooped and slipped his hand in among the grasses. He did not have to search long. "Here it is," he said. "I don't see how you could have missed it, Annette," he added, with a sneer. "You must have had your own reasons."

He withdrew the hatchet from among the grasses and held it up to their view. The head was smeared with blood.

"Are you satisfied now, Jane?" demanded the prince.

"I can't believe it of Brown," she said.

"But you could have believed it of me?"

"Frankly, Alexis, yes."

"Well, you've got plenty of proof now as to who did it.

What are you going to do about it? The fellow ought to be destroyed."

"Who ought to be destroyed?" demanded Brown. He and Tibbs were standing in the doorway.

"The hatchet was found in your bed, Brown," said Jane. "The prince has it; as you can see, it is covered with blood."

"Oh, so you planted that thing in my bed, did you, you lousy little runt? Trying to frame me, eh?"

"I do not understand your talk," said Alexis. "I only know what I heard you say last night and what I found in your bed. Tibbs has already corroborated my report of what you said, and Lady Greystoke and Annette saw me find the hatchet in here right where you had hidden it."

Brown looked from one to another with a questioning expression in his eyes. Could it be that these people believed that he had done this thing? He realized that what slender evidence was at hand pointed to him.

"Well," he said, "don't get it into your heads that you're going to hang me."

13

Treachery

THE little band of Waziri warriors under Muviro had moved steadily westward since their encounter with Tarzan. The ten moved silently along a winding jungle trail; there was no song nor laughter; and when they spoke, which was seldom, their tones were low, for they were in a country strange to them, with the temper of whose people they were not familiar. They moved warily, every sense alert.

Some time during this day they hoped to contact the Bukena, the people who lived nearest to the Kavuru; and here they hoped to have word of Tarzan of the Apes.

Presently, above the subdued noises of the jungle, they heard the excited chattering of a monkey above them; and a moment later a familiar little figure swung downward through the trees.

"It is Nkima," said Muviro. "The big bwana must be near."

Little Nkima jabbered with excitement. He leaped to the shoulder of Muviro and jumped up and down, screaming and chattering. He leaped to the ground and ran ahead very fast, jabbering excitedly in his high, little voice, as he continually looked back at them. He would run ahead until a bend in the trail threatened to hide them from his view; then he would run back and tug at Muviro's legs before starting off again at great speed.

"Something is wrong," said one of the warriors to Muviro. "Little Nkima is trying to tell us."

"He wants us to hurry," said Muviro; "perhaps something has happened to the big bwana." Then he broke into a trot, his fellows following close behind; but still Nkima ran ahead always urging them to greater speed.

Members of a warrior clan that is trained from childhood in feats of endurance, the Waziri could maintain for hour after hour a pace that would soon exhaust an ordinary man.

Their smooth, ebony bodies glistening with sweat, their broad chests rising and falling to their unhurried breathing, their supple muscles rolling easily, they presented a splendid picture of primitive savagery, to which a note of barbaric color was added by anklets and armlets of strange design, their weapons, their shields, and the flowing white plumes that surmounted their heads.

Here, indeed, were men, the very sight of whom would have instilled respect, and perhaps fear, in the hearts of any strange tribesmen who might see them.

And thus it was, when breaking from the jungle into a clearing, little Nkima still in the lead, they burst upon the view of a score of women working in the fields before the village of Udalo, chief of the Bukena.

With terrified cries of warning, the women fled for the village gate.

Bukena warriors inside the kraal seized their weapons and ran to meet their women; and as the rearmost of the latter entered the village, the warriors made haste to close the gate behind them; and as some attended the gate, others manned the barbette inside the palisade over the top of which they could loose their arrows upon an enemy.

At the sight of the village and the fleeing women, Muviro had halted his warriors. He saw the hostile attitude of the Bukena, but he attributed it to the fact that they did not know whether he came in peace or war.

Nkima was very much excited. He waved his hands and jabbered loudly; he was trying so hard to make them understand that his master was a captive in the village. It was always a mystery to Nkima that these gomangani could not understand him. It seemed that no one could understand him except his cousins, brothers, and sisters, and his beloved Tarzan. Everyone else must be very stupid.

77

Muviro left his companions at a short distance from the village and advanced slowly toward the palisade, making the sign of peace that the villagers might know that they did not come with hostile intent.

Udalo, the chief, standing upon the barbette, looked down upon the approaching warrior and his companions. He knew that these were indeed fighting men; and while there were only ten of them he was glad to see the peace sign, for there might be many others back in the forest and this only an advance guard.

As Muviro halted at the foot of the palisade and looked up, Udalo addressed him.

"Who are you? What do you want?" he demanded.

"I am Muviro, chief of the Waziri. We have come here to meet our big chief, Tarzan of the Apes, or to get word of him. Has he been here?"

Gupingu, the witch-doctor, was standing beside Udalo. Searing his heart was the memory of a secret he dared tell no one—the secret of the release of Tarzan upon his promise that the Kavuru would not steal the daughters of Gupingu; and yet almost immediately Naika, his favorite daughter, had been stolen.

Gupingu was confident now that not only was Tarzan a Kavuru, but that it was he who had come back to steal Naika. Resentment and hatred burned in the breast of Gupingu. He recalled that Tarzan had said that he was a Waziri; and, assembling all the facts as he knew them, he conjectured that the Waziri were either the vassals or the allies of the Kavuru.

"Do not trust them, Udalo," he said to the chief; "they are the people of the Kavuru who escaped us. He has sent them back here to be revenged."

Scowling down upon Muviro, Udalo thought quickly.

He would like to be revenged upon the Kavuru but he feared reprisals; and, too, he did not know but what there might be a large body of them back in the forest. The truth or falsity of this he must ascertain before he could make any definite plans.

Annoyed because he had received no answer, Muviro spoke again, this time impatiently. "We come in peace," he said, "to ask a question. Is Tarzan, our master, here?"

"There," whispered Gupingu to Udalo, "he admits that the Kavuru is his master."

"He is not here," said Udalo; "we know nothing of him, and I do not know that you come in peace."

"You are not speaking true words," said Muviro. "Little Nkima, the monkey, is Tarzan's friend. He brought us here, and he would not have done so had Tarzan not been here."

"I did not say that Tarzan had not been here," retorted Udalo; "I say that he is not here, and that I know nothing of him. I do not know where he went after he left here. If

"We do not fear ten men," said Udalo! "the ten may enter the village; then we may talk. If you come in peace, you will do this; if you do not do it, Udalo will know that you have come to make war. As you can see, he has many warriors. We are not afraid of you, but we do not want war."

"We have come in peace," replied Muviro, "but warriors do not lay aside their weapons. If you have so many brave warriors, why should you fear ten men?"

"We do not fear ten men," said Udalo; "the ten may enter and bring their weapons, but the rest of your warriors must not approach the village."

"There are no others with us," said Muviro. "We are alone."

This was the information that Udalo wished. "You may come in," he said; "I will order the gates opened." Then he turned and whispered to Gupingu.

Murviro signalled for his men to approach. The gates swung open, and they entered the village of the Bukena.

Udalo and Gupingu had left the barbette and gone together toward the chief's hut. They were whispering volubly with many gesticulations, Gupingu explaining, Udalo assenting and giving orders. At the chief's hut they separated, Udalo remaining to await the coming of the visitors, while Gupingu hastened to his own hut.

As the Waziri entered the village street, they were surrounded by warriors and conducted to the hut of the chief, where Udalo awaited them.

Here commenced one of those long palavers so dear to the hearts of African natives. With endless circumlocution they iterated and reiterated, and in the end nothing had been said by Udalo other than that Tarzan was not in his village and that he knew nothing whatsoever about him; nor did he know anything concerning the Kavuru or the location of their village, none of which Muviro believed.

And while the palaver progressed, Gupingu was busy in his hut grinding herbs and boiling them in water to extract their juices. He constantly muttered and mumbled to himself, but it is doubtful that he was chanting an incantation over the mess that he was brewing and for the same reason that he did not lay out amulets before him or make passes over the brew with magic sticks or the tail of a zebra—he had no audience.

While the Bukena warriors and their visitors palavered and Gupingu concocted his brew, the women were busy preparing a feast at the orders of Udalo; and in the trees beyond the clearing, a little monkey waited, whimpering and desolated—waited for the release of his master whom he thought to be still confined in a hut in the village.

At last Gupingu left his hut, carrying his brew in a small gourd, and made his way directly to the women who were preparing the native beer for the feast.

The women were already filling the gourds that would be passed around among the warriors. Gupingu went to the one who was filling the large ceremonial gourd that would be passed first to the chief and then to the visitors. They held a whispered conversation and then Gupingu walked away, leaving behind him the small gourd containing his brew. He approached the palaver from the rear of the Waziri, and catching Udalo's eye he nodded. Then the chief clapped his hands and ordered the feast served.

The women came, bringing food and drink; and in the lead was one carrying the ceremonial gourd of native beer.

Udalo took it from her and in silence raised it to his lips. His throat moved, as in the act of swallowing; but none of the liquor passed his lips; then he passed it to Muviro, who took a long drink and handed the gourd to the Waziri next beside him; and so it passed among them all, but when the last of the ten had drunk, the woman was waiting to take the gourd, though it was not yet empty, and the other women brought other gourds of beer to the Bukena warriors; nor did Muviro nor any of his companions suspect that anything was wrong, for had they not seen Udalo drink from the same gourd as they?

Now food was brought, but Muviro did not partake of it. He was looking, strange and glassy-eyed, at his fellow Waziri. What had gone wrong with his eyes? Everything was blurred. He saw his men sitting there with stony stares, their bodies weaving drunkenly; then Muviro, the chief of the Waziri, staggered to his feet. He seized his long knife and drew it from his loin-cloth. "Kill!" he cried. "We have been poisoned." Then he lurched and fell.

Several of the remaining Waziri tried to rise; but the brew of Gupingu worked quickly and well; and though the Bukena warriors had leaped to their feet at a word from Udalo, following Muviro's command to his followers, their ready spears were not needed, as one by one the Waziri collapsed upon the ground.

The Bukena gazed in astonishment upon this strange sight, for only Udalo and one woman knew what Gupingu had done.

The witch-doctor leaped among the fallen Waziri and beat his chest.

"The medicine of Gupingu is strong," he said. "It lays

80

low the enemies of the Bukena; even the great Kavuru it lays low."

"Kill!" shouted a woman, and others took up the refrain. "Kill! Kill! Kill!"

"No," said Udalo. "Bind them securely so that they cannot escape and put them in the hut where the other Kavuru was confined. I shall send runners to the other villages of the Bukena; and when the moon is full on the second night, we shall dance and feast and eat the hearts of our enemies."

Shouts of approval met this announcement, as warriors fell to the work of binding the prisoners and carrying them to the hut where Tarzan had been confined.

In a tree at the edge of the jungle, a little monkey sat gazing disconsolately at the gates of the village. He brightened momentarily when he saw some warriors emerge; lithe young men these, who started off at a brisk gait in different directions; but they were not his beloved Waziri, and he sank again into despondency.

It was many hours before the Waziri recovered from the effects of the narcotic. After they commenced to regain consciousness it was some little time before they could realize their plight. Their heads ached and they were very sick. When they tried to move, they discovered that they were fast bound.

"I knew," said Muviro, after they were able to talk among themselves, "that the chief lied to me. I should have been more careful. I should not have drunk his beer or allowed you to."

"I saw him drink it, and so I thought it was safe," said another.

"He only pretended to drink it," said Muviro. "This Udalo is a very bad man."

"What do you think he will do with us?"

"I do not think," said Muviro; "I know."

"And what do you know?"

"I have heard about these Bukena. I have heard that while they are not cannibals, they do eat the hearts of their enemies, thinking that this will make them brave, for they are great cowards."

"They will eat our hearts?"

"Yes."

"When?"

"That we may not know until we are led out; but if we see that they are preparing for a great feast, we shall know that our end is near."

"And we must lie here and be slaughtered like goats?"

"If one of us can loosen his bonds, we may die as Waziri should—fighting," replied Muviro.

"If only the big bwana could know," said a young man; "he would save us."

"I think perhaps that the big bwana is already dead," said Muviro. "I think that Udalo has killed him, and eaten his heart; and if that is so, I am ready to die, too; for I do not care to live if the big bwana be dead."

"Nor I," said another. "I am so sick and my head hurts so, that I shall be glad to die."

Night came, but no one approached the hut to bring them water or food. They were very miserable, and Muviro was chagrined to think that he had been led into such a trap. He was ashamed of himself, and he felt that only death could atone for his great fault.

Miserable as they were, however, there was one even more miserable—a little monkey that shivered and trembled in a tree beyond the clearing that surrounded the village of Udalo, the Bukena. He heard the roar of Numa, the lion, and the cry of Sheeta, the leopard; and he climbed as high as he dared and hung there shivering and trembling waiting for the thing that he knew was about to leap upon him and devour him. For such was the life of little Nkima.

14

Nkima Forgets

NAIKI, the daughter of Gupingu, the witch-doctor, accompanied her new captor because the only alternative was to be left alone in the jungle, a prey not only to wild beasts but to the numerous demons that infest the grim forest. At first, she momentarily expected the worst; but as time went on and no harm befell her, she gained confidence in the tall, bronzed warrior who accompanied her. Eventually all fear of him vanished.

But if she were no longer afraid of Tarzan, she was far from being without fear; for the jungle night was very black and she conjured in that Stygian gloom all manner of horrifying creatures lying in wait to spring upon her. She could not understand how he travelled so surely through the darkness, and she marvelled at his great courage.

She knew that few men are so brave, and therefore it occurred to her that he must be a demon.

Here, indeed, was an adventure, one that she, Naika, could boast about as long as she lived; for had she not travelled at night through the jungle with a demon? She should have liked to ask him point-blank, but of course there was always the danger of offending a demon. Perhaps if she questioned him adroitly, he might accidentally reveal the truth.

It took quite a little will-power to screw up her courage to the point where she might ask him any question at all; but finally she succeeded. "What country are you from?" she asked.

"I am from the land of the Waziri."

"What sort of men are they?"

"They are black men."

"But you are white."

"Yes," he replied, "but many years ago, when I was much younger, I was adopted into the tribe."

"Have you ever met a demon?" she asked.

"No, there are no such things."

"Then you are not a demon?"

"I am Tarzan of the Apes."

"Then you are not a Kavuru?"

"I told you I am from the land of the Waziri. When you are back among your people, tell them that Tarzan of the Apes is not a Kavuru. Tell them also that he rescued you from the Kavuru, and that they must always be friends with Tarzan and the Waziri."

"I will tell them," said Naika; and, after a moment, "I am very tired."

"We will stop here the rest of the night," said the ape-man.

Picking her up, he carried her high among the trees until she was very much afraid; and when he set her down upon a branch she clung frantically to the bole of the tree.

Here the moon was filtering through the foliage, and it was much less dark than on the ground. In this semi-light, Tarzan cut branches and built a platform upon which Naika could lie during the night.

In the early morning, Tarzan gathered food for himself and the girl; and after they had eaten, they resumed their journey toward the village of the Bukena.

Feeling that she was approaching her home, and with all her fears dissipated, Naika's spirits rose. She laughed and chatted happily; and so at last they came to the edge of the clearing that encircles the village of the Bukena.

"You are safe now, Naika," said the ape-man. "Return to your people and tell them that Tarzan of the Apes is not their enemy." Then he turned and disappeared into the forest, but not before a pair of sharp little eyes had seen him; and as Naika ran shouting toward the gates of the village,

83

little Nkima swung through the trees screaming at the top of his voice, as he pursued his lord and master into the forest.

The diminutive monkey soon overtook the ape-man, and with a final ecstatic yelp leaped to one of his broad shoulders.

Tarzan reached up and took the little fellow in his hand. "So Nkima is back again," he said; "Sheeta did not get him."

"Nkima is not afraid of Sheeta," boasted the monkey. "Sheeta came into the trees hunting for little Nkima; crouching, he crept; he came close. Little Nkima took a stick and beat Sheeta on the head. Sheeta was afraid, and ran away."

"Yes," said Tarzan, "little Nkima is very brave."

Thus encouraged, the monkey became enthusiastic and still more imaginative. "Then came the gomangani, many gomangani; they were going to kill little Nkima and eat him. Little Nkima took two sticks and beat them on the head. They were afraid; they ran away."

"Yes," said Tarzan, "everyone is afraid of little Nkima."

Nkima stood up in the palm of Tarzan's hand and beat his chest. He grimaced, showing his teeth, and looked very fierce. "Everyone is afraid of Nkima," he said.

Back along the trail to the north, in search of the village of the Kavuru went Tarzan and Nkima; and in the village of the Bukena Naika was the center of an admiring and curious throng.

She told her story well, omitting nothing, adding considerable embroidery; it was a good story and it held her listeners spell-bound. She told it many times, for the blacks like repetition; and always she stressed the fact that Tarzan had saved her, that he was the friend of the Bukena and that they must never harm Tarzan or the Waziri; and at that time she did not know that ten Waziri lay bound in a nearby hut waiting for the orgy that would spell their doom.

The Bukena warriors looked at one another and at Udalo, their chief. Udalo was slightly disconcerted; his runners had long since reached their destinations, and by this time the inhabitants of several villages must be on their way toward his kraal. Udalo did not know what to do about it.

Gupingu was troubled, too. He realized now that the giant white, whom he had liberated, had not stolen his daughter as he had thought, but had rescued her and returned her to him. Udalo looked at him questioningly, but Gupingu did not know what to say.

At last the chief spoke, for he saw the question in the eyes of his warriors. "You said, Naika, that you thought this Tarzan of the Apes was a demon; you said that he was fearless in the dark, and that he did things that no man could do; you said also that he went through the trees even more easily than the Kavuru. All these things we believe, but we could not believe them if we knew that he were a man like ourselves. He must therefore be a demon. None but a demon could have escaped from his bonds and left the village as easily as he did."

"If he were a demon, why did he save me from the Kavuru and return me to the village?" demanded Naika.

"The ways of demons are strange," said Udalo. "I think that he wanted to make our fears dead, so that he could come safely into our village and harm us as he pleases. No, I am sure that he is a demon and a Kavuru, and that the prisoners we have taken are Kavuru. We shall not let them escape; they might come back and kill us, and furthermore the Bukena are coming from every village to dance and feast and eat the hearts of our enemies."

Thus did the highest court of the Bukena uphold itself and place its final seal upon the death warrant of Muviro and his warriors.

Through the brooding forest, moving northward, went the Lord of the Jungle, ignorant of the impending fate of his people; and on his shoulder rode Nkima, his little mind fully occupied with his boasting and the present.

Short is the memory of Manu, the monkey. Great is his egotism and his selfishness. Little Nkima had not meant to forget the Waziri; they were his friends and he loved them.

But being wholly occupied with thoughts of himself and with relief at being safe again in the arms of his master, the plight of the Waziri had been crowded into the background of his consciousness. Eventually he would think of them again, but perhaps only after it was too late to be of any benefit to them.

And so the afternoon was half gone, and Nkima was happy, and Tarzan was satisfied; for once again he was on the trail of the Kavuru, concerning whom his curiosity had been intrigued by his brief contact with Ydeni and the suggestion of mystery that Kavuru's few words had lent to the manners and customs of this strange and savage tribe.

Tarzan had not forgotten the Waziri; but his mind was at rest concerning them for he felt that now, because of his rescue of Naika, they would be welcomed in the village of Udalo and directed on their way toward the Kavuru country.

The ape-man seldom spoke unless that which he had to say warranted expression. Ordinarily he kept his thoughts to himself, especially in the presence of men; but he often relaxed with little Nkima and with Tantor, the elephant, for of such were the friendships of his childhood; and deep-rooted within him was the sense of their loyalty and sympathy.

Thus it happened that while he was thinking of the Waziri, he spoke of them to Nkima. "Muviro must be close to the village of the Bukena," he said; "so he and his warriors will not be far behind us when we reach the village of the Kavuru. Then little Nkima will have many good friends to defend him from Sheeta, the leopard, and from Hista, the snake, and from all the gomangani who would catch and devour him."

For a moment Nkima was silent. He was gathering his thoughts and his memory. Then suddenly he began to leap up and down upon Tarzan's shoulder and screech in his ear.

"What is the matter with you, Nkima?" demanded the ape-man. "Are your brains chasing one another around in your head? Stop screaming in my ear."

"Tarzan, the Waziri! the Waziri!" cried the little monkey.

Tarzan looked quickly around. "What of them?" he demanded. "They are not here."

"They are there," cried Nkima. "They are back there in the village of the gomangani. Their feet and their hands are wrapped with cord; they lie in the hut where Tarzan lay. The gomangani will kill them and eat them."

Tarzan halted in his tracks. "What are you saying, Nkima?" he demanded, and then as best he could in the simple language that is common to the greater apes, and the lesser apes, and the little monkeys, and to their cousin Tongani, the baboon, and to their friend Tarzan, he narrated all that he had witnessed since he had met the Waziri in the forest.

The ape-man turned about then, and started back toward the village of the Bukena. He did not ask Nkima why he had not told him this before because he knew full well; nor did he scold the little monkey, nor reproach him, for he knew that it would do no good. Little Nkima would always be a monkey; he was born that way; and he would never have the mind of a man, even though in many other respects he was more admirable than man.

The sun had not been long down when Tarzan came to the village. From a tall tree at the edge of the clearing, he looked down at the scene beyond the palisade. He saw that there were many people there, many more than there had been before; and he guessed that they were gathered for a feast. But his knowledge of the customs of the blacks told him that it would not be this night. Doubtless they were awaiting others that would come upon the morrow; perhaps then the feast would be held, and he guessed that the Waziri were being saved for sacrifice at that time.

When boldness is necessary, the ape-man acts boldly. No spirit of bravado animates him; and when no emergency confronts him, his acts reflect only the caution and stealth of the wild beasts who, impelled by instinct, avoid all unnecessary risks and dangers.

Tonight he reasoned that if the Waziri were already dead he could accomplish nothing by boldly entering the kraal of the Bukena; if they were still alive there was little likelihood that they would be harmed before the following night; but if he were wrong, and this night were the night set for their destruction, he would know it in ample time; for they would be brought out into the open where they would be tortured and killed for the edification of the assembled Bukena. Then he would have to do something about it; in the meantime, he would go closer where he could see and hear what transpired in the village.

"Tarzan goes into the village," he whispered to Nkima. "If Nkima comes, he will make no noise. Does Nkima understand?"

"No noise, no talk," repeated the monkey.

Moving quietly through the trees, Tarzan circled the village; and close beside him, silent as he, moved little Nkima.

At last the two came opposite the rear of the kraal. That part of the village seemed dark and deserted, for all were congregated in the wide street before the hut of Udalo, the chief.

Tarzan dropped to the ground and moved toward the palisade. When a few paces from it, he sprang swiftly forward, leaped into the air, and ran up the barrier with all the agility of little Nkima, who followed close behind him. Then the two dropped silently into the shadows among the huts in the rear of the village.

Creeping stealthily, noiseless as the shadow of a shadow, the two crept toward the hut of the chief. Separated biologically by countless ages, one a little monkey, the other a peer of England, yet there was little difference in the way they passed through the night and swung nimbly into the tree that overshadowed Udalo's hut.

As Tarzan looked down at close range upon the dancing, shouting blacks, he realized that they had been partaking too freely of their native beer; and he knew that under such circumstances anything might happen.

A big black, half drunk, was haranguing Udalo. The man was evidently a sub-chief from another village.

"Bring out the Kavuru," he said; "let us have a look at them; we'll give them a taste of what they are going to get tomorrow night."

"The others are not here," said Udalo; "we should wait for the rest of the tribe."

"Bring them out," demanded another; "we have not seen them; we want to see the Kavuru who steal our girls."

"Bring them out," shrieked a woman. "They stole my

87

daughter; let me burn out their eyes with a red-hot coal, that they may suffer as I have suffered."

Then Tarzan heard the voice of a child. "Do not harm the Waziri," she said; "they are the friends of Tarzan, and Tarzan is a friend of the Bukena. He saved me from the Kavuru and brought me back to my village."

"You cannot trust the Kavuru or a demon," said Udalo. He turned to some of his warriors. "Bring the prisoners," he said, "but see that they are not killed tonight."

Already Tarzan of the Apes was on the ground behind the hut of the chief. Here was an emergency. Every danger, every risk, must be faced without hesitation, boldly, after the manner of the Lord of the Jungle.

He moved quickly to the hut where he had been confined; and as he stooped and entered it, his sensitive nostrils told him that the Waziri were there.

"Silence," he whispered; "it is I, Tarzan. They are coming for you. I will cut your bonds. We will fall upon the warriors who come and take their weapons from them; bind and gag them; let them make no noise. Then bring them where Tarzan leads, to the rear of the chief's hut."

He worked quickly as he talked; and when the three warriors came to fetch the prisoners, all of them were free and waiting, waiting in silence in the darkness.

15

A Bit of Cloth

DON'T get it into your heads that you are going to hang me." There was a challenge in Brown's tone that sounded to Jane like the defiance of a guilty man; and yet she could not believe that it was he who had killed the Princess Sborov.

"We shall hang no one," she said. "We cannot take the law into our own hands; we must all be equally under suspicion until a properly constituted court of law determines our guilt or innocence. There is but one thing to do; we must try to reach the nearest established civilized authority, tell our story, and let the law take its course."

"I quite agree with you, Milady," said Tibbs.

"Well, I don't," grumbled Alexis; "it wouldn't be safe to

travel through this lonely country with a murderer who might easily kill all of us and thus dispose of all the witnesses who could testify against him."

"And what do you suggest?" asked Jane.

"That we leave the murderer here, make our way to the nearest post, report the affair, and leave it to the authorities to apprehend the guilty man and arrest him."

Jane shook her head. "But we don't know who the murderer is; in the eyes of the law, we are all equally suspects. No, the only proper thing to do is to find a magistrate or a commissioner, tell our story and request an investigation."

"Not for me," said Brown. "I wouldn't have a chance in one of these foreign ports. There ain't anybody in Europe got any use for an American anyway, but they sure knuckle down to titles. What chance would an American without money have against a prince with millions? Nix, Miss, there ain't nobody goin' to railroad my neck into a noose!"

"You see, Jane," said Alexis, "he practically admits his guilt. An innocent man would not be afraid to stand trial."

"Listen, Miss," said Brown, turning appealingly to Jane, "I ain't never bumped anyone off yet; but if you don't want another killing around here, make that fool shut up and keep shut up."

"Then you refuse to come with us, Brown?" demanded Jane. "I think you are very foolish."

"I may be foolish, Miss; but I ain't taking no chances with no foreign court. An English court might be all right, but we are not in English territory. No, I came out here with these people in the hopes I could get hold of that formula for perpetual youth. That would be worth millions back home; and now that I am here, I am going ahead and try to find it. I don't know how, but I am going to try."

"There are so few of us," said Jane, "and we are so poorly armed that we really ought to stick together, at least until we contact some friendly natives."

"I didn't plan on leaving you cold, Miss," said the pilot. "I'll stick until you and Annette are safe."

"I was sure you would, Brown; and now that that's settled, we've something else to do—a very unpleasant duty. The princess must be buried. I guess you men will have to dig the grave."

The only implement they had with which to dig was the hatchet that had been used to kill the princess; and thus a task, sufficiently gruesome in itself, was rendered incalculably more so.

While one of the men loosened the earth with the hatchet, the other two scooped it out with their hands; and while the men were thus occupied, Jane and Annette prepared the body for burial as best they might by wrapping it in articles of the victim's clothing taken from her baggage.

Annette wept continually; but Jane, even though she felt the loss infinitely more than the little French maid could have, remained dry-eyed. She had work to do, a duty to perform; and she could not permit her personal sorrow to interfere.

When all was in readiness and the body lowered into the grave, Jane recited as much of the burial service as she could recall, while the others stood about with bowed heads, the men uncovered.

"I think," said Jane, when it was all over and the grave filled, "that we had better break camp immediately; no one will want to remain here."

"Have you any plan?" asked Alexis. "Do you know where we are going?"

"There are only two things we can do," said Jane. "One is to follow this trail toward the west, and the other is to follow it toward the east. The toss of a coin could decide that as intelligently as any of us. Not knowing where we are, it is impossible to know in which direction lies the nearest friendly village. Personally, I should prefer going toward the east because there lies the country with which I am familiar, the country where I have many friends among the natives."

"Then we go to the east," said Brown. "You're boss; what you say goes."

"I doubt the wisdom of your decision, Jane," said Alexis. "The Belgian Congo must lie to the west, if we are not already in it, which I believe; and in that event, we shall strike civilization sooner by going in that direction."

"It's all guess-work at best, Alexis," said Jane. "It really doesn't make much difference which way we go. Let's leave it to a vote. How about you, Tibbs?"

"I—ahem—I beg pardon, Milady, I shall cast my lot with the majority."

"You're a lot of help," said Brown.

"And you, Annette?" asked Jane.

"Oh, if you and Mr. Brown wish to go to the east, I wish to go to the east also."

"That's settled," said Jane; "we go to the east then."

"I still object," demurred Alexis. "As the financial head of the expedition, the one who has paid and must pay all the bills, I believe that some consideration should be shown my wishes."

"Alexis," said Jane, "you make it very difficult. Like the rest, you will have to follow my orders, or when there is a question, accept the will of the majority. As for financing the expedition, each of us has the necessary wherewithal if we care to use it, and it's not money; it's cooperation and loyalty, courage and endurance."

Alexis had been watching her closely as she spoke, and suddenly his whole attitude changed. "I am sorry, Jane," he said, "I spoke thoughtlessly. You must understand that I am terribly upset by what has happened. I have lost my dear wife, and I am heart-broken."

Brown turned away disgustedly and held his nose with a thumb and forefinger.

"All right, Alexis," said Jane. "Now let's gather up what necessities we can carry and get going."

"How about breakfast?" demanded Brown.

"Oh, I had forgotten all about breakfast," said Jane. "Well, it will have to be bush-buck again."

"I don't believe I can eat a mouthful," said Annette to Brown.

"Oh, yes you can, girlie," replied the pilot; "you gotta eat whether you want it or not. We've probably got a lot of hard days ahead of us and we got to keep up our strength."

"I'll try," she said, "for you."

He squeezed her arm. "And say," he said, "you don't believe I done it, do you?"

"No, Mr. Brown, I do not believe it."

"Aw, can the mister, girlie."

"All right—Neal, but I do not see how he could have done it; I do not see how a man could kill his wife. She was such a nice lady."

"Yeah, she was sort of nuts, but she was all right at that. She was a whole lot better than him. As a matter of fact, the old dame killed herself."

"What do you mean? How could she kill herself so horribly with a hatchet?"

"Well, she done it all right; she done it when she told him she was going to change her will."

"Oh! What a terrible man."

"I've known of fellows that was bumped off for less than what this guy will get," said Brown. "Back in the land of the free and the home of the brave, you can get it done to almost any guy for a hundred smackers."

"One hundred smackers? What is a smacker? My English, she is not so good."

"I've noticed that, kiddo, but don't worry; I'll learn you."

"Now I must cook the meat for our breakfast," said Annette, "if you will cut off a few slices for me from the hind quarters."

"Sure." He felt in his pockets. "Where's my knife? Oh,

yes, I remember," and he turned to Jane. "Say, Miss," he called, "let me have my knife if you are through with it."

"You haven't any knife," laughed Jane, "but I'll loan you mine."

Brown rubbed his chin. "That's right; I did lose, didn't I?"

While Annette was cooking the antelope, the others busied themselves selecting such things as they thought they would need and could carry on the march. Tibbs was busy repacking suitcases under the direction of Alexis. Jane gathered her weapons together and then fastened a small hand-bag to the belt that supported her shorts. It was such a bag as a woman uses to carry her money, keys, lipstick, and such odds and ends. Other than this and her weapons, Jane selected nothing more than what she wore.

Brown, who was wearing aviator's boots, chose to take along an extra pair of shoes and several pairs of socks. He also crammed the contents of a carton of cigarettes into various pockets and inside his shirt. These things, with a supply of matches, and the fateful hand-axe, constituted his entire equipment. He knew the bitterness of heavy packs.

As Annette grilled the meat over the coals, her eyes were attracted by something at the edge of the fire, among the cooling ashes. It was a bit of burned fabric to which three buttons remained attached. With a piece of stick, she turned it over. As it had been lying flat on the ground near the edge of the fire, the underneath portion of the fabric was not burned; the color and pattern remained.

A look of recognition entered her eyes; then they half closed in brooding, speculative contemplation of her find.

Brown wandered over toward the fire. "I'll finish the meat," he said; "you go and gather together what you are going to take."

"I don't know what to take," said the girl. "I can't carry very much."

"Take whatever you need, girlie," he said; "I'll help you carry the stuff. Take extra shoes if you have them and plenty of stockings and a warm wrap. Unless I'm mistaken, we are going to need a lot of shoes and stockings, especially you. Them things you are wearing was never meant to walk in nohow."

"I have two pair of low-heeled shoes," said the girl.

"Then throw them things away and take the low-heeled ones."

"All right," she said; "I'll go and get my things together. While I am gone, you might like to look at this," and she touched the piece of burned fabric with the stick she was holding.

Brown picked the thing up and looked at it; then he

whistled as he raised his eyes to the person of Prince Alexis Sborov. Annette walked away to make up her bundle. Tibbs was still busy packing. Jane was seated on a rotting log, deep in thought. Brown was whistling; he seemed very much pleased about something. Presently he looked up at the others.

"Come and get it," he called.

"Beg pardon," said Tibbs, "come and get what?"

"Chuck," explained Brown.

" 'Chuck'!" sneered Sborov.

Jane rose. "I guess we eat," she said, "and after all, I am hungry. I didn't think I should be."

They all gathered around the fire where Brown had laid strips of cooked meat on a little bed of clean twigs close beside the coals.

"Come ahead folks; pitch in," said Brown.

"Tibbs," said Alexis, "you may fetch me a piece not too rare nor too well done—about medium."

Brown looked up in undisguised disgust. He jabbed a stick into a piece of meat and tossed it at Alexis. "Here, Napoleon," he said, "we are sorry we ain't got no gold platters; but the keeper of the imperial pantry ran out on us and no one else ain't got no key."

Alexis gave Brown a venomous look, but he picked up the sorry-looking piece of meat and took a bite of it.

"This is terrible," he said; "it's burned on the outside and raw on the inside. My stomach will never be able to stand such cooking as this. I shall not eat it."

"Well, ain't that just too bad!" said Brown. "Let's all cry."

"You better eat it, Alexis," said Jane. "You'll get awfully hungry before night."

"Tibbs will prepare my food hereafter," said Alexis haughtily. "I shall eat apart."

"That will suit me," Brown assured him, "and the farther apart, the better."

"Come, come," said Jane, "don't start that all over again; we've had enough of it."

"O.K. Miss," assented Brown; "but there is something I'd like to ask the grand duke. I notice that he's changed his coat. That was a mighty nice coat he was wearing last night, and I thought if he wasn't going to use it no more, I'd like to buy it from him—that is, if nothing ain't happened to it."

Alexis looked up quickly, his face paling. "I do not sell my old clothes," he said. "When I am through with it, I'll give it to you."

"That's mighty nice of you," said Brown. "May I see it now? I'd like to find out if it fits me."

"Not now, my man; it's packed with my other things."

"All of it?" demanded Brown.

"All of it? What do you mean? Of course it's all packed."

"Well, here's one piece you forgot, Mister," and Brown held up the charred remnant of the sleeve with the three buttons still remaining on it.

Sborov's face took on a ghastly hue; his eyes stared wildly at the bit of cloth, but almost as quickly he regained his self-possession.

"Some more American humor?" he asked. "That thing doesn't belong to me."

"It looks a powerful like the coat you was wearing last night," said Brown. "Annette thinks so, too; but Tibbs ought to know; he's your valet. Ever see this before, Tibbs?"

The valet coughed. "I—er——"

"Come over and take a good look at it," said Brown.

Tibbs approached and examined the piece of fabric carefully, turning it over and wiping the ashes from the buttons.

"When did you see that last, Tibbs?" demanded Brown.

"I—really—" He glanced apprehensively at Sborov.

"You're a liar, Tibbs," shouted the prince. "I never had a coat like that; I never saw it before. It's not mine, I tell you."

"Tibbs didn't say nothing," Brown reminded him; "he ain't opened his trap except to say 'I—er.' He never said it was off your coat; but you're going to, ain't you, Tibbs?"

"It looks very much like it, sir," replied the Englishman. "Of course, I couldn't exactly take oath to it, seeing as how it's so badly burned."

Brown turned his gaze upon Alexis. "The blood must have spattered some when you hit her."

"Don't!" screamed Alexis; "my God! don't. I never touched her, I tell you."

"Tell it to the judge," said Brown. "You'd better hang on to that evidence, Annette," he added; "the judge might like to know about that, too."

Alexis had quickly gained control of himself. "It was my coat," he said; "someone stole it out of my luggage; it's what you call in America a frame."

"Let's leave this whole terrible matter to the courts," said Jane; "it's not for us to try to decide, and constantly harping on it only makes our situation all the more bitter."

Brown nodded. "I guess you're right, Miss, as usual."

"Very well, then. If you have all finished eating, we'll start. I've left a note stuck up in the shelter telling about our accident and the direction we are taking, and giving the names of all in the party, just on the chance, the very remote chance, that someone might pass this way some day—some white hunter who could take our message out in case we never get out ourselves. Are you all ready?"

"All ready," said Alexis. "Tibbs, my luggage."

Tibbs walked over to where his small handbag, a large Gladstone, and two suitcases were stacked.

"Where's your luggage, Jane?" asked Alexis. "Brown could carry that."

"I'm carrying my own," replied Jane, "what little I'm taking."

"But you haven't any," said the prince.

"I am carrying all that I am going to take. We are not travelling de luxe."

They were all standing silently watching Tibbs trying to gather up the four pieces of baggage so that he could carry them.

"Beg pardon, sir," he said, "but if I may make so bold as to say so, I don't think that I can carry them all."

"Well, let Annette carry that small bag of yours, then. You certainly ought to be able to manage three pieces. I've seen porters carry twice that much."

"Not across Africa," said Jane.

"Well," said Alexis, "I've only brought along what I actually need; I've left nearly all of my stuff behind. Tibbs will have to manage somehow. If Brown were the right sort he'd help him."

Only by the exercise of all his will-power had Brown remained silent; but now he exploded. "Listen, mister," he said, "I ain't going to carry none of your stuff, and neither is Annette, and if Tibbs does, he's a damned fool."

"I fancy I rather agree with you, Mr. Brown," said Tibbs, and dropped all three of the pieces of baggage.

"What?" demanded Alexis. "You refuse to carry my luggage? Why, you impudent upstart, I'll——"

"No you won't, sir," said Tibbs; "I know just what you are going to say, sir, if I may make so bold as to say so; but it won't be necessary, sir." He drew himself up haughtily. "I am giving notice, sir; I am leaving your employ now, immediately."

"Lady Greystoke," said Alexis, with great dignity, "you have assumed command here. I demand that you compel these people to carry my luggage."

"Nonsense," said Jane. "Take an extra pair of shoes and some socks and whatever else you can carry, and come along. We can't waste any more time here."

And thus the unhappy party started upon the trail toward the east. They had had but two guesses; and they had guessed wrong, but fortunately they could not know the dangers and the terrors that lay ahead of them on the trail toward the east.

16

The Message

THE three Bukena warriors crept into the hut where Tarzan and the ten Waziri warriors lay waiting for them in silence.

As the last of the three entered, Tarzan leaped upon him. Powerful fingers closed about the fellow's throat; and simultaneously the other two were dragged down by Muviro and a couple of his warriors. There was no outcry; there was only the subdued sound of the shuffling feet of struggling men, and that for but a moment.

Quickly the three were bound and gagged; then the Waziri, headed by Tarzan, carried them to the tree beside the chief's hut, where a corner of the latter concealed them from the sight of the drunken natives assembled in the street in front.

Shouldering one of the warriors, Tarzan swarmed up into the tree; then after he had deposited his burden safely where it would not fall, the Waziri handed the other two up to him.

Taking his victims up into the denser foliage where they would not be visible from the ground, Tarzan laid them side by side across the huge branch that projected out over the Negroes assembled below.

Tarzan ran his rope through the bonds that encircled the ankles of one of the prisoners. Then he removed the gag from the fellow's mouth and lowered him, head foremost, toward the ground; but before the fellow's head broke through the foliage and came in sight of those below, Tarzan voiced the warning cry of the bull ape. Instantly the dancing stopped; the natives looked around them in evident terror; the sound was very close; it seemed right beside them, but as yet they had been unable to locate it.

Silence followed; and then the head of one of their fellows broke through the foliage above them, and slowly his body descended.

The blacks were already on the verge of panic, for this was a mysterious, supernatural occurrence for which they could find no explanation in their past experience; yet they hesitated, perhaps fascinated and momentarily incapable of movement.

The deep voice rang out above them. "I am Tarzan of the Apes. Let those beware who would harm Tarzan or his Waziri. Open the gates and let my people go in peace, or many of you shall die by the hand of Tarzan."

The victim hanging head downward found his tongue. "Open the gates," he screamed. "Let them go before they kill me."

Still the blacks hesitated.

"The time is short," said Tarzan, and then he started to drag the warrior back up into the tree again.

"Do you promise that none of us will be harmed if we open the gates?" demanded Udalo.

"None will be harmed if you open the gates and let us go in peace, returning their weapons to my Waziri."

"It shall be done," said Udalo. "Fetch the weapons of the Waziri; open the gates; let them go, and may they never return."

Tarzan drew the warrior back up into the tree and laid him beside his fellows.

"Keep still," he warned them, "and I shall kill none of you." Then he dropped to the ground and joined the Waziri.

Fearlessly they walked around the end of the hut; and the blacks gave way fearfully, opening a path before them. Some little boys ran timidly forward with their weapons, for the warriors had not dared to do so. The gates were opened, and Tarzan led his Waziri toward them.

"Where are my three warriors?" demanded Udalo. "You have not kept your word."

"You will find your three warriors alive in the tree above your hut," replied the ape-man. He halted and turned toward the chief. "And now, Udalo, when strangers come to your kraal, treat them well, and especially Tarzan and the Waziri." A moment later the black jungle night beyond the palisade had swallowed them.

Little Naika, the daughter of Gupingu, the witch-doctor danced up and down and clapped her hands. "It is he!" she cried. "It is the white warrior who saved me. I am glad that he and his Waziri got away before we killed them. I told you not to do it."

"Shut up," cried Udalo, "and go to your hut. I never want to hear that white man spoken of again."

"I thought that it was the end," said Muviro, as they crossed the clearing toward the forest.

"Thanks to Nkima's bad memory, it came very near being the end," replied the ape-man. Then he voiced a strange, weird note; and an answer came from the blackness of the jungle trees.

"He is still there," said the ape-man to Muviro.

"Hurry, hurry," cried the monkey. "Little Nkima is fighting with Sheeta, the panther; he is beating him on the head with a stick; he is pounding him on the nose. Sheeta is very frightened."

Tarzan grinned and walked on slowly through the forest, and when he came under the first tree, the little monkey dropped down upon his shoulder. "Where is Sheeta?" demanded Tarzan.

"Little Nkima beat him so hard on the face that he ran away."

"Little Nkima is very brave," said the ape-man.

"Yes," replied the monkey, "little Nkima is a mighty fighter, a mighty hunter."

The following day, Tarzan and the Waziri moved slowly toward the north, resting often, for the latter were still suffering from the effects of the drug that had been administered to them by Gupingu, the witch-doctor. Finally, when Tarzan realized their condition more fully, he ordered a halt; and the party went into camp upon the banks of a river.

As time had never been a matter of consequence to the ape-man, delays, except in cases of immediate emergency, gave him no concern. He could wait there for one day, or two days, or as long as was necessary while his warriors recuperated; nor would he leave them while they needed someone to hunt for them. He made them rest therefore while he foraged for food.

The day after they had left the village of Udalo, a lone warrior trotted into the clearing and approached the gates of the kraal. The white plume of the Waziri waved above his head; and in his hand he carried a split stick, in the end of which an envelope was inserted.

When warriors met him at the gates, he asked to see the chief; and they took him to Udalo, but not without misgivings; for he bore a marked resemblance to the ten prisoners who had escaped them.

Udalo eyed the warrior sullenly. "Who are you?" he demanded, "and what do you want in the village of Udalo?

"I am a Waziri," replied the man. "I bear a message for the big bwana, Tarzan. The sun has risen many times since he left his country to come here in search of the Kavuru. I have followed to bring this message to him. Have you seen him?"

"He has been here, but he has gone," said Udalo, sullenly.

"When did he go, and in which direction?" asked the messenger.

"He went away yesterday with ten Waziri warriors. They took the trail toward the north. You will follow him?"

"Yes."

"I will give you food before you go, and when you find Tarzan tell him that Udalo treated you well." The fear of the Lord of the Jungle was in the heart of Udalo, the chief.

It was mid-day of the following day. The Waziri lay resting in their camp beside the river. Tarzan squatted at the base of a tree fashioning arrows for his quiver. Little Nkima perched upon one of his shoulders, busily occupied by that age-old simian pastime of searching for fleas upon his belly. He was vastly contented.

Presently the ape-man raised his head and looked toward the south where the trail debauched upon the clearing where they were encamped.

"Someone comes," he said.

The Waziri stirred themselves. Some of them seized their weapons and started to rise, but Tarzan reassured them.

"There is no danger," he said; "there is only one. He comes boldly, and not by stealth."

"Who could it be?" asked Muviro. "We have seen no one in all this lonely country since we left the Bukena village."

The ape-man shrugged. "We shall have to wait," he said, "until our eyes tell us, for he is down-wind from us."

Little Nkima, noting the listening attitudes of the others, abandoned the pursuit of a singularly notable specimen and following the example of the Waziri, stared intently toward the south.

"Something comes?" he asked Tarzan.

"Yes."

Little Nkima slipped quickly down behind Tarzan's back, and peered anxiously across his left shoulder. "Something is coming to eat little Nkima?" he demanded.

He glanced up into the tree behind him, gauging the distance to the lowest branch, and debated in his little mind the wisdom of discretion. However, feeling reasonably safe in his present sanctuary; he stood his ground; and a moment later a lone warrior trotted into the clearing. At sight of the party encamped there, he voiced his pleasure in a series of savage whoops; and the Waziri returned his greeting in kind, for he was the runner bearing a message for Tarzan.

As he came forward with the message in the split stick to deliver it to Tarzan, little Nkima evinced great interest and as the message was handed to his master he seized the stick and commenced to scold and jabber when Tarzan took the envelope from it.

The ape-man removed the message and dropped the envelope to the ground, whereupon little Nkima sprang upon it and occupied himself in a futile endeavor to make it remain upright on the end of the stick as the messenger had carried it.

The Waziri were looking expectantly at Tarzan as he read the message, for messages delivered in the depths of the forest were rare indeed.

As he read, Tarzan's brow clouded; and when he had finished he turned to Muviro.

"There is bad news, bwana?" asked the black.

"The mem-sahib left London for Nairobi in an aeroplane," he said; "that was just before the big storm. You remember, Muviro, that after the storm broke we heard an aeroplane circling above?"

"Yes, bwana."

"We thought then that it was in great danger. Perhaps that was the ship in which the mem-sahib rode."

"It went away," Muviro reminded him, "and we did not hear it again. Perhaps it went on to Nairobi."

"Perhaps," said the ape-man, "but it was a very bad storm and the pilot was lost. Either that, or he was in trouble and looking for a landing place; otherwise he would not have been circling as he was."

For some time Tarzan sat in thought, and then the silence was broken by Muviro. "You will go back at once to Nairobi, bwana?" he asked.

"What good would it do?" asked the ape-man. "If they reached Nairobi, she is safe; if they did not, where might I search? In an hour an aeroplane might fly as far as one could travel on the ground in a day; perhaps, if they had trouble, it flew for many hours after we heard it before it came down; and if the pilot were lost, there is no telling in what direction it went. The chances are that I should never find it; even if I did, it would be too late. Then, too, it may as easily be that it came down in the direction we are going as in any other direction."

"Then we may continue to search for my daughter, Buira?" asked Muviro.

"Yes," said Tarzan. "As soon as you are rested and well again, we shall go on toward the country of the Kavuru."

Little Nkima was becoming more and more excited and irritable. Notwithstanding all his efforts, the envelope would not remain upright upon the end of the stick. He chattered and scolded, but it availed him nothing; and then Tarzan noticed him, and taking the stick from him spread the slit end open and inserted the envelope.

Nkima watched him intently, his head cocked upon one side. Tarzan repeated the operation several times, and then he handed the envelope and the stick to Nkima.

An adept in mimicry, the monkey re-enacted all that he had watched Tarzan do; and after a few trials succeeded in inserting the envelope into the end of the stick.

His achievement filled him with enthusiasm and pride. Jabbering excitedly, he leaped from Waziri to Waziri until all had examined the marvel that little Nkima had wrought; nor did his excitement soon subside, and in the exuberance of his spirits he went racing through the trees clinging tightly to the stick that bore the envelope in its end.

Tarzan and the Waziri laughed at his antics.

"Little Nkima is proud because he has learned a new trick," said one.

"He thinks now he is a great witch-doctor among the monkeys," said Muviro.

"It is like many of the useless things that man learns," said Tarzan. "It will never do him nor anyone else any good; but if it makes him happy, that is enough."

For three days more the Waziri rested, and then Muviro said that they were ready to continue on toward the north.

In the meantime, Tarzan had dispatched the runner back to Nairobi with a message for Jane and also one to the authorities there, asking them to make a search for the ship in the event that it had not already arrived.

Little Nkima was still intrigued by his new accomplishment. He would sit for an hour at a time taking the envelope out of the stick and putting it back in, and he never permitted it out of his possession. Wherever he went, he carried the stick and the envelope with him.

Having been several days in this camp, and having seen no danger, Nkima, always restless, had formed the habit of wandering farther and farther away. He found some other little monkeys of his own species with whom he tried to make friends; but in this he succeeded only partially; the males bared their teeth and chattered at him, scolding; and sometimes when he came too close, they chased him away. But handicapped though he was by his stick and his envelope, he always succeeded in eluding them; for Nkima was an adept in escaping danger.

But there was one who did not bare her teeth and scold. However, it was difficult for Nkima to find her when there was not an old male hanging around; and old males can be very disagreeable.

This last day in camp, however, he was more successful; he discovered her some little distance from her fellows.

The young lady was coy; she did not repulse him but she led Nkima a merry chase through the trees. It was all in fun; and they were enjoying it greatly, for she was not really trying to escape from Nkima, nor was he seriously intent upon capturing her, for he knew that eventually she would stop and let him come close.

And so, thoughtless of time or direction or distance, they swung through the trees, a little lady monkey and Nkima with his stick and his envelope.

They had had a glorious time and thoroughly understood one another when the little lady finally came to rest upon a broad branch. That they might permanently cement this friendship, each was soon searching for what he might find upon the head of the other, and certainly that is almost the last word in intimacy—the final proof of trust and confidence and friendship.

They were very happy, and only once did a shadow momentarily becloud this bliss. That was when the young lady sought to snatch the stick and envelope from Nkima. He bared his teeth in a terrible grimace, and gave her a resounding box on one of her shell-like ears. She lowered her head sheepishly then and cuddled closer to him, and it was plain to see that she liked this dominant male and his cave-man tactics.

What a day for little Nkima! They hunted for fruit and nuts; they ate together; they scampered through the trees; they sat enfolded in each other's arms; and little Nkima was entirely unaware that Tarzan and the Waziri had broken camp and started north again. Perhaps if he had known, it would have made no difference at the moment for the alchemy of love works strange metamorphoses in the minds of its victims.

To their consternation, while they were still far away, night overtook them; and they were afraid to return through the menacing darkness of the glowering forest. They were afraid; but they were happy, and when the moon rose it looked down upon two little monkeys clutched tightly in each other's arms. Above their heads rose a little stick bearing an envelope in its split end.

17

The Snake

I T WAS with feelings of relief that the five left the scene of the tragedy that had cast a pall of gloom and horror over them; and while the future held out little of encouragement to them, the very fact of being on the move raised their spirits to some extent.

Brown had insisted upon marching at the head of the little column, and Jane had acceded to his request. Annette stayed as close to Brown as she could. Jane brought up the rear and Alexis walked with her. Tibbs plodded along behind Annette.

Either because he tired more quickly than the others, or because he wanted to get out of earshot of those whom he considered servants and beneath him, Alexis lagged.

"We shouldn't fall so far behind the others," said Jane. "We must not become separated. You will have to walk a little faster, Alexis." Her tone was just a little impatient.

"I thought it would be nice for us to be alone together, Jane," he said. "You see, you and I have nothing in common with those others; and it must be as much of a relief to you as to me to have the companionship of one of your own class."

"You will have to get over that," said Jane; "there are no class distinctions here."

"I am afraid you do not like me, dear lady."

"You have been very annoying at times, Alexis."

"I have been terribly upset," he replied, "and most of all by you."

"By me? What have I done?"

"It is not that you have done anything; it is just that you are you. Can't you understand, Jane? Haven't you noticed?"

"Noticed what?"

"From the first, you attracted me strangely. There seemed to be no hope, though, and I was desperately blue; but now I am free, Jane." He seized her hand. "Oh, Jane, can't you like me a little?"

She jerked her hand from his. "You fool!" she exclaimed. His eyes narrowed menacingly. "You are going to regret that," he said. "I tell you I'm in love with you, madly in love. I'm desperate, and I won't stand idly by and see an illiterate aeroplane pilot get the woman I want."

"Just what do you mean by that?" The girl's eyes and voice were level and cold.

"It's too obvious to need explanation. Anyone can see that you are in love with Brown."

"Alexis, did you ever hear a man referred to as an unspeakable cad? I have; but until this minute I never knew what it meant. I never could have conceived the sort of man it describes until now. Move on now. Get away from me. Get up there with Tibbs."

Instantly his manner changed. "Oh, Jane," he pleaded, "please don't send me away. I don't know why I ever said that; I was just mad with jealousy. Can't you understand that it is because I love you so? Can't you understand and forgive me?"

She made no reply but started ahead, increasing her gait to overtake the others.

"Wait!" he exclaimed, huskily. "You've got to listen to me. I'm not going to give you up." He seized her by the arm and pulled her toward him, endeavoring to throw his arms about her. Then she struck him; and, jumping back, levelled her spear to hold him off.

For a moment they stood there facing one another in silence; and in that moment she saw something in his eyes, in the expression on his face, that made her fear him for the first time. She knew then how really dangerous he was, and it was no longer difficult for her to believe that he had murdered his wife.

"Go up there now as I told you," she said, "or I will kill you. There is no law here but the law of the jungle."

Perhaps he, too, read something in her narrowed lids and icy tone, for he did as she bid, and went on ahead of her in silence.

By mid-afternoon, Tibbs and Alexis and Annette were almost exhausted; and when the party reached a favorable spot, Jane called a halt.

The trail by which they had come had followed the meanderings of the stream upon which they had been camped, and thus the water problem had been solved for them.

"What now, Miss?" demanded Brown. "Hadn't we better rustle some grub?"

"Yes," she replied. "I'll go out and see what I can bring in."

"I'm going to have a look-see myself," said Brown. "We can go in different directions and maybe one of us will find something."

"All right. You go on up the trail, and I'll take to the trees and follow the river. I may run across a drinking hole." She turned to the others. "And while we are gone, the rest of you can be building a boma and gathering firewood. All right, Brown, let's get going."

The three that remained in camp seemed physically unable to drag themselves to their feet, but Alexis was resourceful.

"Tibbs," he said, "go out and gather material for the boma and get some firewood."

Motivated by years of servile obedience, the Englishman rose painfully to his feet and started away.

"I'll help you, Tibbs," said Annette, and started to rise.

Alexis laid a restraining hand on her arm. "Wait," he said, "I want to talk with you."

"But we must help Tibbs."

"He can do very nicely by himself. You wait here."

"What do you want, Prince Sborov? I've got to go and help Tibbs."

"Listen, my dear," said Alexis, "how would you like to have a hundred thousand francs?"

The girl shrugged. "Who would not like to have a hundred thousand francs?" she demanded.

"Very well, you can earn them—and very easily."

"And how?" Her tone was skeptical.

"You have something that I wish. I will pay you one hundred thousand francs for it; you know what it is."

"You mean the burned sleeve of your coat, Prince Alexis?"

"You won't let them frame me, Annette? You won't let them send me to the guillotine for something I didn't do, when everybody in this party hates me; they will all lie about me, and when they bring that piece of burned cloth into court, I shall be convicted in spite of my innocence. Give it to me. No one need ever know; you can say that you lost it, and as soon as we get back to civilization I will give you one hundred thousand francs."

The girl shook her head. "No, I could not do that. It may be all that will save Mr. Brown."

"You are wasting your time on Brown," he said, nastily. "You think he loves you, but he doesn't. Don't be fooled."

The girl flushed. "I have not said that he loves me."

"Well, you think so; and he's trying to make you think so; but if you knew what I know, you wouldn't be so anxious to save his worthless head."

"I do not know what you mean. I do not care to talk about it any more. I will not give you the piece of cloth."

"Well, I'll tell you what I mean, you little fool," snapped Alexis. "Brown's in love with Lady Greystoke, and she's in love with him. What do you suppose they've gone off into the jungle for? Why, to meet each other, of course."

"I do not believe it," said Annette. "I will not listen to any more."

She started to rise; and as she did so, he leaped to his feet and seized her.

"Give me that piece of cloth," he demanded, in a hoarse whisper. The fingers of his right hand encircled her throat. "Give it to me or I'll kill you, you little fool."

Quick as a cat, and with surprising strength, she tore herself away from him and screamed.

"Help, Tibbs! Help!" she cried.

The Englishman had not gone far, and he came running back.

"If you tell on me," cried Sborov in a low whisper, "I'll kill you. I'll kill you as I killed her."

Annette looked into his eyes, as Jane had, and was frightened.

"What's wrong, sir?" demanded Tibbs, as he approached them.

"It wasn't anything," said Alexis, with a laugh. "Annette thought she saw a snake."

"I did see a snake," she said.

"Well, it's all right now, Tibbs," said Alexis; "you can go back to your work."

"I shall need a little help, sir," said the Englishman. "I cannot do it all alone."

"I'll come with you, Tibbs," said Annette.

Alexis followed them. He walked very close to Annette and whispered, "Remember, if you tell them."

"I don't fancy having a snake around the camp," said Tibbs, "the nasty beggers. I don't like 'em."

"Neither do I," said Annette, "but I won't be afraid when Mr. Brown comes back. If a snake tries to harm me then, he will kill it." She did not look at Tibbs as she spoke, although she seemed to be addressing him, but at Alexis.

"I think I would not tell the others about the snake," said Sborov; "it might frighten Lady Greystoke."

"My word, sir, I don't believe she's afraid of anything, sir."

"Nevertheless, see that you don't mention it," cautioned Alexis.

"Why, here's Mr. Brown now," cried Tibbs. "He's running. Something must have happened."

"What's wrong?" demanded Brown. "I heard someone scream. Was that you, Annette?"

"Annette saw a snake," said Alexis. "Did you not, Annette?"

"Where is it?" asked Brown. "Did you kill it?"

"No," replied the girl, "I had nothing with which to kill it; but if it frightens me again, you will kill it."

"You bet your life I will, girlie. Where is it now?"

"It got away," said Alexis.

Annette looked straight into his eyes. "Next time it will not get away," she said.

Brown's pockets were bulging with fruit which he took out and laid on the ground.

"I hope this ain't poison," he said. "I had a heck of a time getting it. Lady Greystoke will know whether or not we can eat it."

"Here she comes now," said Annette.

"What luck, Jane?" asked Alexis.

"Not so good," she replied, "just a little fruit. I didn't see any game." Her eyes fell on the fruit that Brown had gathered. "Oh, you found the same thing," she said. "Well, it won't taste very good, but it's safe and it's food. I thought I heard a scream a few moments ago. Did any of you hear it?"

"It was Annette," said Brown; "she seen a snake."

Jane laughed. "Oh, before Annette gets out of Africa, she'll be used to snakes."

"Not this one," said the girl.

A puzzled expression crossed Brown's face. He started to speak, and then evidently thinking better of it remained silent.

Not much had been accomplished toward the building of the boma and collecting the firewood; so Jane and Brown lent a hand in the work which moved much more rapidly with the aid of the hand-axe.

It was dark before the work was completed, and then they felt that they could take their ease around the fire that Jane had built.

Jane showed them how they might make the fruit that constituted their sole food supply more palatable by roasting it on the end of a stick. So hungry were they that even Sborov ate without complaining; and as they ate, a pair of eyes watched them from behind the concealing foliage of a nearby tree.

Brown had insisted that the three men assume the duty of guarding the camp; and though Jane and Annette insisted upon doing their share, the pilot was firm in respect to this matter and would not be moved.

"Two hours on and four off won't hurt nobody," he insisted, "and you girls are going to need all the sleep you can get if you're going to keep up with us."

The statement made Jane smile, for she knew that she could endure more than any of them, not excepting Brown; but she appreciated the spirit that animated him; and knowing how jealous men are of their protective prerogative she bowed to his will rather than offend him.

The three men matched coins to determine the order in which they should stand guard.

"I wish you'd let me be a sentry," said Annette.

"No, that ain't no work for a girl," said Brown.

"Oh, please, Neal, just once," she begged. "Oh, please."

"Nothing doing."

"Oh, just one little hour. You are on from two to four, Neal. Wake me at four and let me stand guard until five. Then I will wake the prince. It will be almost morning, anyway."

"Let her do it, if she wants to," said Jane.

"All right," said Brown, "but it ain't goin' to be the regular thing."

All were stretched out around the fire, apparently sleeping, when Tibbs woke Brown for his first tour of duty at eight o'clock.

Tibbs was so exhausted that he was asleep almost as soon as he lay down. Then Annette raised on one elbow and looked around. A moment later she came over and sat down beside Brown.

"You better get back to bed, kid," he said.

"I just wanted to talk with you for a minute, Neal," she said.

"What's on your mind, girlie."

She was silent for a moment. "Oh, nothing in particular," she replied. "I like to be alone with you; that is all."

He put an arm about her and pressed her closer, and thus they sat in silence for a moment before Brown spoke again.

"You know, I've been thinking a lot about that snake business, Annette," he said. "It sounded sort of fishy to me. You sure you wasn't stringin' me?"

"Stringing? I don't know what stringing is."

"Well, skip it. I seen funny looks pass between you and the grand duke when you was handing me that line about snakes. On the level now, kiddo, give me the low-down."

"The low-down?"

"The facts—truth. What was it all about?"

"I am so afraid of him, Neal. Promise me that you won't tell him that I told you. I think of what he did to her; he would do the same to me; he said so."

"What? He said he'd kill you?"

"If I told."

"If you told what?"

"That he had tried to take that piece of coat sleeve away from me."

"That was when you screamed?" he asked.

"Yes."

"I'll get him for that," said Brown.

"Please don't say anything about it; please promise me," she begged. "Only don't leave me alone with him again."

"All right, then," he promised; "but if he ever makes another break like that, I'll sure get him. You needn't be afraid of him."

"I am not afraid when you are with me. I do not know what I should do if it were not for you."

"You like me a little, kid?"

"I like you a great deal, Neal."

He pressed her closer to him. "I guess I like you a lot, too—more than I ever liked anyone else."

She nestled closer to him. "Tell me how much that is," she whispered.

"I'm not much good at saying things like that. I—I—well, you know what I mean."

"I want to hear you say it."

He cleared his throat. "Well—I love you, kid."

"And you don't love Lady Greystoke?"

"Eh? What!" he exclaimed. "What put that into your head?"

"He said so; he said that you loved her, and that she loved you."

"The dirty rat! Imagine that dame, the wife of an English viscount, falling for me. That is to laugh."

"But you might—what you call it—fall for her."

"Not on your life, kid; not while I've got you."

She put her arms around his neck and drew him down toward her. "I love you, Neal," she murmured, before their lips met.

They felt that they had the night and the world to themselves, but that was because they were not aware of the silent watcher in the tree above them. She sat with him until he awoke Sborov.

The camp was sleeping soundly when Tibbs finished his tour of duty at two in the morning and called Brown again.

At four Brown hesitated to awaken Annette, but he had given his word that she might stand guard for an hour; so he shook her gently.

"It's four o'clock and all's well," he whispered. Then he kissed her ear. "And now it's better."

She raised herself to an elbow, laughing. "Now you lie down and sleep," she said, "and I'll stand guard."

"I'll sit along with you for awhile," he said.

"No, that was not in the bargain," she insisted. "I want to watch alone. I shall feel very important. Go on, and go to sleep."

Then quiet fell upon the camp—a quiet that was unbroken until Jane awoke after daylight. She sat up and looked about her. No one was on guard. Alexis, who should have been, was fast asleep.

"Come on, sleepy heads," she cried; "it's time to get up."

Brown sat up sleepily and looked around. He saw Alexis just awakening.

"I thought the grand duke was on guard," said Brown. "Did you take his place?"

"There wasn't anyone on guard when I woke up," said Jane, and then she noticed. "Where is Annette?"

Brown sprang to his feet. "Annette!" he cried. There was no answer. Annette was gone.

18

A Bit of Paper

W HEN morning broke, Nkima, had he been a man, would have said that he had not slept a wink all night; but that was because when he was awake he was so worried and frightened that the time had dragged interminably. During the night, he regretted that he had not stayed with Tarzan and determined to return to the camp the first thing in the morning; but when morning came, dispelling the gloom with brilliant sunshine, his little monkey mind forgot its good resolution and concerned itself only with the moment and his new playmate.

Off they went, racing through the jungle, swinging from limb to limb, scampering high aloft, dropping again to lower levels.

Nkima was very happy. The sun was shining. It would always shine. He could not vision that another night of cold and dread was coming quickly.

Farther and farther toward the west they scampered, farther and farther away from camp; and in one hand Nkima clutched the little stick with the split end, topped by the soiled and crumpled envelope. Through all the playing and the love-making and the long night, little Nkima had clung to his sole treasure.

The little she, who was Nkima's playmate, was mischievous. She was also covetous. For long had she looked upon the stick and the envelope with envy, but she had been cuffed once for trying to take them; so she was wary, yet the more she saw them, the more she wished them.

Nkima was running along a branch holding the envelope on high. The little she was following in his wake when she saw her chance—just ahead, a limb beneath which Nkima would have to pass. Quickly she sprang upward and raced ahead along this limb; and, as Nkima passed beneath her, she reached down and seized the envelope. She was disappointed because she did not get the stick, too; but even a part of this wonderful thing was better than nothing.

Having achieved her design, she scampered on ahead as fast as she could go. Nkima witnessed the theft, and his heart was filled with righteous anger and indignation. He pursued her, but fear lent her a new speed.

On they raced; but the little she always seemed to have the advantage, for she steadily outdistanced Nkima until she was lost to his sight; and then his indignation and sorrow at the loss of his treasure was submerged in a fear that he had lost the little she also.

But he had not. He came upon her perched innocently in a high-flung crotch, contentedly eating a piece of fruit. As Nkima approached her, he looked for the envelope. It was gone. He wanted to pound her, but he also wanted to hug her; so he compromised by hugging her.

He asked for his bit of paper. Of course, he had no name for it; but he made her understand. It seemed that she had become frightened and thrown it away.

Nkima went back a little way to look for it, but he became interested in some fuzzy caterpillars that he passed on the way; and when he had eaten all that he could find, he had temporarily forgotten the paper.

A little river flowed beneath them. Rivers always intrigued Nkima. He liked to follow them; so he followed this one.

Presently he espied something that brought him to a sudden stop. In a small, natural clearing on the bank of the river was a flimsy man-made hut.

Nkima thought that there must be gomangani around; and he was wary, but he was also very curious. He watched and listened. The place seemed deserted. Finally he mustered sufficient courage to drop to the ground and investigate.

Followed by the little she, he crept toward the entrance to the hut. Cautiously he peeked around a corner of the door frame and peered within. There was no one there. Nkima entered. Luggage and clothing were strewn about the floor. He looked things over, seeking what he might appropriate. Then his eyes fell upon a piece of paper fastened to the wall with a sliver of wood. With a yelp of delight, Nkima leaped for it. Then he scampered out of the hut with his prize, raced across the clearing, and swarmed up to the topmost branches of a giant tree. Behind him came the little she.

By the time Nkima had succeeded in inserting the piece of paper in the notch at the end of the stick, his interest in the other things that he had seen in the hut had, monkey-like, waned.

Now he recalled the tall warrior who had brought the piece of paper in the end of the stick to Tarzan. Nkima decided that he would do likewise. He felt very important and was only sorry that he did not have a white plume to wave above his head.

Holding to this single idea for an unusually long time, Nkima raced back in the direction of the camp where he had left Tarzan and the Waziri.

It was late in the afternoon when he got there, and his little heart leaped into his throat when he discovered that his friends were gone.

He was very sad and a little frightened, although it was not yet dark; but when his lady friend came and sat close beside him, he felt better.

Unfortunately, this respite from despair was all too brief. The little band of monkeys to which his playmate belonged came trooping through the trees. They saw Nkima and the shameless young creature who had run away with him.

Jabbering, chattering, scolding, several of the males of the clan came swinging through the trees toward Nkima and his light-of-love. For a moment, just a fleeting moment, Nkima had visions of standing his ground and doing battle; but the leading male was an old fellow, very large and strong. His fangs were bared in a most disconcerting manner; and he voiced terrifying threats that made Nkima's heart quail, so that on second thought he determined to go elsewhere and go quickly; but his lady friend clung to him tightly, hampering his movements, for she, too, was frightened. Perhaps she did not want to lose Nkima who, after all, had a way with him.

The terrifying old monkey was approaching rapidly, and then Nkima did a most ungallant thing; he struggled to free himself from the lady's embrace, and when she only clung more tightly he tore at her arms to disengage himself, and then struck her in the face until she finally released him.

By now, Nkima was screaming in terror. The little she was screaming, and so were all the other monkeys. Bedlam reigned in the jungle; and to the accompaniment of this din of rage and terror, little Nkima broke away and fled; but through it all he had clung to his stick with its fluttering bit of paper, and now toward the north he bore it away like a banner, but scarcely triumphantly.

Some of the males pursued him for a short distance; but when terror impelled little Nkima only a bird on the wing might hope to overtake him; and so his pursuers soon gave up the chase.

For some time thereafter, Nkima did not reduce his speed; he continued to flee, screaming at the top of his voice.

It was only after he had almost reached the point of exhaustion that he slowed down and looked back, listening. In his mind's eye was the picture of the snarling visage of the old male; but he was nowhere to be seen, nor was there any

112

sound of pursuit; so little Nkima took heart and his courage commenced to return. He even swaggered a little as though he were returning triumphant from a well-earned victory. Had he had a wife, he would have gone home to her and bragged of his exploits; there are men like that; so who may censure little Nkima who was only a monkey.

Presently he found the trail of Tarzan and the Waziri. He knew that they had been travelling north, and so he came down and sniffed the earth in the game trail that they had been following. Clear in his nostrils was the scent spoor of his friends. This heartened him, and he hurried on again.

Little Nkima moved through the trees many times faster than a man on foot. His fear of the coming jungle night held him to his purpose, so that he did not stop along the way to chase butterflies and birds.

That night he perched high among the smaller branches where Sheeta, the panther, cannot go.

19

Hate and Lust

T HE discovery that Annette was missing from the camp momentarily stunned the remaining members of the ill-fated expedition.

"What could possibly have become of her?" demanded Jane. "I know that she wouldn't just have wandered off into the jungle. She was too much afraid of it."

Brown advanced slowly upon Sborov. There was murder in his heart and it was reflected in his eyes. "You know where she is, you rat," he said. "Tell me what you've done with her."

Sborov fell back, instinctively raising his hands in defense. "I know nothing about her," he said; "I was asleep."

"You lie," said Brown, still advancing.

"Keep away from me," cried Sborov; "don't let him get me, Jane; he'll kill me."

"You're right I'm going to kill you," growled Brown. It was then that Sborov turned and ran.

Brown sprang forward. In a dozen steps he had over-taken the terrified man and seized him by the shoulder. Screaming, Sborov wheeled to fight with all the mad ferocity of the cornered rat fighting for its life. He pounded and scratched and bit, but the American bore him to the ground and closed his fingers upon his throat.

"Where is she?" demanded the American. "Where is she, you——"

"I don't know," gasped Sborov. "As God is my judge, I don't know."

"If you don't know, you might as well be killed anyway, for you ain't no good for anything then nohow."

Brown's fingers tightened upon the throat of the terrified Sborov, who still struggled and fought furiously to free himself.

All that it takes so long to tell happened in the span of a few brief seconds.

Nor during this time was Jane idle. The instant that she realized the gravity of the situation and that Brown was really intent upon destroying Sborov, she seized her spear and ran toward them.

"Stop it, Brown," she commanded. "Let the prince up."

"Not 'til I've given him what's coming to him," cried the pilot; "and he's going to get it, even if I hang for it."

Jane placed the point of her spear beneath Brown's left shoulder-blade and pushed until he felt the sharp point against his flesh.

"Drop him, Brown," demanded Jane; "or I'll run this spear straight through your heart."

"What do you want to kill me for, Miss?" demanded Brown. "You need me."

"I don't want to kill you, Brown," she said; "but that fact won't do you any good unless you obey my command and remember that I am leader of this expedition. You are doing a foolish thing, Brown; you haven't any evidence to uphold your judgment. Remember, we haven't made the slightest investigation. We should do that first to determine the direction in which Annette left camp, and whether she left alone or was accompanied by another. We can also tell by examining the spoor if she went willingly or was taken by force."

Slowly Brown's fingers relaxed upon the throat of the struggling, gasping prince; then he released him and rose slowly to his feet.

"I guess you're right, Miss," he said; "you're always right; but poor little Annette—what she told me yesterday about that rat made me see red."

"What did she tell you?" asked Jane.

"He waylaid her yesterday and tried to take that piece of coat sleeve away from her, and then he threatened to kill her if she told. It wasn't no snake that made her scream yester-

114

day, Miss, leastways not an honest-to-God respectable snake; it was him. She was terribly afraid of him, Miss."

Alexis was gasping his breath back slowly. He was trembling from head to foot from terror.

"Is this true, Alexis?" demanded Jane.

"No," he gasped. "I just asked her for the coat sleeve so that I could see if it was really mine, and she commenced to scream just to get me in trouble. She did it just for spite."

"Well," said Jane, "we're not accomplishing anything this way. The rest of you stay where you are while I look for some kind of tracks. If we all wander around looking for them, we'll obliterate any that there may be."

She started to circle the camp slowly, examining the ground carefully. "Here they are," she said presently; "she walked out this way, and she went alone."

Jane walked slowly for a few yards, following the footprints of the missing girl; then she stopped. "They end here," she said, "right under this tree. There is no indication of a struggle, no sign that she was forced. As a matter of fact, she walked very slowly. There are no other footprints near hers. It is all very strange."

Jane stood for a moment, looking first at the footprints that ended so mysteriously and then up into the branches of the tree above. Suddenly she sprang upward, seized a branch and drew herself up into the tree.

Brown came running forward and stood beneath her. "Have you found anything, Miss?" he asked.

"There's only one explanation," she replied. "People do not vanish in thin air. Annette walked from the camp to the spot where her footprints ended beneath this tree; she did not return to the camp. There is only one place that she could have gone, and that is up here where I am."

"But she couldn't have jumped up there the way you did," protested Brown. "She just couldn't have done it."

"She didn't jump," said Jane. "Her tracks would have shown it, if she had jumped. She was lifted up."

"Lifted up! My God, Miss, by what?" Brown's voice was trembling with emotion.

"It might have been a snake, Miss, if you'll pardon me for suggesting it," said Tibbs; "it could have reached down and wound itself around her and pulled her up into the tree."

"She would have screamed," said Brown; "we'd have heard her."

"Snakes charm their victims so that they are helpless," said Tibbs.

"That is all poppycock, Tibbs," said Jane, impatiently. "I don't believe snakes do anything of the sort, and it wasn't a snake that got her anyway. There has been a man up here.

He has been in this tree for a long time, or if not a man some sort of a man-like creature."

"How can you tell that?" demanded Brown.

"I can see where he squatted on this big branch," she replied. "The bark is scuffed a little, for he must have remained in the same position for a long time; and then in a line between where his eyes would have been and the camp, some small twigs have been cut away with a knife, giving a less obstructed view of the camp. Whatever it was, sat here for a long time watching us."

Sborov and Tibbs had approached and were standing nearby. "I told you I had nothing to do with it," said the former.

"I can't figure it out," said Brown; "I just can't figure it out. If she had been frightened, she would have screamed for help and some of us would have heard her."

"I don't know," said Tibbs, "but I saw something like it once before, sir. His Grace had a castle on the east coast up in Lincoln. It was a most lonely place, overlooking the North Sea. We only went there once a year for about six weeks; but that was enough, and what happened there the last time was why I gave notice. I couldn't stand the place any longer. Her Grace, the Duchess, was murdered there one night, and that was 'arrowing enough; but what 'appened three days later was, to my way of thinking, even worse.

"Her Grace had a maid she was very fond of, and three nights after the duchess was murdered, the maid disappeared. She just vanished in thin air, as it were, sir. There was never a trace found of her from then until now, and the country folk round said that Her Grace had come back for her—that it had 'appened before in the Castle of the Duke of Doningham—so I was thinking——"

"For Pete's sake, shut up!" cried Brown. "You'll have us all nuts."

"Horrible," muttered Alexis.

"Well, whatever it was, it wasn't a ghost," said Jane. She dropped to the ground beside Brown and laid a hand on his arm. "I'm sorry, Brown," she said; "I know you were very fond of her, but I don't believe that there is anything we can do, except to try to reach some outpost of civilization and report the matter. Then a search will be made."

"It will be too late then," said Brown. "I reckon it's too late now. She was so little and delicate. She couldn't have stood very much. She probably is dead by this time." He stopped speaking and turned away. "Perhaps she's better off dead," he added.

In silence the four ate of what little they had to eat, and then set out once more on their seemingly hopeless journey. There were few attempts at conversation. The four seemed stunned by the series of calamities that had overtaken them. Suspicion, fear, and distrust dogged their footsteps; and beside them stalked the shadow of the nameless menace that had snatched Annette away.

Brown suffered more than the others, so much so that his mind was numb even to his hatred of Alexis. So completely did he ignore him that it was as though the man did not exist.

Jane walked at the rear of the column. Her tread was firm and light; but Alexis, who was directly in front of her, was footsore and weary. He was, however, no worse off than Tibbs for whose soft muscles continued exercise was little better than torture.

"Jane," said Sborov, after they had walked a long way in silence, "haven't you any idea what it was took Annette away?"

Jane shook her head. "All I know is that I don't believe in ghosts, and that no animal could have done it; therefore it must have been a man, but what sort of man, I have no idea. Whatever it was must have been as agile as a monkey, and for that reason I cannot bring myself to believe that it was a member of any native tribe—they are, as a rule, far from being excellent climbers; and I never heard of one who travelled through the trees as this—creature must have to reach our camp and depart again with Annette without leaving any spoor on the ground."

"But you are willing to believe now, that it was not I?" queried Sborov.

"There is no reason to believe that you did it," replied Jane.

"Then why not give me the benefit of the doubt in the other matter. You must know that I couldn't have killed Kitty."

"What does it matter what I think?" asked Jane. "That is a matter for the court to decide."

"Your opinion matters a lot to me, Jane. You have no idea how much."

She looked at him shortly. "I have no desire to know."

The note of finality in her tone was lost on Sborov. "But I want you to know," he persisted. "I've never known anyone like you; I'm mad about you, Jane. You must have seen it."

The girl shook her head impatiently. "That will be about enough of that, Alexis," she said. "Our situation is sufficiently difficult without your making it any worse."

"Does it make it any worse for you to know that someone is with you who loves you very much?" he demanded. "Oh,

117

Jane," he cried, "I could make you very happy." Then he seized her arm and tried to draw her to him.

Once again she wrenched herself free; once again she struck him heavily in the face with her open palm. Instantly his expression changed. His face became contorted with rage.

"I'll get you for this, you little——"

"You'll do what?" demanded a man's voice angrily.

The two looked up. Brown was striding toward them, followed by Tibbs. The hand-axe swung at the pilot's side in his right hand. Sborov cowered and backed away.

"I'm going to finish you now, once and for all," said Brown.

Jane stepped between the two men. "No, Brown," she said, "we can't take the law into our own hands, as much as we'd like to."

"But you're not safe as long as he's alive; none of us is."

"I can take care of myself," replied Jane; "and if I can, I guess the rest of you can."

Brown hesitated, but finally he acquiesed. "Very well," he said, "I can wait." There seemed a world of meaning in those few words, nor was it lost on Sborov.

That night they camped again near the little river whose winding the trail followed.

The instant that they stopped, Sborov and Tibbs threw themselves upon the ground thoroughly exhausted.

"If I may say so, Milady," said the latter, "I fancy I couldn't carry on for another half hour if my life depended upon it. Tomorrow you had better go on without me; I'm afraid I can't keep up, ma'am; and I'm only delaying the rest of you."

"You're doing splendidly, Tibbs," said Jane, encouragingly. "I know it's hard on you now; but you'll be surprised how quickly your muscles will toughen as they get accustomed to the work, and then you'll be able to keep up with any of us."

"I 'ope so, Milady, but the way I feel now I don't believe I'll be able to go on."

"Don't worry, Tibbsy, we'll stick by you," said Brown, reassuringly.

"It's mighty good of you, Mr. Brown, but——"

"But nothing," said Brown. "We could get along with one less member in this outfit," and as he spoke, he stared straight at Sborov, "but it ain't you, Tibbsy."

"Now," said Jane, "I'm going out to look for meat. I want you men to promise me that you will not quarrel while I'm gone. We have already had too much bloodshed and disaster."

"Tibbsy don't never fight with no one," said Brown, "and I won't be here; so you won't have to worry."

"You won't be here?" demanded Jane. "Where are you going?"

"I'm going with you, Miss."

"But you can't. I can't hunt with you along."

"Then you won't do no hunting," said Brown, "because I'm going with you. You may be boss, but there's one thing you ain't going to do no more."

"What is that?" asked the girl.

"You ain't going off alone by yourself, again, after what happened to Annette."

"If I may say so, Milady, I think Mr. Brown is quite right. We can't take any chances with you, Milady."

Jane shrugged. "Perhaps you're right," she said, "from your point of view, but really I'm much better able to take care of myself in the jungle than any of you."

"That ain't neither here nor there," said Brown. "You just ain't going into the jungle alone, and that's that."

"All right," said Jane, with a laugh. "I suppose I'll have to give in. Come ahead then, Brown; we'll see what we can find."

Tibbs and Alexis watched them depart, and then the former turned to the prince. "Beg pardon, sir," he said, "but hadn't we better start building a boma and gathering firewood?"

"Yes, you had," said Alexis; "and you'd better hurry up about it as it will soon be dark."

"You're not going to help me, sir?" demanded Tibbs.

"Certainly not, my man. I'm far too tired."

"And 'ow about me, sir? I'm tired, too." Tibbs was surprised at his own temerity.

"You've no business to be tired. I'm not paying you to be tired. I'm paying you to work. Come, get busy; and don't be impudent. You seem to be forgetting yourself, Tibbs."

"If I may make so bold as to say so, your 'ighness, if you're not careful, I shall."

"What do you mean, you impertinent puppy?" demanded Alexis.

Tibbs sat down on the ground and leaned his back against the tree. "I mean, sir, that if you don't help and do your share there won't be any boma and there won't be any firewood when Lady Greystoke and Brown come back to the camp. I daresay they'll both be very angry, especially Brown. If I were you, sir, I wouldn't antagonize him any more. I suspect that he does not like you; and out here in the jungle sir, where there ain't no laws nor no Bobbies, he wouldn't need much more of an excuse to kill you."

For a minute or two Alexis sat in silent thought; then he

rose painfully and slowly. "Come on, my man," he said, "and I'll give you a hand with the boma."

It was almost sunset when Jane and Brown returned with a small antelope, slices of which Tibbs was soon grilling before a cooking fire, while the others sat silently waiting.

There was little conversation as they ate their slender meal. It was an ill-assorted company, with little in common among them other than the grim disasters which had befallen them and which made such depressing conversation that they were taboo as though by a tacit understanding. The girl and Brown each found the other the most congenial member of the party; and what little talk there was passed between these two; but very soon even they were silent; and presently all slept, except Tibbs who had the first watch.

The long night wore on to the accompaniment of savage, jungle sound, usually remote but sometimes so close as to arouse the sleepers—stealthy sounds, weird sounds, fierce and savage sounds, sometimes whispering, sometimes thundering, died softly, dying into nothingness, or reverberated through the jungle until the earth trembled.

Each in his turn, the men stood guard. At four in the morning, Tibbs completing his second tour, awoke Alexis who was to follow him.

Shivering in the chill of early morning, Sborov piled more wood upon the fire. Then he stood with his back toward it gazing out into the night.

Just beyond the farthest reaches of the firelight rose a black, impenetrable wall of darkness—a mysterious world filled with nameless terrors; when a tongue of flame leaped higher in the air than its fellows its light glanced momentarily from the bole of a tree or from a cluster of leaves giving the impression of movement out there beyond the rim of his little world.

There were noises, too, sounds that he could not interpret. His fear and his imagination put strange interpretation upon the things that he saw and heard. A moaning woman floated at the border line of reality. He could swear that he saw her.

Sborov recalled the ghost of the murdered woman that came back for her maid, and cursed Tibbs. A beast screamed and Sborov shuddered.

He turned away from the forest and sought to concentrate his mind upon other things. His eyes wandered over the figures of his sleeping comrades. They fell upon the hand-axe lying close beside Brown. Sborov breathed an imprecation and tore his gaze away. It fell on Jane and rested there. How beautiful she was. Why did she spurn him? He had always had luck with women. He fascinated them, and he knew it. He could not understand why Jane repulsed him; and so he blamed Brown, whom he hated, assuring himself that the fellow had talked against him and embittered Jane's mind.

His eyes wandered back to Brown and the hand-axe. How he hated the man and feared him. The fellow would kill him. He had threatened him more than once.

Alexis felt that if the man were dead, his own life would be safer and—there would be no one to stand between him and Jane.

He rose and walked nervously to and fro. Every once in awhile he shot a glance at Brown and the axe.

He walked closer to Tibbs and listened. Yes, the fellow was already asleep, sound asleep. He must have been asleep almost at the instant he touched the ground. Jane was asleep, too, and so was Brown. Sborov assured himself of both of these facts.

If Brown were only dead! The thought repeated itself monotonously, drumming on his tired brain. If Brown were only dead! Presently Alexis Sborov seemed galvanized by a sudden determination. He moved directly, though stealthily, toward the sleeping Brown. He paused beside him and kneeled upon one knee. Listening intently, he remained there silent, motionless; then cautiously one hand crept out toward the axe.

Brown moved and turned in his sleep, and Sborov froze with terror; then the pilot resumed the regular breathing of sleep. Sborov reached out and seized the axe handle. His mad eyes glued upon the forehead of the sleeping man, he raised the weapon aloft to strike.

20

Nkima Plays a Game

TARZAN AND the Waziri moved on in search of the village of the Kavuru. It was yet early in the morning; the dawn mists still defied the efforts of a low-swinging sun to dispel them. The spirits of the searchers were low, for they were many long marches from their homeland; and with each passing day a sense of the futility of their quest had been increasingly impressed upon them, for not once since they started had they seen any sign or clue to suggest that they were on the right track; only vague rumors based upon tribal legend had suggested the fate of Buira, the daughter of Muviro.

Several of the warriors felt that they were chasing a myth; and only great courage and loyalty kept them, uncomplaining, on the trail.

It was true that Tarzan had met Ydeni, the Kavuru, and that he had rescued Naika, the daughter of Gupingu, and heard her story; yet these things had occurred at such a remote distance from the land of the Waziri that even Muviro was commencing to doubt that it had been a Kavuru who had been responsible for the disappearance of Buira, for why should these strange men go so far afield when they could find young girls much closer to their mysterious village.

But upon this chill and misty morning, it was not the Waziri alone who were depressed and discouraged. Upon the trail behind them, a damp and bedraggled little monkey swung through the trees. In one hand he carried a stick in the end of which fluttered a bit of paper; that he still clung to it was a miracle, for Nkima was not particularly tenacious of purpose. Perhaps it had become a fixed idea, for the stick was often an encumbrance to him; yet it never occurred to him to discard it.

There was however another thought that was forming in his mind—it was the thought that he was very far from his own country, that he had lost Tarzan and could never find him again, and that he was very much afraid. It made him wish to turn around and start for home. He was almost upon the verge of turning about, when he recollected the grimacing visage of the disagreeable old male whom Nkima was certain thirsted for his life-blood somewhere upon the back trail; and then there were Sheeta, and Hista, the snake, and the bad gomangani. All these lay behind him; and until he encountered some of their like upon the trail he was following, his little mind so functioned that he could not anticipate their presence there—what little Nkima did not know did not bother him. And so he continued on his way into a land that seemed free from inhospitable monkeys and bloodthirsty beasts and men.

As the ascending sun warmed him, his spirits rose; and after he had discovered and robbed a bird's nest, sucking the eggs, he felt equal to any adventure.

Then came the crowning moment of happiness. In the trail ahead of him, he saw a file of ten ebon warriors led by the giant white man who was his god. With a loud scream of joy that attracted the attention of the men below him, Nkima fairly flew through the trees to drop upon one of Tarzan's broad shoulders.

"Where has Nkima been?" asked the ape-man. "Tarzan thought that at last Sheeta had caught him."

"Little Nkima has been fighting with all the Manus in the forest," replied the monkey. "They tried to stop little Nkima from coming through their trees, but he scratched them and bit them and hit them with a stick; then he chased them into the country where Kudu, the sun, lies down at night. That is where little Nkima has been; that is what he has been doing; that is why he has been away from Tarzan."

The ape-man smiled. "Little Nkima is very brave," he said, as he stroked the little head nestled in the hollow of his neck.

Tarzan noticed that Nkima still carried the message stick, and was surprised that his little friend should have been constant to one idea for so long a time; and then he noticed that the paper in the end of the stick was not the same as that which Nkima had taken away with him. The ape-man's curiosity was aroused.

"What is that in the end of your stick, Nkima?" he asked. "Where did you get it? It is not the thing that Tarzan gave you. Let me see it." And he reached for it.

Now Nkima had forgotten just why he had clung to the stick. He had forgotten that he had been mimicking the Waziri warrior who had carried the message to Tarzan. Also, he was very happy and wanted to play; so when Tarzan tried to take the paper from the end of the stick, Nkima saw therein a challenge and an invitation to a new game; and so he leaped nimbly from Tarzan's shoulder and scampered away, waving the stick with its bit of fluttering paper above him.

The ape-man called to him to come back; but Nkima's thoughts were wholly centered upon play; and he only climbed the higher, grimacing and chattering in great good humor, as he challenged the ape-man to catch him.

Perhaps if Tarzan had guessed the message that fluttered from the end of the cleft stick and all that it meant to him and one dear to him he would not have laughed so lightly and let Nkima go his way unrebuked, but he did not know. Upon such trivial things may hinge the lives and happiness of men.

Seeing that Tarzan did not pursue him, nor even pay any further attention to him, Nkima soon lost interest in the game and started to descend again to his master. But once more Fate intervened, this time in the form of a fledgling bird trying its wings for the first time in short, uncertain flights.

Little Nkima espied it, and forthwith forgot all else in the excitement of the chase. When the bird rested upon a twig he crept toward it; but when he would have seized it it flew away just eluding his grasp. Again and again was this repeated, and as long as the bird remained in sight the excitement of the chase held Nkima enthralled.

Farther and farther north he followed the fledgling, bearing with him the message that would have meant so much to Tarzan of the Apes; but at length, in a flight much longer sustained than any it had previously attained, the bird disappeared; and that was the last that Nkima saw of it.

For no good reason he had pursued it, for thus his little monkey mind functioned. He had wasted his time, he had missed an opportunity to accomplish something worth while; and he had nothing to show for his pains. But then we have seen men do likewise. We have all chased chimeras.

For some time Nkima continued on toward the north, impelled by the rapidly fading vestiges of the urge that had been driving him; but presently he noticed the paper in the end of the stick that he had been carrying mechanically because he had been carrying it for so long. This recalled Tarzan to his mind and the fact that he was again alone in a strange land. He decided to return to the ape-man and the Waziri, but even as the determination was forming he heard something to the north of him that aroused his curiosity, demanding investigation. It was the voice of a human being.

Now, by nature Nkima is curious; and in addition Tarzan has trained him to investigate unusual occurrences; so it was not at all strange that he swung on through the trees in the direction of the voice that had attracted his attention, for the moment wholly absorbed in this new interest.

From a lofty height he at last looked down upon the objects of his interest, two Tarmangani, a he and a she. And when Nkima saw the he-Tarmangani he was glad that he was perching safely out of reach, for here was indeed a terrifying Tarmangani. Nkima had never before seen a white man like this one. He had seen the Gomangani, the black men, thus arrayed, but never a white man.

The fellow was large and powerful, with a fierce, evil face, the ferocity of which was surely not lessened by the straight piece of bone or ivory six or eight inches long that pierced the septum of his nose, nor by the feathers in his head dress, nor the paint on his face, the rings in his ears, and the necklace of human teeth lying against his massive chest.

Nkima noted all these things and more—the loin cloth of gorilla skin, the armlets, wristlets, and anklets, the fibre rope wound many times about the waist, the dagger, and the spear.

This was indeed a Tarmangani to avoid. He filled little Nkima with fear, but not so his companion. She was of a far different mold—small, dainty, and with no indications of barbaric ornamentation. Had Nkima been accustomed to making intelligent deductions from his perceptions he would have guessed immediately that the she was not of the same tribe, perhaps not of the same race as the man; but he could not have guessed that she was a French girl named Annette. No more could he know that the man was her captor, nor that he was a Kavuru. The mind of Nkima had its limitations.

However, his curiosity was once more aroused. For this reason and another, he followed them. The other reason presupposes imagination, a characteristic that little Nkima possessed, as must all creatures that know how to play; for play is often make-believe, and make-believe requires imagination of no mean order.

So now little Nkima pretended that he was stalking the two Tarmangani; he pretended that they were afraid of him and that presently he would leap upon them and destroy them. It was great fun for Nkima of whom almost nothing in the whole jungle was afraid, little Nkima who could destroy so few creatures in his teeming world, from whom nothing more important than a fledgling bird might seek to escape. It gave him a fleeting sense of superiority. There are men like that. Often one sees them strutting, clothed in a shred of tenuous, evanescent authority, play-acting at importance.

Pursuing this exciting game, he lost all sense of time, of which, at best, he had little or no conception. Presently night would come; and then he would know that time had passed, but while it was passing he gave it no thought.

The afternoon waned. The quarry passed out of the forest into an open plain at the foot of a tall mountain. The distance from the forest to the mountain was not great. Nkima could see across the plain, cut with little ravines, cluttered with huge boulders, to a village that lay at the foot of a perpendicular cliff.

A little river wound down toward the forest from the village, as though it rose in the village itself and flowed out beneath the gates of the lofty palisade. These things Nkima saw. He also saw the two he had been stalking cross the plain toward the village, but he did not follow them. After all a game is a game; there is no use carrying one too far.

He saw the gates open to admit the couple. He saw them close behind them. Then, for the first time, he realized that night was falling; and suddenly he became very lonely and afraid.

He thought of Tarzan and the safety of that bronzed shoulder; then he turned and scampered through the trees back into the south, clutching the forked stick tightly in his little fist, whimpering as he went.

21

Only Two Left

TIBBS AWOKE suddenly out of a sound sleep, and as he opened his eyes he saw Sborov with upraised hatchet kneeling above Brown. With a cry of warning, he leaped to his feet. Sborov hesitated an instant and looked quickly toward Tibbs. It was that momentary hesitation that saved Brown's life.

Tibbs' cry awakened him, and almost instinctively he recoiled and rolled to one side; perhaps it was a natural reaction to the note of warning and the terror in the voice of the Englishman.

Sborov struck, but the sharp blade missed Brown by a fraction of an inch and was buried in the earth where his head had lain but a brief instant before.

At Tibbs' cry Jane leaped to her feet, fully awake on the instant. Sborov, on one knee, reached his feet before Brown, and clinging to the hatchet fled into the jungle.

Brown started in pursuit, but Jane called him back. "Don't follow him," she said. "What's the use? We are well rid of him; he won't dare come back now. If you followed him, he might lie in wait for you and kill you. We can't spare any more; we are all too few now."

Brown turned back. "I hate to let him get away with anything like that. But I suppose you're right. He could hide and get me in that mess of trees and undergrowth before I knew what it was all about." He shook his head ruefully. "But I still hate to let him go; he ought to get what's coming to him."

"He will—out there alone," prophesied Jane.

"Hi 'opes 'e does before hever Hi lays eyes on 'im again, the bounder, if you'll pardon me, Milady."

"I think you're quite right, Tibbs; we all feel the same about the man. But now we are only three—though he never was much good to us."

" 'Much good'!" exploded Brown. "Migawd, Miss, he wasn't *no* good. He never done a thing except make trouble. If I don't never see the sight of him again that will be twenty years too soon."

126

"Prince!" There was a world of contempt and irony in the American's tones. "If they was all like him I don't wonder they been kickin' 'em out."

Jane smiled. "There have been some pretty good ones, Brown; and there still are. Princes like Sborov are not really princes at all—it is often just a courtesy title, as meaningless as a colonelcy in Kentucky. They don't rate very high in their own countries."

Brown grinned. "They sure are the fair haired boys in America, though. It was that title the poor old lady fell for, and look what it cost her. American women are fools, the way they go for titles."

Jane smiled good naturedly. "I'm an American, you know, Brown."

The pilot flushed. "Heck, no, Miss, I didn't know it. I'm sorry."

"You needn't be, because you're right about some American women—the climbers. It's not as bad as it used to be; but Americans still buy titles, and they don't often get very much for their money beside the titles. Oftentimes even the titles are as spurious as their owners.

"I recall reading a book written a number of years ago by a French count who had married a daughter of one of America's richest railroad families. He made fun of his wife's people, their poor taste, their love of money. Yet nothing that they were accused of could have been in such rotten taste as this book, nor was their love of money any greater than his by his own admission; for he bragged of having sold his title for their money. In the same breath he spoke of the honor of his house and his ancient lineage. He and his kind are sickening.

"I grow more and more to agree with my husband's appraisal of beasts and men—he prefers the beasts."

Brown shook his head dubiously. "I ain't got much use for men, myself," he admitted; "leastwise some men, but if your husband was in our fix I reckon he'd be doggone glad to get out of this jungle back where there were plenty of men and no beasts."

"You don't know my husband."

"Well, perhaps he'd rather be here than in good old Chi; but I wouldn't."

"Then we'd better start getting out," suggested Jane. "There's nothing to keep us here any longer."

"Quite right, Milady, if you'll pardon my saying so," agreed Tibbs.

"I'm for hopping off right away," said Brown. "Perhaps—well, perhaps——"

"Perhaps what?" asked Jane.

"I was just thinking of Annette. I know there ain't no chance of running across her, but I can't help hoping."

"We're all hoping, Brown. That's about all we can do, I'm afraid." Jane laid a sympathetic hand on the man's arm.

As the three set out once more upon the trail toward the east, a pair of eyes watched them from the foliage of a nearby tree, sinister, unblinking eyes that appraised the two men casually but were most often centered upon Jane.

Brown took the lead, setting a pace that would not be too hard on Tibbs; he had learned that whatever pace he set, the girl was equal to it; perhaps even more. He often wondered at her strength, endurance, and nerve. She was not at all the sort of person that he had imagined a titled English woman would be. He had always thought of women of her class as pampered, helpless creatures. It seemed strange to him now that he should look up to one as a trusted, dependable leader; that is, it seemed strange when he gave the matter any thought; otherwise, it appeared perfectly natural. He had never followed a man in whom he had greater confidence, or for whom he had more respect, than this slender, beautiful lady of quality.

Behind Brown came Tibbs. The night's rest had refreshed him. His muscles were already becoming inured to the hardships of the trail. He swung along this morning like a veteran.

"Hit's a grand day, Milady," he remarked, "if you don't mind my saying so. I feels as 'ow things was goin' to be a little bit of all right, you know, from now on."

"I hope so, Tibbs. Perhaps the worst is over. If we only knew just where we were, it would make things so much easier. We may be headed straight for some friendly village where we can get guides, or we may be headed into a wilderness. That is what troubles me most. If we only *knew*."

"The Duke of Doningham used to say that what we don't know won't never harm us, Milady."

"It won't do us any good, either," laughed Jane.

"But maybe 'e wasn't ever lost in Africa," suggested Tibbs. "Hi never 'ad no idea Africa was such a large place."

"It covers quite a lot of territory, Tibbs. It's no place to be lost."

"Hi'd 'ate to be lost in it all alone, milady—like 'is 'ighness. My word, milady, but 'e must be frightened back there all alone—nothin' only his thoughts to keep 'im company."

"And such terrible thoughts, Tibbs. I shudder to think what they must be; but I'm not worrying about him—it's poor little Annette."

Tibbs was silent. He too was thinking of Annette.

Gliding silently through the trees behind them followed a

tireless stalker. Seldom now were those cruel eyes allowed to wander from the slender figure of the girl swinging along behind the two men.

As the hours passed, Tibbs commenced to tire again. He lagged a little and dropped farther behind Brown. He no longer sought to converse with Jane. He was too tired to talk. The last couple of times that he had glanced back to see if the girl were coming he had stumbled because his muscles were so weary and his feet seemed so heavy; so he gave it up, and set his mind wholly upon plodding steadily ahead.

He thought that Brown would never stop. What was the man made of, anyway—iron? His legs and feet seemed to be mechanical things that must go on and on, forever. They no longer seemed a part of him. Yet he realized that he had done better today, that he had tired less quickly than on previous days. That was something; but—sitting down would be Heaven. Would Brown never stop?

But at last Brown did stop. "This looks like as good a place as any to stop for the night," he said. "Tired, Tibbsy?"

The Englishman staggered up and threw himself to the ground. "Tired!" he echoed. "Mr. Brown, there ain't no word in the whole bloomin' Hoxford Hinglish Dictionary that's as tired as Hi am."

Brown laughed. "Well, I don't feel so chipper myself," he admitted. "I'll bet the lady's the freshest one of all. Say, where is she?"

Tibbs looked back along the trail. "She was right behind me the last time I looked. Doubtless she'll be along in a second."

'She shouldn't get so far behind," grumbled Brown. It was evident that he was becoming apprehensive. Then he called aloud. "Hi, there! Lady Greystoke!"

There was no answering call. The two men stared expectantly along the trail. Tibbs rose wearily to his feet. Brown called again. There was only silence. Brown looked at Tibbs. There was an expression on the American's face that Tibbs had never seen there before. It was fear; but it was not fear for himself.

At a run Brown started along the back trail. Tibbs staggered after him. Occasionally Brown would stop and call the missing girl's name aloud, but there was never any answer. They kept on until darkness overtook them.

Tibbs was exhausted; he could go no farther. Brown, too, was almost at the limit of his powers. They threw themselves to the ground.

"It ain't no use," said Brown wearily. "She's gone—just like Annette—and I think in the same way. Why didn't she let me kill him? Why didn't I kill him anyway? I knew I should of."

"You think it was the prince?"

"Sure it was, the dirty—. Oh, what's the use? It's all my fault for lettin' a woman tell me what to do. She's a grand woman, but women are all alike when it comes to a job like that; they're too soft hearted. I ought to of killed him when I first wanted to. We'd of had Lady Greystoke and Annette both with us now if I had."

"Hit ain't your fault, Mr. Brown," said Tibbs soothingly. "You only done what any man would 'ave done. We hall of us promised to hobey Lady Greystoke, hand she told you not to kill 'im. Though, if you'll pardon my saying so, Hi think the blighter ought to have been killed long ago."

The rumble of a lion's roar echoed through the darkening forest awakening the men to the dangers of the coming night. Brown groaned.

"If I only knew where they were! If I just knew they was alive. If he hasn't killed 'em; just think of 'em back there somewheres in the dark with only that—that pansy to look after 'em." The gloom of Brown's mood was reflected in his voice.

"You don't really think 'e'd kill Lady Greystoke, do you?" demanded Tibbs, horrified. It was quite one thing to kill a lady's maid, but another, an unthinkable thing, to kill a titled lady. Tibbs' viewpoint on such matters was largely a matter of heredity (his people had been serving people as far back as any of them knew) and training and habit of thought. His snobbishness was the snobbishness of the serving class, ingrained and ineradicable.

"No, I don't think he'd kill her, unless she resisted him; and there ain't no question about that. But he did have good reason to want to kill poor little Annette. If it was him that got her, she's dead all right. God, if I could only lay my hands on him! What say we back track tomorrow and keep on huntin' 'till we find him. We may never find them, but it would be some satisfaction to find him. What do you say, Tibbsy? I'll let you help me kill him."

"Hi've never been one that believed in bloodshed, Mr. Brown; but Hi do say, hand Hi'm not ashamed of hit, that hif 'e killed Lady Greystoke and Annette Hi'd like nothing better than to do 'im in all by my bloomin' self; but, Mr. Brown, Hi don't think we ought to turn back. Hi think we should carry on just like milady told us to, hand get 'elp to come back 'ere hand search for them—some one that knows the country."

"I suppose you're right, Tibbsy. We couldn't find the Empire State building if it was wandering around in this man's jungle, let alone a couple of girls."

A lion roared again, nearer this time.

130

"I reckon we'd better climb a tree, Tibbsy, and wait for daylight. It don't look like sleepin' on the ground was goin' to be very healthy."

"My father always said it was most un'ealthy. 'E got rheumatism something terrible sleeping on the ground in the Crimea."

"Then let's climb," said Brown. "I don't want to get rheumatism."

22

Stalked by Numa

NKIMA SPENT a night of terror. Sheeta, the leopard, prowled on the ground, climbed through the trees. Nkima clung to the loftiest branch that would support his weight and shivered from cold and terror throughout the long night. But at last day dawned, and with the first lessening of the terrifying darkness he swung off through the trees in search of Tarzan and the Waziri. And still he clung to the little cleft stick with the bit of paper fluttering from its tip.

He had not gone far when he heard the voices of men. His little heart beat wildly as he sped in the direction of the sound. So anxious was he to find Tarzan that he had no place in his mind for any doubt that the voices he heard might be those of others than his friends.

Nor were they.

Chattering and screaming, Nkima dropped plummetlike from high branches to alight upon the shoulder of his friend. One arm encircled Tarzan's neck, and from the little clenched paw the cleft stick brought the fluttering bit of paper directly in front of the ape-man's eyes. He saw writing upon it, handwriting that even in a brief glance he recognized. Yet he could not believe. It was incredible, preposterous to even imagine that little Nkima bore a message penned by Jane. The remarkable similarity between this handwriting and hers could be nothing more than a fantastic coincidence.

Before Nkima could again escape him Tarzan slipped the message from the stick; and, while the monkey chattered and scolded, scanned it hurriedly. The Waziri, watching him, saw sudden concern mirrored in his expression.

"Where did you get this, Nkima?" demanded the ape-man. "Who gave it to you?"

Nkima stopped scolding and scratched his head. Where did he get it? He could not recall. Many things had happened since then. His memory was a long, dim corridor; and this event a tiny thing at the far end.

"Something is wrong, Bwana?" asked Muviro. "Nkima has brought you bad news?"

"It is a message from Lady Greystoke. She and a party of friends were forced down in an aeroplane. They are lost somewhere without provisions or weapons."

He turned his attention again to Nkima. "Who gave you this?" he demanded. "Was it a she?—a Tarmangani?"

Slowly Nkima was recollecting. "It was not a Tarmangani," he said.

"A Gomangani?"

"It was not a Gomangani."

"Who did give it to you, then?"

Now Nkima recalled. "No one gave it to Nkima. Nkima found it in a wala."

"What does he say, Bwana?" asked Muviro; for Nkima had spoken in the language of his people, which only Tarzan, among men, understands.

"He says he found it in a 'nest'," explained the Lord of the Jungle. "That might mean a house, or a hut, or a shelter, the lair of a wild beast, or the nest of a bird. I will find out."

"Nkima, what built the nest in which you found this?"

"Tarmangani. The Gomangani do not build a wala like it."

"Where is it? Try to recall. You must take me to it. Where was it?"

Nkima waved a paw loosely in the general direction of the West.

"You will take Tarzan to this nest," said the ape-man.

Instantly Nkima was all excitement. He felt quite important. He hopped to the ground and pulled on Tarzan's leg.

"Come with Nkima," he begged.

"Lead your warriors toward the north until you find the village of the Kavuru," Tarzan directed Muviro. "If they are unfriendly, and you cannot enter their village to recover Buira, wait for me there. If you find her and take her away, leave some sign that will tell me so. You understand?"

"Yes, Bwana."

"Then Nkima and I go to search for Lady Greystoke."

It was not by a direct route that Nkima led Tarzan toward the shelter in which he had found the message, but a circuitous one that retraced his wanderings. Each of his mischances and adventures of the preceding days was a landmark on the back trail, and thus slowly he found his way back toward the shelter.

At one point he told Tarzan he had seen a strange Tarmangani with a she-Tarmangani; and Tarzan was almost convinced that it might have been Jane, the captive of a Kavuru. He was tempted to give up the search for the shelter where the message had been found and attempt to trail the man and the woman; but Nkima could not tell him in which direction they had gone, the spoor had disappeared, and his judgment told him that the place to start his search for Jane was at some point at which he might be positive she had been.

It required infinite patience to endure the vagaries of Nkima's memory and his inability to hold for long to a fixed continuity of thought; but most beasts are patient, and in this respect Tarzan was like his fellows of the jungle. His reward came eventually when Nkima proudly led him down through the trees to the camp that the marooned fliers had made—the camp where Nkima had found the note.

Here Tarzan found indisputable evidence that Jane had indeed been a member of the ill-starred company, and plain before him lay the trail that they had taken toward the east. No longer was he dependent upon Nkima, and with renewed hope he swung off into the unknown country that had swallowed his mate.

* * *

Retribution is seldom swift or well directed, yet perhaps in his terror Prince Alexis Sborov was tasting the immediate fruits of his misdeeds through a punishment scarcely less drastic than death itself; for Sborov was an arrant coward, and he was suffering as only a coward might as he trembled alone in the menacing silence of the mysterious jungle.

And he was torn between two terrors, one of which almost cancelled the other. He was afraid of the denizens of the jungle and the thought of facing a jungle night alone, and it was this fear that almost submerged another—his fear of Brown. But not quite. As much as he longed to return to the companionship of those he had persistently sought to offend or injure, the knowledge that Brown would kill him if he did, exiled him to the torture of his terror-stricken loneliness.

When he had finally been forced to definitely abandon any thought of returning to the others, he determined to follow the plan that he had originally suggested to them, the plan that had been voted down in favor of Jane's suggestion that they search toward the east for friendly tribes; and so he set his face toward the west in the hope that he might stumble upon a white settlement in the Belgian Congo.

One ordeal that he dreaded lay ahead of him on this route, for in retracing his steps he must pass the grave of his murdered wife. He had no regrets for his deed; but his superstitious mind was terror ridden by imaginings induced by Tibbs' story of the murdered Duchess of Doningham, who returned from the grave to carry away her maid.

As Tibbs had, so did Sborov see a parallel in the mysterious disappearance of Annette, a disappearance that he could not account for logically in any other way.

But there was no alternative. He must pass close to the grave and the scene of the murder. Once again he would wield the hand-axe in the fullness of his imagination, and once again the warm blood of his victim would splatter upon his hand and his clothing.

The first night he spent among the branches of a tree, too terrified to sleep. He heard the hunting beasts prowl beneath him. He heard the screams of stricken prey. The earth trembled to the roar of the king of beasts; and there were other sounds, stealthy, mysterious sounds that were even more terrifying because he could not identify them.

But at last the night passed and dawn came to look down upon a haggard, unkempt creature that started at its own shadow, a creature exhausted by fright, by sleeplessness, and by hunger, a very different creature from the Prince Sborov of the Paris boulevards.

His hands and arms, his unshaven face, his matted hair were caked with dirt and dried sweat, cut down his shrunken cheeks by muddy rivulets of tears. His mind was tottering. He talked to himself, and then cautioned himself to silence lest his voice might attract the attention of some beast of prey.

Thus he stumbled on through the day, without food and without water—hopeless victim of his own avarice, a sorry contrast to the proud beasts he feared, a sad commentary upon the theory of evolution.

It was midafternoon when the thing that he had dreaded occurred. He was walking a broad and, for a short distance, straight trail. As he had been constantly doing, he glanced behind him. His knees trembled. He thought that he must fall. For a moment he was paralyzed.

For where the trail turned to disappear among the underbrush stood a great lion. He was eyeing Sborov appraisingly. What he was doing abroad at that hour of the day when he should have been lying up waiting for evening and the hunting hours is a matter of his own concern, but there he was. He merely stood and contemplated Sborov.

134

Presently the man regained control of his muscles. He started to move slowly along the trail. He had heard that if one ran, almost any beast of prey would pursue—and overtake; for man is of the slowest of animals.

As Sborov moved away, the lion moved after him. It came slowly, just keeping pace with the man. It was stalking him. When it was ready to do so, it would charge; and that would be the end.

Sborov knew little of the habits of lions; but he had gleaned this much from yarns spun around the camp fires, to which he had listened, even though he had never been encouraged to take part.

He wondered how long it would be before the lion would rush at him and drag him down. He wanted to run. It was with difficulty that he restrained the impulse. He looked longingly at the trees that he was too weak to climb.

A turn in the trail hid the lion from him, and then Sborov broke into a run. An instant later an angry growl sounded behind him. It seemed very close. The man threw a glance back across his shoulder. The lion was advancing at a trot. Its eyes were blazing, terrible yellow-green eyes that shrivelled the last vestige of his self-control.

Sborov voiced a piercing scream of terror.

23

Captive

TARZAN SWUNG through the trees not far from a jungle trail that led toward the east. Nkima scampered sometimes ahead sometimes above his master. He was very brave and truculent, for the sanctuary of a bronzed shoulder was always near.

Usha, the wind, was blowing in Tarzan's face. To his nostrils it brought messages from the jungle ahead. It spoke of Hista, the snake, of Wappi, the antelope, and of Sheeta, the leopard. Faintly from a great distance, it told of water it had passed upon its journey. Thus could Tarzan direct his course and select his camp sites far ahead when he passed through country that was unfamiliar to him.

There came also upon the breath of Usha the pungent odor of Numa, the lion; and a moment later Tarzan heard the angry growl of the king of beasts. Almost simultaneously he caught the scent spoor of man, of a lone Tarmangani.

Tarzan could almost picture the scene that was being enacted somewhere along that trail ahead of him, and he increased his speed; for a white man in this particular district might well be a member of the party that Jane had accompanied; he might know where she was or what fate had befallen her. It would not do to let Numa destroy him; at least not until Tarzan had questioned him.

No considerations of humanity prompted Tarzan of the Apes to hasten to the aid of this unknown man, nor would it have been selfish callousness to the suffering of another that would have left him more or less indifferent but for the thought of Jane. He was a jungle animal, a fellow to the lion; and he knew that the lion must eat, even as he must. If it did not feed upon this man, it would feed upon some other living creature whose life was as precious to it as the man's was to him; and in the philosophy of the jungle one life is no more valuable than another, unless it be that of one's self or a friend.

Tarzan knew that the two were not far ahead of him. The odor of Numa told him that the lion was not empty and that therefore he was probably stalking the Tarmangani with no immediate likelihood that he would attack unless provoked.

Then the quiet of the jungle was shattered by a scream of terror, and Tarzan guessed that the lion's short temper had been aroused. Instantly the ape-man swung forward at terrific speed, and so swiftly he sped through the middle terrace of the forest that even little Nkima had difficulty in keeping pace.

Sborov thought that the lion was charging, but it was not. It was merely keeping its prey in sight, but the angry growl of annoyance was a warning against attempted escape and a threat of what the quarry might expect if it forced the king to exert himself unnecessarily at this hour of the day when heat lay heavy and humid upon the jungle and royalty should be taking its siesta.

But Sborov would have been deaf to all warnings now even had he understood them. He was crazed with terror. His one, his only impulse was to escape; and so he ran on, his legs staggering from exhaustion and fear, his heart pounding in his throat, choking the screams that trembled there unborn.

Now indeed did Numa wax wroth. This pitiful thing was trying to escape him, and it was making him trot when he wished only to loaf along the trail at his ease until he was again ready to kill and feed. He would put an end to it; and that, quickly. He voiced another warning roar as he prepared to charge—a roar that half paralyzed the man.

136

Thinking the end had come, Sborov fell to his knees, turning so that he faced the lion; and as he did so a strange thing happened, a thing so remarkable that it surprised the lion quite as much as it did Sborov. A white man dropped from above into the trail between them.

Sborov had never seen a man such as this, a bronzed giant, almost naked; a handsome giant with grim, stern features; a giant who faced a lion with as little apparent concern as one might reveal in shooing away an alley cat. He just stood there facing the lion and waiting; and the lion stopped in its tracks, eyeing the intruder but with evidently growing displeasure.

As Sborov looked at the man he realized that he was really not of gigantic proportions, yet he conveyed the impression of great size. Perhaps it was the suggestion of power and majesty in his mien that gave him the appearance of towering over other creatures. He stood, perhaps, a couple of inches over six feet; rounded muscles flowed smoothly beneath clear, bronzed skin; his proportions were as perfect for his kind as were those of the great lion he faced. It occurred to Sborov that these two were very much alike, and he began to be as afraid of the man as of the other beast.

They stood thus facing each other for but a moment; then the lion growled, lashing its tail, and took a step forward. The man growled, and Sborov shuddered. Now, indeed, was he terrified. Above them a little monkey danced up and down upon the limb of a tree, chattering and scolding. He loosed upon the lion a vocabulary of rich invective, but to Sborov it was only the silly chattering of a monkey.

The bronzed giant moved slowly forward to meet the lion; from the mighty cavity of his deep chest rolled savage growls. Numa halted. He glanced quickly from side to side. He shook his head and, holding it upon one side, snarled; then he wheeled about and stalked majestically away without a backward glance. The man had outbluffed the lion.

Suddenly the newcomer wheeled upon Sborov. "Who are you?" he demanded. Had the lion spoken, Sborov would have been little less surprised than he was to hear excellent English fall from lips that had just been voicing the hideous growls of a beast. He was so surprised that he did not reply; then the man repeated the question. This time his tone was peremptory, brooking no delay.

"I am Prince Alexis Sborov."

"Where are the rest of your party—Lady Greystoke and the others?"

Sborov's eyes went wide. How did this man know about them? Who could he be?

"I don't know. They left me alone to die in the jungle."

"Who left you alone?"

"Only Lady Greystoke, myself, my valet, and the pilot, Brown were left of the original party when they abandoned me."

"Why did they abandon you?"

"Brown wanted me to die. He did not want me to reach civilization and accuse him of murder."

Tarzan scrutinized the man closely. There was nothing about him to arouse the ape-man's admiration or liking. "Whom did he murder?" he asked.

"He killed my wife, because he thought that she could not keep up with the rest of us and would thus prevent Brown's escape from the jungle. He knew that I would not leave her, and he did not want to lose any of the men—he was afraid to travel alone."

"Then why did he abandon you?" demanded Tarzan.

Sborov realized the inconsistency of his two statements; but his explanation came quickly, glibly. "He was in love with Lady Greystoke—they ran off together."

Tarzan's face darkened, and his fingers moved as though closing upon something—a throat, perhaps. "Which way did they go?" he asked.

"Along this same trail toward the east," replied Sborov.

"When?"

"Yesterday, I think, or perhaps the day before. It seems very long that I have been alone in the jungle—I have lost track of time."

"Where are Tibbs and Annette?"

Again Sborov was astonished. "Who are you?" he asked. "How do you know so much about us?"

Tarzan did not reply. He just stood looking at the man. What was he to do with him? He would delay his search for Jane, yet he could not leave him alone to die, as he most assuredly would, because he believed that he was a friend of Jane. In her note she had given no details of the mishaps that had befallen them. She had only enumerated the members of the party, explained that their ship had crashed and that Princess Sborov had died. He naturally assumed that Jane was a guest of the Sborovs and that therefore the man must be her friend.

"What became of Tibbs and Annette?"

"Annette disappeared," explained the prince. "We do not know what became of her. She just vanished in thin air. Her footprints led to a point beneath a tree. They stopped there."

"How long ago was that?"

"I think it was the day before Brown ran away with Lady Greystoke."

"And Tibbs?"

"Tibbs went with them."

"Why did he take Tibbs and not you?"

"He was not afraid of Tibbs. He knew that I would protect Lady Greystoke and also bring him to justice if we ever reached civilization."

Tarzan's level gaze held steadily upon Sborov as he appraised the man. He mistrusted him, but no hint of what was passing in his mind was betrayed by any changing expression of his inscrutable face. He was repelled by Sborov's face, by his manner, by the suggestion of contradiction and inconsistency in several of his statements; yet he realized that in the latter must lie some germ of fact.

At least the fellow had definitely assured him that he was on Jane's trail; and convinced him that the girl Nkima had seen with the Kavuru must have been Annette, as Jane must still have been with Brown and Sborov at the time that Nkima had seen the other woman.

"Come," he said to the man, "we shall go and find Lady Greystoke and Brown."

"Brown will kill me," said Sborov. "He has threatened to many times."

"He will not kill you while I am with you."

"You do not know him."

"I do not need to know him," replied the ape-man; "I know myself."

"I am too weak to travel fast," explained Sborov. "If you know this country, you had better take me to some village and then go on after Brown yourself. I have not eaten for a long time. I doubt that I could walk another mile, I am so weak from hunger."

"Stay here," directed Tarzan. "I will get food; then we will go on after—Brown."

Sborov watched the man move off into the forest, a little monkey perched upon one broad shoulder.

24

Down into Darkness

Jane's thoughts had been far away as she swung along the trail behind Tibbs and Brown that afternoon; they had been far to the west where a little, time worn cabin stood near the shore of a landlocked cove on the west coast. There had centered many of the important events and thrilling adventures of her life; there she had met that strange demi-god of the forest whom she had later come to know as Tarzan of the Apes.

Where was he now? Had he received her cablegram? If he had, he was already searching for her. The thought gave her renewed hope. She longed for the sanctuary of those mighty arms, for the peace and safety that his strength and jungle-craft afforded.

As her thoughts re-explored the winding back-trail of time her pace slowed and she dropped still farther in the rear of her companions. For the moment they were forgotten; she was alone in the great jungle of her memories.

But she was not alone. Eyes watched her every move; from the foliage of the trees above, they watched her, ever keeping pace with her.

Presently she felt an unaccountable urge to turn back. She wondered why. Was it a woman's intuition directing her for her best good? Was it a beneficent or a malign influence? She could only wonder.

At first this peculiar urge was only a faint suggestion; then it became more pronounced, became a force beyond her power to deny. At last she ceased to wonder or to question. Tibbs and Brown seemed very far away. She thought of calling to them, but she knew that it would be useless. For just an instant longer she hesitated, striving to force her will to drive her along the trail in an effort to overtake them; then she surrendered. A power stronger than she controlled her, and she turned docilely back away from them.

It was as though some one was calling to her in a voice that she could not hear but that she must obey. It offered her nothing, nor did it threaten her. She had neither hope nor fear because of it.

When the noose of the Kavuru dropped about her she felt no surprise, no terror—her sensibilities were numbed. She looked into the savage, painted face of the white man who drew her to a limb beside him and removed the noose from about her. It all seemed perfectly natural, as though it were something that had been foreordained since the beginning of time.

The man lifted her to a shoulder and started off through the trees toward the east away from the trail that ran in a northeasterly direction at that point. He did not speak, nor did she. It all seemed quite in order.

This state of mind persisted for a matter of an hour or

140

so; then it gradually commenced to fade as she slowly emerged from the state of hypnosis that had deadened her sensibilities. Slowly the horror of her situation dawned upon her. She realized that she was in the clutches of a strange, savage creature that was also a white man. She knew now that she had been hypnotized, the victim of a strange power that turned her will to its own purposes yet left her conscious of all that transpired.

She felt that she must do something about it, but what was there to do? From the ease with which the man carried her, she knew that his strength was abnormal—far beyond any that she could pit against it in an effort to escape. Her only hope lay in evolving some stratagem that would permit her to elude him when he was off guard. This she could never hope to do as long as he carried her.

She wondered where he was taking her and to what fate. If she could only carry on a conversation with him she might discover, but what language would such a creature speak? Well, she could only try.

"Who are you?" she asked in English. "What are you going to do with me?"

The man grunted and then mumbled in a Bantu dialect with which she was familiar, "I do not understand."

Jane experienced a moment of elation that was great by contrast with the hopelessness of her situation when she realized that he spoke a language she was familiar with.

"I understand you," she said in the same dialect that he had used. "Now tell me who you are and why you have taken me. I am not an enemy of your people, but if you keep me or harm me my people will come and destroy your village; they will kill many of you."

"Your people will not come. No one ever comes to the village of the Kavuru. If any did, they would be killed."

"You call yourselves Kavuru? Where is your village?"

"You will see."

"What are you going to do with me?"

"I take you to Kavandavanda."

"Who is Kavandavanda?" she demanded.

"He is Kavandavanda." The man spoke as though that were sufficient explanation. It was as though one said, "God is God."

"What does he want of me? What is he going to do with me? If he wants ransom, if you want ransom, my people will pay much to have me back unharmed."

"You talk too much," snapped the Kavuru. "Shut up."

For a while Jane was silent; then she tried again, spurred

141

on by the discomfort of the position in which she was being carried.

"Put me down," she said. "I can travel through the trees quite as well as you. There is no reason why you should carry me. It will be easier for us both if you let me walk."

At first the Kavuru appeared to ignore the suggestion; but at last he put her down. "Do not try to escape," he warned. "If you do try to, I may have to kill you. No one must ever escape from a Kavuru."

Jane stretched her cramped muscles and surveyed her captor. He was indeed a savage appearing specimen; but how much of that was due to his natural countenance and how much to the paint, the nose ornament and the ear rings she could not guess. Like many savage or primitive people, his age was undeterminable by his appearance; yet somehow she felt that he was a young man.

"What is your name?" she asked.

"Ogdli," he replied.

"You are a chief, of course," she said, hoping to make a favorable impression by flattery.

"I am not a chief," he replied. "There is only one chief, and that is Kavandavanda."

She tried to draw him on into a conversation; but he was short and taciturn at first, finally becoming ugly.

"Shut up, or I will cut your tongue out," he snapped. "Kavandavanda does not need your tongue."

Thereafter, Jane was silent; for there was that about her captor and the tone in which he made the threat that told her it was no idle one.

That night he bound her securely with his rope while he lay down to sleep, and the next morning they were on their way again. At the halt he had gathered some fruit and nuts, and these formed the only breakfast that they had.

In the middle of the forenoon they came suddenly to the end of the forest and looked out across a narrow plain to a lofty mountain at the foot of which Jane thought that she discerned what appeared to be a palisade built close to a perpendicular cliff.

The plain was strewn with large boulders and cut by several washes; so that as they advanced across it toward the mountain the palisade was sometimes in view and sometimes hidden from their sight.

As they approached more closely, Jane saw that the palisade was a massive affair of stone and that it formed three sides of a rectangle the rear wall of which was evidently the face of the mighty cliff that loomed high above them.

A small river followed a winding course across the plain from the very foot of the palisade, as though it were born there; though when she came closer she saw that it flowed from beneath the stone wall through an opening left for that purpose.

Her captor shouted as he approached the palisade, and a moment later one of the two massive gates swung open a little way to admit them. Beyond was a narrow street flanked by small stone houses, the flat roofs of which suggested that this was a country of little rain. They were houses similar in design to those built of stone and adobe by the prehistoric builders of the ancient pueblos of southwestern America.

Savage warriors loitered before tiny doorways or tended cooking fires built in little out-door ovens. Like Ogdli, they were all young men, their ornaments, apparel, and weapons being almost identical to his.

Some of them gathered around Jane and her captor, examining her and asking questions of Ogdli.

"You and Ydeni have all the luck," grumbled one. "He captured a black girl and a white girl all during the full of the moon."

"The black girl got away from him," said another.

"Yes, but he went right back into the forest and caught a white girl."

"He will get no teeth for the black girl."

"No, but he will get a fine string for the white one; and Ogdli will get another row of teeth—that will make four for Ogdli. Kavandavanda will think well of him."

"He should," said Ogdli. "I am the greatest warrior among the Kavuru."

A big fellow grunted derisively. "You have but three rows of teeth," he taunted. "I have seven," and he tapped his chest where it joined his throat.

Jane, listening to this strange conversation, made little of it until this gesture of the speaker called her attention to the necklaces of human teeth about his throat; then she saw that there were seven rows of them and that about Ogdli's neck were three similar strands. She glanced at some of the other warriors. Some had one or two, others had none. These necklaces were evidently a sign of greatness, evidencing the prowess of the individual and his success in capturing women.

Suddenly she became aware of a marked peculiarity of her surroundings—here she was in an isolated village of a war-like people far removed from other villages, a village in which there were many men in the prime of life; yet she had seen neither women nor children.

What could it mean? Did some strange custom require that women and children remain indoors at certain hours or upon certain occasions, or were there no women nor children? If the latter were true, then what became of the women captives of which they boasted? But it could not be true; there must be women and children. But if there were women, why did the men attend the cooking fires? That was no fit work for warriors.

These observations and thoughts passed quickly through Jane's mind as she was led along the narrow street by Ogdli. At an intersection her captor turned into a narrow alley and led her to a low, circular building that lent to her surroundings a still greater similtude to the ancient villages of the pueblos; for this was a windowless structure against which leaned a primitive wooden ladder leading to the roof. If it were not a ceremonial kiva its appearance belied its purpose.

With a grunt, Ogdli motioned her to precede him up the ladder; and when she gained the roof she found still further evidence of kivalike attributes, for here the top of a second ladder protruded from a small, rectangular opening.

Ogdli pointed to it. "Go down," he commanded; "and stay down. Do not try to escape. It will be worse for you if you do try."

Jane looked down through the aperture. She could see nothing—just a black pit.

"Hurry!" admonished Ogdli.

The girl placed a foot upon a rung of the ladder and started slowly down into the black, mysterious void. She was no coward, but her courage was tested to its utmost as she forced her unwilling feet down that shaky, primitive ladder. Uppermost in her mind was the fact that she had seen no women in the village of the Kavuru. What had been the fate of the captives of which the warriors had boasted? Had they, too, descended this ladder? Had they gone down into this dark abyss never to return?

25

Defeat

Muviro and the Waziri came to the end of the forest. Before them stretched a narrow plain that lay at the foot of a lone mountain.

One of the warriors pointed. "There is a village built at the foot of that high cliff. I see the palisade."

Muviro shaded his eyes with his hand. He nodded. "It must be the village of Kavuru. We have found it at last. Perhaps we shall not find Buira, but we will punish the Kavuru. We will teach them to leave the daughters of the Waziri alone."

The other warriors assented with savage growls; for they were Waziri, known for ages as mighty warriors. Who might dare encroach upon their rights? Who might steal their women with impunity? None.

Other tribes suffered similar losses. They made big noise with tom-toms and shouting. They danced their war dances. And then, when there was little chance of overtaking their enemy, they set out in pursuit; but always they abandoned the chase before they overhauled the quarry. Not so the Waziri. What they undertook, they pursued relentlessly whether it brought victory or defeat.

"Come!" said Muviro, and led his warriors out upon the plain toward the village of the Kavuru. Suddenly he halted. "What is that?" he demanded.

The Waziri listened. A low droning sound that at first barely commanded the attention of their ears was growing steadily in volume. The warriors, standing in silence, looked up toward the heavens.

"There it is," said one, pointing. "It is a canoe that flies. I saw one pass low over the country of the Waziri. It made the same sound."

The ship came rapidly into view, flying at an altitude of three or four thousand feet. It passed over the plain and the Waziri; then it banked steeply and turned back. With motor throttled, the ship descended gracefully in wide spirals. At a few hundred feet from the ground the pilot gave it the gun, but still he continued to circle low over the plain. He was searching for a landing place. For two hours he had been searching for one, almost hopelessly.

Lost, and with only a little fuel remaining in his tanks, he welcomed the sight of this open plain and the village with heartfelt thanks. He knew that he couldn't get fuel here, but he could get his position, and at least he was saved from making a forced landing over the forest.

Flying low, he saw the Waziri, white plumed savages evidently coming from the forest; and he saw natives emerging from the village, too. He saw that these were different in a most surprising way, and he dropped lower and circled twice more to make sure.

His companion, in the front cockpit, scribbled a note and

handed it back to him; "What do you make of them? They look white to me."

"They are white," wrote the pilot.

Owing to the washes and boulders there were not many safe landing places available on the plain. One of the best, or perhaps it would be truer to say least impossible, was directly in front of the village; another, and perhaps a better one, lay across the plain, near the forest. Muviro and his Waziri stood near the edge of it, a band of primitive savages; and the sight of these and the implications their presence suggested determined the pilot to set his ship down nearer the village and its white inhabitants. Tragic error.

Once again the ship circled the plain, rising to an altitude of a thousand feet; then the pilot cut his motor and glided toward a landing.

Muviro resumed his advance upon the village; and as the way led him and his men down into a deep wash they did not see the actual landing of the ship, but when they again reached higher ground they saw two men climbing from the cockpits of the plane, while advancing from the open gates of the Kavuru village was a swarm of savage, white warriors, whose hostile intent was all too apparent to Muviro.

They were white! No longer was there any doubt in the mind of the Waziri chieftain; now he knew that these were indeed the Kavuru. They were shouting and brandishing their spears as they ran toward the two aviators. Apparently they had not as yet discovered the presence of the Waziri; or, if they had, they ignored them.

Muviro spoke to his men in low tones, and they spread out in a thin line and moved silently forward at a trot. They did not yell and prance as do many native warriors, and because they did not they seemed always to inspire greater fear in the hearts of their enemies. There were only ten of them, yet they charged the savage Kavuru, who out-numbered them ten to one, with all the assurance that they might have been expected to have had the odds been reversed.

The fliers, seeing that the natives were hostile, fell toward their ship. One of them fired a shot over the heads of the advancing Kavuru; but as it had no deterrent effect, the man fired again; and this time a Kavuru fell. Still the savage white warriors came on.

Now both the fliers opened fire, yet on came the Kavuru. Soon they would be within spear range of their victims. The men glanced behind them as though seeking temporary shelter, but what they saw must have been disheartening—a thin line of black warriors trotting silently toward them from the rear.

146

They did not know that these would have been friends and allies; so one of them raised his pistol and fired at Muviro. The bullet missed its mark; and the Waziri chieftain sought cover behind a boulder, ordering his men to do likewise; for he knew better than the Kavuru the deadly effectiveness of firearms.

Then he called to the two fliers in English, telling them that the Waziri were friendly; but the harm had already been done—the delay permitted the Kavuru to close in upon the two men before the Waziri could join forces with them to repel the enemy. Perhaps it would have done no good, so greatly did the Kavuru out-number them all.

With savage yells they bore down upon the fliers, though several of their number dropped before the fire that the two poured into their ranks. Now they were close; but close too were the Waziri, who were moving forward again, now at a run.

Presently the Kavuru spears began to fly. One of the strangers fell with a weapon through his heart. Now a volley of spears leaped from the hands of the Waziri, momentarily checking the advance of the Kavuru, who seemed to fear spears more than they did firearms.

They did not retreat, but merely paused a moment; then they launched another flight of spears; and this time the second flier fell, and with him three Waziri. A moment later the Kavuru and Waziri closed in hand-to-hand struggle.

Now there were but seven of the latter; and though they fought valiantly, they were no match for the hundred Kavuru warriors that overwhelmed them.

Fighting close to the bodies of the slain fliers, Muviro and one of his warriors, Balando, salvaged the pistols and ammunition of the dead men. At close quarters the firearms had a more definite effect on the morale of the Kavuru, stopping them temporarily and permitting Muviro and his remaining warriors to fall back in search of shelter. Now there were but four of them, Muviro, Balando, and two others.

The Waziri chief sought to reach a pile of granite rising spire-like from the plain; and at last he was successful, but now only Balando remained alive to carry on the unequal struggle with him. Together they fell back to the rocky sanctuary Muviro had chosen, and while Muviro held the Kavuru at bay Balando clambered to the summit safely out of effective spear range; then he fired down upon the enemy while Muviro climbed to his side.

Again and again the Kavuru hurled their spears aloft; but the height was too great for any but the most powerful muscles, and even the weapons of these had lost so much speed and momentum by the time they reached the level at which their targets stood that they ceased to constitute a menace. The revolvers and bows of the two Waziri, however, still did effective work—so effective that the Kavuru fell back toward their village; and with the coming of the swift equatorial twilight Muviro saw them definitely give up the attack and file back toward the village gate.

As they passed the grounded ship, Muviro saw that they avoided it and guessed that they were afraid of it as of something supernatural; then night fell, blotting out the scene.

Sorrowfully Muviro and Balando descended from the rock that had afforded them sanctuary. They sought shelter and a place to sleep in the forest, the impenetrable gloom of which seemed no darker than their future. But they made no plans; they were too exhausted, too overcome by grief and disappointment to think clearly.

"If only the Big Bwana would come," sighed Balando.

"Yes," agreed Muviro. "If he had been here, this would not have happened."

26

Tarzan Stalks Brown

THE morning mist floated lazily in the still air, the soul of the dead night clinging reluctantly to earth. A strange hush lay on the jungle, a silence as poignant as a leopard's scream. It awakened Brown. He moved gingerly in the crotch of the tree into which he had wedged himself the evening before. He was stiff and lame and sore. Every muscle ached. He looked up at Tibbs, a couple of feet above him, and grinned. The Englishman was spread-eagled across two parallel branches to which he was clinging tightly in restless slumber.

"He looks like he was goin' to be grilled," mused the pilot. "Poor old Tibbsy." He spoke the last words half aloud.

Tibbs opened his eyes and looked around. For a moment his expression was surprised and troubled; then he discovered Brown below him, and full consciousness returned.

"My word!" he exclaimed with a shake of his head. "Hi was just drawing 'is Grace's bawth."

"You even wait on 'em in your sleep, don't you, Tibbsy?"

"Well, you see, sir, hits been my life, always; and Hi wouldn't hask for a better one—peace and orderliness. Heverything clean and straight; heverything always in its place. Hand not 'ard work, sir. Hand you're always treated well—that is, by gentlemen. It's been my good fortune to be in the service mostly of gentlemen."

"Like this Sborov guy?" inquired Brown.

"'E was not a gentleman."

"But he was a prince, wasn't he? Don't that make him a gentleman?"

Tibbs scratched his head. "It should but it doesn't; not always. Hi sometimes think when Hi see a bounder with a title that possibly at some time his mother may have been indiscreet."

Brown laughed. "I guess there must of been a lot of indiscretion in high places," he remarked, and then: "How about pullin' our freight, Tibbsy? We got a long ways to go on a pair of empty stomachs."

Wearily the two men plodded on through the jungle. All the forces of nature and the laws of chance seemed to have combined against them from the first. Now they were sad, disheartened, almost without hope; yet each tried bravely to keep up the spirits of the other. It was oftentimes a strain, and occasionally one of them voiced the morbid doubts and fears that assailed them both.

"Do you believe in black magic, Tibbsy?" asked Brown.

"Hi 'ave seen some strange things hin my life, sir," replied the Englishman.

"You know what the old dame come down here to look for, don't you?"

"Yes, something that would renew youth, wasn't it?"

"Yes. I know a lot about that. I knew a lot I didn't tell her. If I had she might not have come, and I sure wanted her to. I wanted to get that formula. Cripes, Tibbsy! It would be worth a million back in civilization. But it's well guarded. A few men have tried to get it. None of 'em was ever heard of again."

"Well, we ain't trying to get it now. We got troubles enough trying to find our way out of this jungle to be bothering with any helixir of life. If we just go along and mind our own business, we'll be all right."

"I don't know about that. I never took much stock in black magic, but it is funny all the things that's happened to this expedition ever since it started out. Just like somebody or something had put a jinx on it. It started right off the bat with that zero-zero flyin' weather; then come the forced land-

149

in'; then the old dame's murdered; then Annette disappears; now Lady Greystoke's gone.

"Do you realize, Tibbsy, that of the six that took off from Croyden there's only two of us left? It's just like something was following us, pickin' off one at a time. It sure gets my goat when I stop to think about it. It's doggone funny, Tibbsy, that's what it is."

"Hi see nothing amusing in it, sir," objected Tibbs; "but then Hi've always 'eard that you Americans had a strange sense of humor."

"The trouble is that you Englishmen don't understand English," explained Brown. "But let's skip it. The question is, which one of us will be next?"

"Don't," begged Tibbs. "That's just what Hi've been trying not to think about."

Brown turned again and looked back at his companion who was following along a narrow trail. The American grinned. "Wasn't Lady Greystoke walkin' behind when it got her?" he reminded.

* * *

Tarzan, following the trail toward the east, found Sborov a problem. The man was too exhausted to move faster than a snail's pace, and even so he was compelled to rest often.

Tarzan was anxious to overtake Brown and Tibbs with whom he believed Jane to be. He would kill Brown. The very thought of the man caused the scar across his forehead to burn red—the scar that Bolgani, the gorilla, had given him years ago in that first life and death struggle that had taught the boy Tarzan one of the uses of his dead father's hunting knife and thus set his feet upon the trail that led to the lordship of the jungle.

Ordinarily the life of a strange tarmangani would have weighed as nothing as against a delay in his search for Jane; but Alexis had given the impression that he had been Jane's friend and protector, and Tarzan could not desert him to the certain fate that would have claimed such as he alone in the jungle.

So the Lord of the Jungle decided to remain with Sborov until he could turn him over to the chief of some friendly tribe for protection and guidance to the nearest outpost of civilization, or place him in the hands of his own Waziri.

Seemingly imbued with many of the psychic characteristics of the wild beasts among which he had been reared, Tarzan often developed instinctive likes or dislikes for individuals on first contact; and seldom did he find it necessary to alter his decisions.

He had formed such a conviction within a few moments after his meeting with Sborov, a conviction which made it doubly distasteful to him to be in the company of the man and waste time befriending him. He mistrusted and disliked him, but for Jane's sake he would not abandon him. Little Nkima seemed to share his mistrust, for he seldom came near the stranger; and when he did he bared his teeth in a menacing snarl.

Chafing under the delay forced upon him by Sborov's physical condition, which bordered on complete exhaustion, the ape-man at last swung the surprised Sborov to his shoulder and took to the trees with the agility and speed of a small monkey.

Alexis voiced a cry of remonstrance that carried also a note of fear, but he was helpless to escape the situation into which he had been snatched as though by the hand of Fate. Should he succeed in wriggling from that vise-like grasp, it would only lead to injury in the resultant fall to the ground below. So Alexis shut his eyes tight and hoped for the best.

He knew that they were moving rapidly through the trees; the swift passage of foliage and twigs across his body told him that. He remonstrated with the bronzed savage that was carrying him, but he might as well have sought conversation with the Sphinx. At last he gained sufficient courage to open his eyes; then, indeed, did he gasp in horror; for at that very moment Tarzan leaped out into space to catch a trailing liana and swing to another tree upon his arboreal trail. Fifty feet below the eyes of the thoroughly terrified Sborov lay the hard ground. He screamed aloud, and then he found articulate voice.

"Take me down," he cried. "Let me walk. You'll kill us both." Overcome by terror, he struggled to free himself.

"It will be you who will kill us if you don't lie still," warned the ape-man.

"Then take me down."

"You are too slow," replied Tarzan. "I cannot be held to the pace of Kota, the tortoise, if I am ever to overtake the man you call Brown. If I take you down I shall have to leave you alone here in the jungle. Would you prefer that?"

Sborov was silent. He was trying to weigh the terrors of one plan against those of the other. All that he could think of was that he wished he were back in Paris, which really didn't help at all in this emergency.

Suddenly Tarzan came to an abrupt halt on a broad limb. He was listening intently. Sborov saw him sniffing the air. It reminded him of a hound on a scent trail.

"What do those two men look like?" demanded Tarzan.

"Describe them to me, so that I may know Brown when I see him."

"Tibbs is a small man with thin hair and a pinched face. He is an Englishman with a slight cockney accent. Brown is a big fellow, an American. I suppose he would be called good looking," added Sborov, grudgingly.

Tarzan dropped to a trail that they had crossed many times as it wound through the jungle, and set Sborov on the ground.

"Follow this trail," he directed. "I am going on ahead."

"You are going to leave me alone here in the jungle?" demanded Alexis, fearfully.

"I will come back for you," replied the ape-man. "You will be safe enough for the short time I shall be gone."

"But suppose a lion—" commenced Sborov.

"There are no lions about," interrupted Tarzan. "There is nothing near that will harm you."

"How do you know?"

"I know. Do as I tell you and follow the trail."

"But—" Sborov started to expostulate; then he gasped and sighed resignedly, for he was alone. Tarzan had swung into the trees and disappeared.

The ape-man moved swiftly along the scent spoor that had attracted his attention. His sensitive nostrils told him it was the scent of two white men. He sought in vain to detect the spoor of a woman, but there was none—if the two men were Brown and Tibbs, then Jane was no longer with them.

What had become of her? The man's jaw set grimly. That information he would get from Brown before he killed him.

A human life meant no more to Tarzan of the Apes than that of any other creature. He never took life wantonly, but he could kill a bad man with less compunction than he might feel in taking the life of a bad lion.

Any living thing that harmed his mate or threatened her with harm he could even find a species of grim pleasure in killing, and Sborov had convinced him that Brown meant harm to Jane if he had not already harmed her.

The man's statement that Jane and Brown had run away together had not carried the conviction that the implication might have provoked, so sure was the Lord of the Jungle of the loyalty of his mate. Her intentions and her voluntary acts he never doubted nor questioned.

What were his thoughts as he swung along the trail of the two unsuspecting men? That inscrutable face gave no suggestion of what passed in the savage mind, but they must have been grim and terrible thoughts of revenge.

Rapidly the scent of his quarry grew stronger as the distance that separated them grew shorter.

Now he went more slowly; and, if possible, even more silently. He moved as soundlessly as his own shadow as he came at last in sight of two men trudging wearily along the trail beneath him.

It was they; he could not mistake them—the small Englishman, the big American. He paid little attention to Tibbs, but his eyes never left the figure of the aviator. Stealthily he stalked, as the lion stalks his prey.

He was quite close above them. Easily now at any moment he could launch himself down upon his victim.

Tibbs mopped the streaming perspiration from his forehead and out of his eyes. "Whew!" he sighed. "Hit all seems so bloody useless. Hit's like lookin' for a needle in a hay stack. We won't never find her anyway. Let's stop and rest. I'm jolly well done in."

"I know how you feel, but we got to keep on lookin' though. We might find her. The more I think about it, the less I think Sborov got away with Lady Greystoke."

"What's made you change your mind?" demanded Tibbs. "Hi thought you was sure he had."

"Well, in the first place, she was armed; and she had the guts to defend herself. He ain't got no guts at all."

"'E 'ad enough to murder his poor wife," objected Tibbs.

"He sneaked up on her in the dark while she was asleep," sneered Brown. "That didn't take no guts."

"But 'ow about Annette?"

Brown shook his head. "I don't know. I can't make it out. Of course, there was a good reason for his wanting to kill Annette. She had the evidence against him—she knew too much; and she wasn't armed.

"But what gets me is the way her footprints disappeared, just like she'd dissolved in thin air. If his footprints had been there too, and gone on, I'd have thought he picked her up and carried her into the jungle to finish her; but hers were all alone."

They had stopped now while Tibbs rested. The ape-man crouched above them, listening. He missed no word, but what effect they had upon him was not revealed by any change of expression.

"But 'e couldn't 'ave picked 'er up and carried her hoff and her not scream," argued Tibbs. "That would have woke some of us."

"She might have been too scared to scream," explained Brown. "Annette was awful scared of him."

"Lady Greystoke wasn't scared of him. Why didn't she call for help?"

"Lady Greystoke wasn't scared of nothing. There was some dame, Tibbs."

"Hi quite agree with you," replied the Englishman. "Lady Greystoke was a most extraordinary person. Hi 'opes as how we find her."

"Yes, and I hope we find Annette. I can't believe she is dead, somehow." The note of yearning in the aviator's voice was not lost on the silent listener above.

"You was rather soft on Annette, wasn't you?" said Tibbs, sympathetically.

"Plenty," admitted Brown, "and that louse, Sborov, told her I was tryin' to make Lady Greystoke. Hell! Can you picture a English noblewoman falling for me?"

"If you'll pardon my saying so, I can't," admitted Tibbs, candidly.

"No more can I. She was a swell dame, but Annette was the only girl I ever seen that had me ga-ga. I'd give—well, all I ain't got to know for sure what became of her."

Softly the ape-man dropped to the trail behind the two men.

"I think I know," he said.

At the sound of his voice they wheeled suddenly and faced him, surprise written large upon the face of each.

"Who the devil are you and where did you come from?" demanded Brown, while Tibbs stood with his lower lip dropped, staring wide-eyed at the strange figure of the ape-man. "And what do you think you know?" concluded the American.

"I think I know how your two women disappeared."

"Say," exclaimed Brown, "what are you, anyway? This country's got me nuts—people disappearing and you jumping out of thin air like a spook. Are you a friend or what?"

"Friend," replied Tarzan.

"What you runnin' around undressed for?" demanded Brown. "Ain't you got no clothes, or ain't you got no sense?"

"I am Tarzan of the Apes."

"Yeah? Well, I'm glad to meet you, Tarzan; I'm Napoleon. But spill what you know about Annette—about both the dames. What got 'em? Was it Sborov? But of course you don't know nothin' about Sborov."

"I know about Sborov," replied Tarzan. "I know about the accident that wrecked your plane. I know the Princess Sborov was murdered. I think I know what happened to Lady Greystoke and Annette."

Brown looked puzzled. "I don't know how you got hep to all this, but you know plenty. Now tell me what happened to the two dames."

"The Kavuru got them. You are in Kavuru country."

"What are Kavuru?" demanded Brown.

"A tribe of savage white men. They make a practice of stealing women, presumably for use in some religious rite."

"Where do they hang out?"

"I don't know. I was looking for their village when I heard about the accident to your ship. I believe I can find it soon. It lies in a very wild country. The Kavuru have secrets they wish to guard; so no one is allowed to approach their village."

"What secrets?" inquired Brown.

"They are believed to have discovered some sort of an elixir of life, something that will make old people young again."

Brown whistled. "So that's it? They were the people we were looking for."

"You were looking for the Kavuru?" asked Tarzan, incredulously.

"The old dame was looking for the formula for that elixir stuff," explained Brown, "and so am I, now that she is dead—someone has to carry on, you know," he added rather lamely. "But say, how did you hear of the accident to the ship? How could you hear about it? We ain't seen or talked to no one." Suddenly Brown ceased speaking. His face darkened in anger.

"Sborov!" he exclaimed.

The prince, rounding a bend in the trail, halted when he saw Brown. The American started toward him, menacingly, an oath on his lips.

Sborov turned to run. "Stop him!" he screamed to Tarzan. "You promised you wouldn't let him harm me."

The ape-man sprang after Brown and seized him by the arm. "Stop!" he commanded. "I promised the man."

Brown attempted to wrench himself free. "Let me go, you fool," he growled. "Mind your own business." Then he aimed a heavy blow at Tarzan's jaw with his free hand. The ape-man ducked, and the clenched fist only grazed his cheek. The shadow of a grim smile touched his lips as he lifted the American above his head and shook him; then he tossed him into the thick underbrush that bordered the trail.

"You forgot Waterloo, Napoleon," he said.

Upon the branch of a tree above, little Nkima danced and chattered; and as Brown was extricating himself with difficulty from the thorny embrace of the bushes, Nkima gathered a ripe and odorous fruit and hurled it at him.

Tibbs looked on in consternation, believing that Brown had made a dangerous enemy in this giant white savage; and when he saw Tarzan step toward the struggling American he anticipated nothing less than death for both of them.

But there was no anger in the breast of the ape-man as

he again seized the aviator and lifted him out of the entangling bushes and set him upon his feet in the trail.

"Do not again forget," he said, quietly, "that I am Tarzan of the Apes or that when I give an order it is to be obeyed."

Brown looked the ape-man squarely in the eyes for a moment before he spoke. "I know when I'm licked," he said. "But I still don't savvy why you wouldn't let me kill that louse—he sure has it coming to him."

"Your quarrels are of no importance," said the ape-man; "but it is important to locate Lady Greystoke."

"And Annette," added Brown.

"Yes," agreed Tarzan. "Also that you three men get back to civilization where you belong. You do not belong in the jungle. The world is full of fools who go places where they do not belong, causing other people worry and trouble."

"If Hi may make so bold as to say so, sir, Hi quite agree with you," ventured Tibbs. "Hi shall be jolly well pleased to get hout of this bally old jungle."

"Then don't any of you start killing off the others," advised Tarzan. "The more of you there are the better chance you will have of getting out, and three are none too many. Many times you will find it necessary for some one to stand watch at night; so the more there are the easier it will be for all."

"Not for mine with that prince guy along!" said Brown, emphatically. "The last time he stood guard he tried to kill me with a hatchet, and he'd have done it if it hadn't been for old Tibbsy. If you say I don't kill him, I don't kill—unless he forces me to it; but I don't travel with him, and that's that."

"We'll get him back here," said Tarzan, "and have a talk with him. I think I can promise you he'll be good. He was in a blue funk when I found him—a lion had been stalking him—and I think he'd promise anything not to be left alone again."

"Well," agreed Brown, grudgingly, "get him back and see what he says."

Tarzan called Sborov's name aloud several times, but there was no answer.

" 'E couldn't have gotten so very far," said Tibbs. " 'E must 'ear you, sir."

Tarzan shrugged. "He'll come back when he gets more afraid of the jungle than he is of Brown."

"Are we going to sit here waiting for him?" asked the American.

"No," replied Tarzan. "I am going on to find the Kavuru village. My own people are somewhere to the east. I'll take

27

Madmen and Leopards

As Jane reached the foot of the ladder leading down into the dark interior of the kivalike structure in the village of the Kavuru her ears caught a faint sound as of someone or something moving at no great distance from her.

Instantly she froze to silent immobility, listening. She thought that she heard the sound of breathing. Dim light from the opening above relieved the darkness immediately about her, and she knew that she must be revealed to whatever was in the room with her. Then a voice spoke, spoke in English with a familiar accent.

"Oh, madame! It is you? They got you, too?"

"Annette! You are here? Then it was not the prince who took you away?"

"No, madame. It was a terrible white man who held me powerless by some black magic. I could not cry out for help. I could not resist. I simply went to him, and he took me up into the trees and carried me away."

"One of them took me in the same way, Annette. They possess a hypnotic power beyond anything that I had ever dreamed might be possible. Have they harmed you, Annette?"

"I have only been terribly frightened," replied the girl, "because I don't know what they intend to do with me."

Jane's eyes had become accustomed to the gloom of the dark chamber. Now she could discern more of the details of the interior. She saw a circular room with a litter of dry grasses and leaves on the hard dirt floor. Against one wall Annette was sitting on a little pallet of these same leaves and grasses that she had evidently scraped together. There was no one else, nothing else, in the room.

"What do you suppose they are going to do with us?" asked Jane. "Haven't they given you any clew at all?"

"None, madame, absolutely none. Nor you? They have told you nothing?"

"The man who captured me was named Ogdli. He told

me that much and that he was taking me to some one called Kavandavanda, who, I gathered, is their chief. When I asked more questions he threatened to cut my tongue out, saying that Kavandavanda did not need my tongue. They are most unpleasant people."

"Ah, madame, that does not describe them—they are terrifying. If only Monsieur Brown was here. You have seen him lately, madame? He is well?"

"Quite well, Annette, in body; but his heart was sick. He was worrying about you."

"I think he loves me very much, madame."

"I am sure of it, Annette."

"And I love him. It is terrible to have this happen now when we might have been so happy. Now we never shall be. I shall never see him again. I have that feeling, madame. It is what you call a—a premonition. I shall die here in this awful village—soon."

"Nonsense, Annette! You mustn't say such things; you mustn't even think them. What we should be thinking about is escape—and nothing else."

"Escape? What chance have we, madame?"

"I saw no guard at the entrance to this hole when they brought me in," explained Jane; "and if there is none posted at night we can certainly get to the roof. From there on will depend upon what obstacles we find in our way, but it will be worth trying."

"Whatever you say, madame."

"Tonight then, Annette."

"S-sh, madame! Some one is coming."

Footsteps sounded plainly on the roof above them now, and then the opening through which they had entered was darkened by the form of a man.

"Come up!" he commanded; "both of you."

Jane sighed. "Our poor little plan," she bemoaned.

"What difference does it make?" asked Annette. "It would not have succeeded anyway."

"We shall have to try something else later," insisted the other, as she started to ascend the ladder.

"It will fail, too," prophesied Annette gloomily. "We shall die here—both of us—tonight, perhaps."

As they stepped out onto the roof Jane recognized the warrior as the one who had captured her. "Now what, Ogdli?" she asked. "Are you going to set us free?"

"Be still," growled the Kavuru. "You talk too much. Kavandavanda has sent for you. Do not talk too much to Kavandavanda."

He took hold of her arm to urge her along—a soft, smooth, sun-tanned arm. Suddenly he stopped and wheeled her about until she faced him. A new fire burned in his eyes. "I never saw you before," he said, in a low voice. "I never saw you before." It was an almost inaudible whisper.

Jane bared her teeth in a flashing smile. "Look at my teeth," she said. "You will soon be wearing them; then you will have four rows."

"I do not want your teeth, woman," growled Ogdli huskily. "You have cast a spell on me; I, who have foresworn women, am bewitched by a woman."

Jane thought quickly. The change in the man had come so suddenly, and his infatuation was so apparent that for an instant it only frightened her; then she saw in it possibilities that might be turned to the advantage of herself and Annette.

"Ogdli," she whispered softly, "you can help me, and no one need ever know. Hide us until tonight. Tell Kavandavanda that you could not find us, that we must have escaped; then come back after dark and let us out of the village. Tomorrow you can come out to look for us; and perhaps, Ogdli, you will find me—find me waiting for you in the forest." Her words, her tones, were provocative.

The man shook his head as though to rid his brain of an unwelcome thought; he passed a palm across his eyes as one who would push aside a veil.

"No!" he almost shouted; then he seized her roughly and dragged her along. "I will take you to Kavandavanda. After that you will bewitch me no more."

"Why are you afraid of me, Ogdli?" she asked. "I am only a woman."

"That is why I am afraid of you. You see no women here. There are none, other than those who are brought for Kavandavanda; and they are here but briefly. I am a priest. We are all priests. Women would contaminate us. We are not allowed to have them. If we were to weaken and succumb to their wiles, we should live in torment forever after death; and if Kavandavanda found it out, we should die quickly and horribly."

"What is he saying, madame?" asked Annette. "What are you talking about?"

"It is preposterous, Annette," replied Jane; "but Ogdli has developed a sudden infatuation for me. I tried to play upon it in order to tempt him to let us escape—and meet me in the forest tomorrow. It offered hope."

"Oh, madame! You would not!"

"Of course not; but all is fair in love and war, and this is both. If we ever get into the forest, Annette, it will just be too bad for Ogdli if he can't find us."

159

"And what does he say to it?"

"Thumbs down. He is dragging me off to Kavandavanda as fast as he can, so that temptation may be removed from his path."

"All our hopes are dashed, madame," said Annette, woefully.

"Not entirely, if I know men," replied Jane. "Ogdli will not so easily escape his infatuation. When he thinks he has lost me, it will tear at his vitals; then anything may happen."

The Kavuru was leading the two girls along the main street toward the rear of the village. Confronting them was a heavy gate across the bottom of a narrow cleft in the cliff that towered ominously above the village.

Ogdli opened the gate and herded them through into the narrow, rocky cleft, beyond which they could see what appeared to be an open valley; but when they reached the far end of the cleft they found themselves in a box canyon entirely surrounded by lofty cliffs.

A small stream of clear water wound down through the canyon and out through the cleft and the village where it was entirely bridged over at the outer gate as well as in the cleft leading into the canyon.

The floor of the canyon appeared extremely fertile, supporting numerous large trees and growing crops. In the small fields Jane saw men laboring beneath the watchful eyes of Kavuru warriors. At first she paid little heed to the workers in the fields, as Ogdli led her and Annette toward a massive pile of buildings standing in the center of the canyon, but presently her attention was attracted to one of the laborers who was irrigating a small patch of Kaffir corn.

Suddenly he threw down the crude wooden hoe he was using and stood upon his head in the mud. "I am a tree," he screamed in the Bukena dialect, "and they have planted me upside down. Turn me over, put my roots in the ground, irrigate me, and I will grow to the moon."

The Kavuru warrior who was guarding the workers in the vicinity stepped up to the man and struck him a sharp blow across the shins with the haft of his spear. "Get down and go to work," he growled.

The worker cried out in pain; but he immediately came to his feet, picked up his hoe, and continued to work as though there had been no interruption.

A little farther on another worker, looking up and catching sight of the two white girls, rushed toward them. Before the guard could interfere he was close to Jane. "I am the king of the world," he whispered; "but don't tell them.

They would kill me if they knew, but they can't know because I tell everyone not to tell them."

Ogdli leaped at the fellow and struck him over the head with his spear just as the guard arrived to drag him back to his work.

"They are all bewitched," explained Ogdli. "Demons have entered their heads and taken possession of their brains; but it is well to have them around, as they frighten away other evil spirits. We keep them and take care of them. If they die a natural death, the demons die with them; if we were to kill them the demons would escape from their heads and might enter ours. As it is, they can't get out in any other way."

"And these workers are all madmen?" asked Jane.

"Each has a demon in his head, but that doesn't keep them from working for us. Kavandavanda is very wise; he knows how to use everything and everybody."

Now they had arrived before closed gates in the wall surrounding the building that they had seen when they first entered the canyon. Two Kavuru warriors stood on guard at the entrance to Kavandavanda's stronghold, but at the approach of Ogdli and his prisoners they opened the gates and admitted them.

Between the outer wall and the buildings was an open space corresponding to the ballium of a medieval castle. In it grew a few large trees, a few clumps of bamboo, and patches of brush and weeds. It was ill-kept and unsightly. The buildings themselves were partially of unbaked brick and partially of bamboo and thatch, a combination which produced a pleasing texture, enhancing the general effect of the low, rambling buildings that seemed to have been put together at different times and according to no predetermined plan, the whole achieving an unstudied disharmony that was most effective.

As they crossed to the entrance to what appeared to be the main building, a leopard rose from a patch of weeds, bared its fangs at them, and slunk away toward a clump of bamboo. Then another and another of the treacherous beasts, disturbed by their passage, moved sinuously out of their path.

Annette, her eyes wide with fright, pressed close to Jane. "I am so afraid!" she said.

"They're ugly looking brutes," agreed Jane. "I wouldn't imagine this to be a very safe place. Perhaps that is why there are no people here."

"Only the guards at the entrance ahead of us," said Annette. "Ask Ogdli if the leopards are dangerous."

"Very," replied the Kavuru in reply to the question that Jane put to him.

"Then why are they allowed to run at large?" demanded Jane.

"They do not bother us much in the day time, partially because they are fairly well fed, partially because only armed men cross this court yard, and partially because they are, after all, cowardly beasts that prefer to sneak upon their prey in the dark. But it is after dark that they best serve the purpose of Kavandavanda. You may be sure that no one escapes from the temple by night."

"And that is all that they are kept for?" asked the girl.

"That is not all," replied Ogdli.

Jane waited for him to continue, but he remained silent. "What else, then?" she asked.

He gazed at her for a moment before he replied. There was a light in his eyes that appeared strange to Jane, for it seemed to reflect something that was almost compassion. He shook his head. "I cannot tell," he said; "but you will know soon enough another reason that the leopards are here in the outer court."

They were almost at the entrance when a weird, wailing scream broke the stillness that seemed to brood like an evil thing above the temple of Kavandavanda. The sound seemed to come either from the interior of the mass of buildings or from beyond them—sinister, horrible.

Instantly it was answered by the snarls and growls of leopards that appeared suddenly from amongst the weeds, the brush, or the bamboo and bounded off to disappear around the ends of the buildings.

"Something called to them," whispered Annette, shuddering.

"Yes," said Jane, "something unclean—that was the impression conveyed to me."

At the entrance there were two more guards to whom Ogdli spoke briefly; then they were admitted. As they passed the portal and came into the interior they heard muffled screams and growls and snarls as of many leopards fighting, and to the accompaniment of this savage chorus the two girls were conducted through the dim rooms and corridors of the temple of Kavandavanda.

Kavandavanda! Who, or what, was he? To what mysterious fate was he summoning them? Such were the questions constantly recurring in the thoughts of the girls. Jane felt that they would soon find answers, and she anticipated only the worst. There seemed to be no hope of escape from whatever fate lay in store for them.

That one hope that had given her strength to carry on

through danger-fraught situations many times in the past was denied her now, for she felt that Tarzan must be wholly ignorant of her whereabouts. How could he know where, in the vast expanse of the African wilderness, the ship had crashed? He would be searching for her—she knew that; for he must have long since received her cablegram, but he could never find her—at least, not in time. She must depend wholly upon her own resources, and these were pitifully meager. At present there was only the frail straw of Ogdli's seeming infatuation. This she must nurse. But how? Perhaps when he had delivered her to Kavandavanda he would return to the village and she would never see him again; then even the single straw to which her hope clung in the deluge of dangers that threatened to engulf her would be snatched from her.

"Ogdli," she said, suddenly, "do you live here in the temple or back in the village?"

"I live where Kavandavanda commands," he replied. "Sometimes in the village, again in the temple."

"And now! Where do you live now?"

"In the village."

Jane mused. Ogdli would be of no good to her unless he were in the temple. "You have lived here all your life, Ogdli?"

"No."

"How long?"

"I do not remember. Perhaps a hundred rains have come and gone, perhaps two hundred; I have lost count. It makes no difference, for I shall be here forever—unless I am killed. I shall never die otherwise."

Jane looked at him in astonishment. Was he another maniac? Were they all maniacs in this terrible city? But she determined to humor him.

"Then if you have been here so long," she said, "you must be on very friendly terms with Kavandavanda. If you asked him a favor he'd grant it."

"Perhaps," he agreed, "but one must be careful what one asks of Kavandavanda."

"Ask him if you can remain in the temple," suggested the girl.

"Why?" demanded Ogdli, suspiciously.

"Because you are my only friend here, and I am afraid without you."

The man's brows knit into an angry scowl. "You are trying to bewitch me again," he growled.

"You have bewitched yourself, Ogdli," she sighed; "and you have bewitched me. Do not be angry with me. Neither of us could help it." Her beautiful eyes looked up at him appealingly, seemingly on the verge of tears.

"Do not look at me like that," he cried, huskily; and then once more she saw the same look in his eyes that she had noticed before they left the village.

She laid a hand upon his bare arm. "You will ask him?" she whispered. It was more a statement than a question.

He turned away roughly and continued on in silence, but on Jane's lips was a smile of satisfaction. Intuition told her that she had won. But what would she do with her success? Its implications terrified her. Then she gave a mental shrug. By her wits she must turn the circumstance to her advantage without paying the price—she was every inch a woman.

As they passed through the temple corridors and apartments, Jane saw a number of black men—fat, soft, oily looking fellows that reminded her of the guardians of a sultan's harem. They seemed to personify cruelty, greed, and craft. She instinctively shrank from them if they passed close. These, she assumed, were the servants of Kavandavanda. What then was Kavandavanda like?

She was soon to know.

28

Kavandavanda

A N IDIOT jibbered beneath the gloomy shadows of the forbidding forest. A little monkey swung low from a branch; and the idiot leaped for it, shrieking horribly.

From high among the foliage of a nearby tree two appraising eyes watched the idiot. What passed in the brain behind those eyes only the creature and its Maker knew.

The idiot suddenly started to run blindly along a trail. He stumbled and fell. It was evident that he was very weak. He scrambled to his feet and staggered on. Through the branches above, the creature followed, watching, always watching.

The trail debouched upon a little clearing, perhaps an acre in extent. A single tree grew alone near the far side. Beneath the tree sprawled three maned lions; young lions, they were, but in the prime of their strength.

As the idiot stumbled into the clearing one of the lions arose and stared at the intruder, more in curiosity than in disapproval. The idiot saw the lions; and with loud screams, hideous screams, he bore down upon them waving his arms wildly above his head.

Now lions are nervous, temperamental creatures. It is difficult to prophesy just what they will do under any given circumstances.

The others had come to their feet with the first scream of the idiot, and now all three stood watching his approach. For just a moment they stood their ground before such an emergency as had never confronted any of them before, nor, doubtless, ever would again. Then the one who had first risen turned and bounded off into the jungle, his two companions close upon his heels.

The idiot sat down suddenly and commenced to cry. "They all run away from me," he muttered. "They know I am a murderer, and they are afraid of me—*afraid of me! afraid of me!* AFRAID OF ME!" His shrieking voice rose to a final piercing crescendo.

The stalker among the trees dropped to the floor of the clearing and approached the idiot. He came upon him from behind. He was Ydeni, the Kavuru. Stealthily he crept forward. In his hand was a coiled rope.

Ydeni leaped upon the idiot and bore him to the ground. The idiot screamed and struggled, but to no avail. The mighty muscles of the Kavuru held him and deftly bound his wrists together behind his back.

Then Ydeni lifted the man and set him upon his feet. The idiot looked at his captor with wide eyes from which terror quickly faded to be replaced by a vacuous grin.

"I have a friend," he mumbled. "At last I have a friend, and I shall not be alone. What is your name, friend? I am Prince Sborov. Do you understand? I am a prince."

Ydeni did not understand, and if he had he would not have cared. He had been scouting for more girls and he had found an idiot. He knew that Kavandavanda would be pleased; for, while there were never too many girls, there were even fewer idiots; and Kavandavanda liked idiots.

Ydeni examined his captive. He discovered that he was weak and emaciated and that he was unarmed.

Satisfied that the man was harmless, the Kavuru released his wrists; then he fastened the rope securely about Sborov's neck and led him off into the jungle along a secret, hidden path that was a short cut to the village.

His mind broken by terror and privation, the European babbled incessantly as he staggered along behind his captor. Often he stumbled and fell; and always Ydeni had to lift him to his feet, for he was too weak to rise without assistance.

At last the Kavuru found food and halted while Sborov ate; and when they started on again Ydeni assisted him, carrying him much of the way until at last they came to the village of the Kavuru beside the lone mountain in the wilderness.

And in the meantime, Tarzan led Brown and Tibbs along the main trail, a much longer route to the same village; for none of them knew where it was located, and at best could only harbor the hope that this trail led to it.

Sometimes Nkima rode upon Tarzan's shoulder; or, again, swung through the trees above the three men. He, at least, was carefree and happy; Tarzan was concerned over the fate of his mate, Brown was worried about Annette, and Tibbs was always sad on general principles when he was away from London. Being hungry and footsore and weary and terrified by the jungle and its savage life in no way lessened the pall of gloom that enveloped him.

They were not a happy company, but none could tell from Tarzan's manner or expression or any word that fell from his lips the bitterness of the sorrow that he held within his breast. He did not know what fate was reserved for the girl captives of the Kavuru, but his knowledge of the more savage tribes of these remote fastnesses offered but faint hope that he might be in time to rescue her. To avenge her was the best that he could anticipate.

And while his thoughts dwelt upon her, recalling each least detail of their companionship, Jane was being led into a large, central room in the temple of Kavandavanda, king, witch-doctor, and god of the Kavuru.

It was a large, low room, its ceiling supported by columns consisting of the trunks of trees, the surfaces of which, stripped of bark and darkened by antiquity, bore a high polish. Toothless skulls hung in clusters from the capitals of the columns, white against the darkened surfaces of the ceiling and the columns, grinning, leering upon the scene below, watching the silly antics of mortal men through the wisdom of eternity out of sightless eyes.

The gloom of the remoter purlieus of the large chamber was only partially relieved by the sunlight shining through a single opening in the ceiling and flooding a figure seated upon a great throne on a dais carpeted with the skins of leopards.

As her eyes rested for the first time upon the enthroned man, Jane was plainly aware of a mental gasp of astonishment. The picture was striking, barbaric; the man was beautiful.

If this were Kavandavanda, how utterly different was he from any of the various pictures of him her imagination had conceived; and it was Kavandavanda, she knew; it would

166

be none other. Every indolent, contemptuous line of his pose bespoke the autocrat. Here indeed was a king—nay, something more, even, than a king. Jane could not rid herself of the thought that she was looking upon a god.

He sat alone upon the dais except for two leopards, one chained on either side of his great throne chair. Below him, surrounding the dais, were Kavuru warriors; and close at hand the soft, fat slaves such as Jane had seen elsewhere in the temple. Upon the floor, on each side of the dais, a dozen girls reclined upon leopard skins. They were mostly black girls, but there were a number with the lighter skins and the features of the Bedouins.

One of the Bedouin girls and a couple of the blacks were reasonably comely of face and figure, but on the whole they did not appear to have been selected with an eye to pulchritude.

Ogdli led his two charges to within a few yards of the dais; then, as he knelt himself, gruffly ordered them to kneel. Annette did as she was bid; but Jane remained erect, her eyes fearlessly appraising the man upon the throne.

He was a young man, almost naked but for an elaborate loin-cloth and ornaments. Many rows of human teeth suspended about his neck, covered his chest and fell as low as his loin-cloth. Armlets, bracelets, and anklets of metal, of wood, and of ivory, completed his barbaric costume. But it was not these things that riveted the girl's attention, but rather the divine face and form of the youth.

At first Jane felt that she had never looked upon a more beautiful countenance. An oval face was surmounted by a wealth of golden hair; below a high, full forehead shone luminous dark eyes that glowed with the fires of keen intelligence. A perfect nose and a short upper lip completed the picture of divine beauty that was marred and warped and ruined by a weak, cruel mouth.

Until she noticed that mouth, hope had leaped high in Jane's breast that here she and Annette might find a benevolent protector rather than the cruel savage they had expected Kavandavanda to be.

The man's eyes were fixed upon her in a steady stare. He, too, was appraising; but what his reaction, his expression did not reveal.

"Kneel!" he commanded suddenly, in imperious tones.

"Why should I kneel?" demanded Jane. "Why should I kneel to you?"

"I am Kavandavanda."

"That is no reason why an English woman should kneel to you."

167

Two of the fat, black slaves started toward her, looking questioningly at Kavandavanda.

"You refuse to kneel?" asked the youth.

"Most certainly."

The slaves were still advancing toward her, but they kept one eye on Kavandavanda. He waved them back. A strange expression twisted his lips. Whether it was from amusement or anger, Jane could not guess.

"It pleases me to discuss the matter," said the youth; then he commanded Ogdli and Annette to rise. "You brought in both of these prizes, Ogdli?" he asked.

"No," replied Ogdli. "Ydeni brought this one." He gestured toward Annette. "I brought the other."

"You did well. We have never had one like her—she contains the seeds of beauty as well as youth." Then he turned his eyes upon Jane once more. "Who are you?" he demanded, "and what were you doing in the country of the Kavuru?"

"I am Jane Clayton, Lady Greystoke. I was flying from London to Nairobi when our ship was forced down. My companions and I were trying to make our way to the coast when this girl and myself were captured by your warriors. I ask that you release us and give us guides to the nearest friendly village."

A crooked smile twisted the lips of Kavandavanda. "So you came in one of those devil birds," he said. "Two others came yesterday. Their dead bodies lie beside their devil bird outside the city gates. My people are afraid of the devil bird; they will not go near it. Tell me, will it harm them?"

The girl thought quickly before she replied. Perhaps she might turn their superstitious fear to her advantage. "They had better keep away from it," she advised. "More devil birds will come, and if they find that you have harmed me or my companion they will destroy your village and your people. Send us away in safety, and I will tell them not to bother you."

"They will not know that you are here," replied the youth. "No one knows what happens in the village of the Kavuru or the temple of Kavandavanda."

"You will not set us free?"

"No. No stranger who enters the gates of the village ever passes out again—and you, least of all. I have had many girls brought to me, but none like you."

"You have plenty of girls here. What do you want of me?"

His eyes half closed as he regarded her. "I do not know," he said in a voice scarce raised above a whisper. "I thought that I knew, but now I am not sure." Suddenly he turned his

168

eyes upon Ogdli. "Take them to the room of the three snakes," he commanded, "and guard them there. They cannot escape, but see that they do not try. I don't want anything to happen to this one. Medek will show you the way," he nodded toward one of the fat blacks standing near the dais.

"What was all the talk about, madame?" asked Annette, as they were being led through the temple by Medek.

Jane told her, briefly.

"The room of the three snakes!" repeated Annette. "Do you suppose there are snakes in the room?" She shuddered. "I am afraid of snakes."

"Look above the doors of the rooms we pass," suggested Jane. "I think you will find the answer to your question there. There is a doorway with a boar's head above it. We just passed one with two human skulls over the lintel; and there, on the other side of the corridor, ahead, is one with three leopards' heads. It is evidently their way of designating rooms, just as we number them in our hotels. I imagine it has no other significance."

Medek led them up a flight of rude stairs and along a corridor on the second floor of the temple and ushered them into a room above the doorway of which were mounted the heads of three snakes. Ogdli entered the room with them. It was a low ceiled room with windows overlooking the courtyard that surrounded the temple.

Annette looked quickly around the apartment. "I don't see any snakes, madame," she said, with evident relief.

"Nor much of anything else, Annette. The Kavuru don't waste much thought on furniture."

"There are two benches, madame, but no table and not a bed."

"There's the bed over in the corner," said Jane.

"That's just a pile of filthy skins," objected the French girl.

"Nevertheless, it's all the bed we'll get, Annette."

"What are you talking about?" demanded Ogdli. "Don't think that you can escape. You haven't a chance; so there's no sense in planning anything of the sort."

"We weren't," Jane assured him. "We can't escape unless you'll help us. I was so glad when Kavandavanda said that you were to guard us. You know, you are the only friend we have, Ogdli."

"Did you see how Kavandavanda looked at you?" the man demanded, suddenly.

"Why no, not particularly," replied Jane.

"Well, I did; and I've never seen him look that way at

169

a captive before. Neither did I ever know him to permit a person to stand before him without first kneeling. I believe that you have bewitched him, too. Did you like him, woman?"

"Not as well as I like you, Ogdli," whispered the girl.

"He can't do it!" exclaimed the man. "He's got to obey the law the same as the rest of us."

"Do what?" demanded Jane.

"If he tries it, I'll—" A noise in the corridor silenced him, and just in time. The door was swung open by a slave, and as he stood aside the figure of Kavandavanda was revealed behind him.

As he entered the room Ogdli dropped to his knees. Annette followed his example, but Jane remained erect.

"So you won't kneel, eh?" demanded Kavandavanda. "Well, perhaps that is the reason I like you—one of the reasons. You two may arise. Get out into the corridor, all of you except this one who calls herself Jane. I wish to speak with her alone."

Ogdli looked Kavandavanda straight in the eyes. "Yes," he said; "yes, high priest of the priests of Kavuru, I go; but I shall be near."

Kavandavanda flushed momentarily in what seemed anger, but he said nothing as the others passed out into the corridor. When they had gone and the door had been closed, he turned to Jane. "Sit down," he said, motioning toward one of the benches; and when she had, he came and sat beside her. For a long time he looked at her before he spoke, his eyes the eyes of a dreamer of dreams. "You are very beautiful," he said, at last. "I have never seen a creature more beautiful. It seems a pity, then; it seems a pity."

"What seems a pity?" demanded the girl.

"Never mind," he snapped, brusquely. "I must have been thinking aloud." Again, for a space, he was silent, sunk in thought; and then: "What difference will it make. I may as well tell you. It is seldom that I have an opportunity to talk with anyone intelligent enough to understand; and you will understand—you will appreciate the great service you are to render—if I am strong. But when I look at you, when I look deep into those lovely eyes, I feel weak. No, no! I must not fail; I must not fail the world that is waiting for me."

"I do not understand what you are talking about," said the girl.

"No, not now; but you will. Look at me closely. How old do you think I am?"

"In your twenties, perhaps."

He leaned closer. "I do not know how old I am. I have

170

lost all track. Perhaps a thousand years; perhaps a few hundred; perhaps much older. Do you believe in God?"

"Yes, most assuredly."

"Well, don't. There is no such thing—not yet, at least. That has been the trouble with the world. Men have imagined a god instead of seeking god among themselves. They have been led astray by false prophets and charlatans. They have had no leader. God should be a leader, and a leader should be a tangible entity—something men can see and feel and touch. He must be mortal and yet immortal. He may not die. He must be omniscient. All the forces of nature have been seeking throughout all the ages to produce such a god that the world may be ruled justly and mercifully forever, a god who shall control the forces of nature as well as the minds and acts of men.

"Almost such am I, Kavandavanda, high priest of the priests of Kavuru. Already am I deathless; already am I omniscient; already, to some extent, can I direct the minds and acts of men. It is the forces of nature that yet defy me. When I have conquered these, I shall indeed be God."

"Yes," agreed Jane, bent upon humoring this madman; "yes, you shall indeed be God; but remember that mercy is one of the characteristics of godliness. Therefore, be merciful; and set my companion and me free."

"And have the ignorant barbarians of the outer world swoop down upon us and rob mankind of its sole hope of salvation by destroying me? No!"

"But what purpose can I serve? If you free us, I promise to lead no one here."

"You can serve the only purpose for which women are fit. Man may only attain godliness alone. Woman weakens and destroys him. Look at me! Look at my priests! You think we are all young men. We are not. A hundred rains have come and gone since the latest neophyte joined our holy order. And how have we attained this deathlessness? Through women. We are all celibates. Our vows of celibacy were sealed in the blood of women; in our own blood will we be punished if we break them. It would be death for a Kavuru priest to succumb to the wiles of a woman."

Jane shook her head. "I still do not understand," she said.

"But you will. Long ago I learned the secret of deathless youth. It lies in an elixir brewed of many things—the pollen of certain plants, the roots of others, the spinal fluid of leopards, and, principally, the glands and blood of women—young women. Now do you understand?"

"Yes." The girl shuddered.

"Do not recoil from the thought; remember that you will

171

thus become a part of the living god. You will live forever. You will be glorified."

"But I won't know anything about it; so what good will it do me?"

"I shall know. I shall know that you are a part of me. In that way I shall have you." He leaned closer to her. "But I should like to keep you as you are." His breath was hot upon her cheek. "And why not? Am I not almost a god? And may not God do as he chooses? Who is there to say him nay?"

He seized her and drew her to him.

29

To What Doom

I T WAS almost dusk when Ydeni led his captive through the village of the Kavuru and to the temple of Kavandavanda. By another trail Tarzan was approaching the clearing before the village. He paused and lifted his head.

"What is it?" asked Brown.

"Is 'is 'ighness coming?" inquired Tibbs.

The ape-man shook his head. "We are nearing a village. It is the village of the Kavuru; but nearer still are friends—Waziri."

"How do you know?" demanded Brown.

Tarzan ignored the question, but motioned for silence; then from his lips came softly the call of the quail—three times he voiced it. For a moment, as he stood listening, there was silence; then once, twice, thrice came the answering call.

Tarzan moved forward again followed by his companions, and a moment later Muviro and Balando came running to drop to their knees before him.

Very briefly and in sorrow Muviro told what had happened. Tarzan listened without comment. No emotion of either sorrow or anger was reflected by his expression.

"Then you think it impossible to gain entrance to the village?" he asked.

"We are too few, Bwana," replied Muviro, sadly.

"But if Buira still lives, she is there," Tarzan reminded him, "and your Mem-sahib and another white girl who belongs to this man." He gestured toward the American. "Much that life holds for us three may be behind the gates of that village, and there is the memory of our slain friends. Would you turn back now, Muviro?"

"Muviro follows where Tarzan leads," replied the black, simply.

"We will go to the edge of the clearing that you speak of, and there we may make our plans. Come." The ape-man moved silently along the trail, followed by the others.

As they came to the edge of the clearing, he halted. Brown smothered an exclamation of surprise. "Well! In the name of—. Say, do you see what I see? That's a ship."

"I forgot to tell you," said Muviro. "Two men came in a ship and landed. The Kavuru killed them. You can see their bodies lying beside the ship."

As Tarzan stood at the edge of the forest beyond the village of the Kavuru it was well for his peace of mind that he did not know what was transpiring in the temple of Kavandavanda on the opposite side of the village, for at that very moment the high priest seized Jane and crushed her to him.

Helpless and hopeless, not knowing which way to turn for help, the girl acted upon what appeared an inspiration. Pushing the man's lips from hers, she raised her voice in a single piercing cry: "Ogdli!"

Instantly the door of the apartment swung open. Kavandavanda released her and sprang to his feet. Ogdli crossed the threshold and halted. The two men stood glaring at one another. Ogdli did not ask why the girl had summoned him. He appeared to know.

Kavandavanda's face and neck burned scarlet for a moment; then went deadly white as he strode past Ogdli and out of the room without a word.

The warrior crossed quickly to the girl. "He will kill us both, now," he said. "We must escape; then you will belong to me."

"But your vows!" cried Jane, clutching at a straw.

"What are vows to a dead man?" asked Ogdli. "And I am as good as dead now. I shall go and take you with me. I know a secret passage beneath the courtyard and the village. Thus sometimes goes Kavandavanda to search in the forest for secret flowers and roots. When it is dark, we shall go."

As Kavandavanda strode through the corridors of his palace, his heart black with rage, he met Ydeni coming with his captive.

"What have you there?" he demanded.

Ydeni dropped to his knees. "One of those into whose

skull a demon has come to dwell. I have brought him to Kavandavanda."

"Take him away," growled the high priest, "and lock him up. I will see him in the morning."

Ydeni rose and led Sborov on through the temple. He took him to the second floor and shoved him into a dark room. It was the room of the two snakes. Next to it was the room of the three snakes. Then Ydeni shot a bolt on the outside of the door and went away and left his prisoner without food or water.

In the next room Ogdli was planning the escape. He knew he could not carry it out until after the temple slept. "I will go away now and hide," he said, "so that Kavandavanda cannot find me before it is time to go. Later I shall return and get you."

"You must take Annette, too," said Jane—"the other girl. Where is she?"

"In the next room. I put her there when Kavandavanda sent us out of this one."

"You will take her with us?"

"Perhaps," he replied; but Jane guessed that he had no intention of doing so.

She very much wished to have Annette along, not alone to give her a chance to escape the clutches of the high priest, but because she felt that two of them together would have a better chance of thwarting the designs of Ogdli once they were in the jungle.

"Do not try to escape while I am gone," cautioned Ogdli. "There is only one way besides the secret passage, and that is across the courtyard. To enter the courtyard would mean certain death." He opened the door and stepped out into the corridor. Jane watched him close the door, and then she heard a bolt moved into place.

In the room of the two snakes Sborov groped around in the darkness. A lesser darkness came from the night outside through the single window overlooking the courtyard. He went to the window and looked out. Then he heard what seemed to be muffled voices coming from an adjoining chamber. He prowled along the wall until he found a door. He tried it, but it was locked. He continued to fumble with the latch.

In the next room Jane heard him and approached the door after Ogdli left her. The warrior had said that Annette was in the next room; that must be Annette, she thought, trying to return to her.

Jane found that the door was secured by a heavy bolt on her side. She was about to call to Annette when she real-

174

ized that the girl evidently realized some necessity for silence, else she had called to Jane.

Very cautiously she slipped the bolt a fraction of an inch at a time. Annette was still fumbling with the latch on the opposite side—Jane could hear her.

At last the bolt drew clear and the door swung slowly open. "Annette!" whispered Jane as a figure, dimly visible in the gloom, came slowly into the room.

"Annette is dead," said a man's voice. "Brown killed her. He killed Jane, too. Who are you?"

"Alexis!" cried Jane.

"Who are you?" demanded Sborov.

"I am Jane—Lady Greystoke. Don't you recognize my voice?"

"Yes, but you are dead. Is Kitty with you? My God!" he cried, "you have brought her back to haunt me. Take her away! Take her away!" His voice rose to a shrill scream.

From the door on the opposite side of the apartment came the sound of running, and then Annette's voice. "Madame! Madame! What is it? What has happened?"

"Who's that?" demanded Sborov. "I know—it's Annette. You have all come back to haunt me."

"Calm yourself, Alexis," said Jane, soothingly. "Kitty is not here, and Annette and I are both alive." As she spoke she crossed the room to the door of the chamber in which the French girl was confined; and, feeling for the bolt, drew it.

"Don't let her in!" screamed Sborov. "Don't let her in. I'll tear you to pieces if you do, ghost or no ghost." He started across the room on a run just as the door swung open and Annette rushed in. At the same moment the door leading into the corridor was pushed open; and the black slave, Medek, entered.

"What's going on here?" he demanded. "Who let that man in here?"

At sight of Annette, Sborov recoiled, screaming. Then he saw Medek in the dim light of the interior. "Kitty!" he shrieked. "I won't go with you. Go away!"

Medek started toward him. Sborov turned and fled toward the far end of the room, toward the window looking out upon the courtyard. He paused a moment at the sill and turned wild eyes back toward the shadowy figure pursuing him; then, with a final maniacal scream of terror, he leaped out into the night.

Medek followed him to the window and leaned out; then from his lips broke the same horrid scream that Jane had heard earlier in the day as she was being led from the

175

throne-room of Kavandavanda. From below came the moans of Sborov, who must have been badly injured by the fall from the second story window; but presently these were drowned by the snarls and growls of leopards.

The two girls could hear them converging from all parts of the grounds upon the moaning creature lying out there in the night. Presently the sounds of the leopards rose to a hideous din as they fought over the flesh of their prey. For a few moments the screams of their victim mingled with the savage mouthings of the beasts, but soon they ceased.

Medek turned away from the window. "It is not well to seek escape in that direction," he said, as he returned to the outer corridor, closing the door behind him.

"How awful, madame," whimpered Annette.

"Yes," replied Jane, "but his sufferings were mercifully brief. Perhaps, after all, it is just as well. His mind is gone. Prince Sborov had become a maniac."

"What a terrible price he paid. But is it not, perhaps, that he deserved it, madame?"

"Who shall say? But we, too, are paying a terrible price for his greed and his wife's vanity. The thing she sought is here, Annette."

"What thing, madame? Not the restorer of youth?"

"Yes. Kavandavanda holds the secret, but neither the princess nor any other could have gotten it from him. We should all have met a terrible fate just the same had the entire party succeeded in reaching the village of the Kavuru—the fate that is reserved for you and me."

"What fate, madame? You frighten me."

"I do not mean to, but you may as well know the truth. If we do not succeed in escaping we shall be butchered to furnish ingredients for Kavandavanda's devilish potion that keeps the priests of Kavuru always youthful."

"S-s-sh, madame!" cautioned Annette, fearfully. "What was that?"

"I don't know. It sounded as though someone in the corridor had tried to scream."

"Then there was a thud, as though someone had fallen. Did you hear that?"

"Yes—and now someone is trying the door. They are slipping the bolt."

"Oh, madame! Some new horror."

The door swung open and a figure stepped into the room. A voice spoke. "Woman! Are you there?" It was the voice of Ogdli.

"I am here," said Jane.

"Then come quickly. There is no time to be lost."

"But how about the slave in the corridor? He will see us go out."

"The slave is there, but he will not see us. Come!"

"Come, Annette! It is our only chance."

"The other woman is here?" demanded Ogdli.

"Yes," replied Jane. "And if I go, she must go."

"Very well," snapped the Kavuru, "but hurry."

The two girls followed the man into the corridor. Across the doorway lay the body of Medek. The dead eyes were staring up at them. Ogdli kicked the black face and gave a short laugh. "He looks, but he does not see."

The girls shuddered and pressed on behind the warrior. He led them cautiously along dark corridors. At the slightest sound he dragged them into pitchblack rooms along the way until he was sure there was no danger of discovery. Thus, much time was consumed in nerve-wracking suspense.

Ogdli advanced with evident trepidation. It was apparent that now that he had embarked upon this venture he was terrified—the shadow of Kavandavanda's wrath lay heavy upon him.

The night dragged on, spent mostly in hiding, as the trio made their slow way toward the secret entrance to the tunnel that led out into the jungle.

Once more they crept on after a long period of tense waiting and listening in a dark chamber; then Ogdli spoke in a relieved whisper. "Here we are," he said. "Through this doorway. The entrance to the tunnel is in this room. Make no noise."

He pushed the door open cautiously and entered the chamber, the two girls following closely behind him. Instantly hands reached out of the dark and seized them. Jane heard a scuffling and the sound of running feet; then she was dragged out into the corridor. A light was brought from another apartment—a bit of reed burning in a shallow vessel.

Annette was there, close to her, trembling. They were surrounded by five sturdy warriors. In the light of the sputtering cresset the men looked quickly from one to another.

"Where is Ogdli?" demanded a warrior. Then Jane realized that her would-be abductor had vanished.

"I thought you had him," replied another. "I seized one of the girls."

"I thought I had him," spoke up a third.

"And so did I," said a fourth, "but it was you I had. He must have run for the tunnel. Come, we'll go after him."

"No," objected the first warrior. "It is too late. He has a good start. We could not catch him before he reached the forest."

177

"We could not find him there at night," agreed another. "It will soon be daylight; then we can go after him."

"We'll see what Kavandavanda says when we take the women to him," said the first warrior. "Bring them along."

Once again the girls were led through the corridors of the temple this time to an apartment adjoining the throne-room. Two warriors stood before the door. When they saw the girls and were told what had happened, one of them knocked on the door. Presently it was opened by a black slave, sleepily rubbing his eyes.

"Who disturbs Kavandavanda at this hour of the night?" he demanded.

"Tell him we have come with the two white girls. He will understand."

The black turned back into the apartment, but in a few moments he returned.

"Bring your prisoners in," he said; "Kavandavanda will see you."

They were led through a small antechamber lighted by a crude cresset to a larger apartment similarly illuminated. Here Kavandavanda received them, lying on a bed covered with leopard skins.

His large eyes fixed themselves upon Jane. "So you thought you could escape?" he asked, a crooked smile twisting his weak lips. "You were going to run off with Ogdli and be his mate, were you? Where is Ogdli?" he demanded suddenly, as he realized that the man was not with the others.

"He escaped—through the tunnel," reported a warrior.

"He must have thought Kavandavanda a fool," sneered the high priest. "I knew what was in his mind. There are only six men beside myself who know about the tunnel. Ogdli was one of them; the other five are here." He was addressing Jane. "I sent these five to wait at the entrance to the tunnel until Ogdli came, for I knew he would come." He paused and gazed long at Jane; then he turned to the others. "Take this other one back to the room of the three snakes," he ordered, "and see that she does not escape again." He indicated Annette with a gesture. "This one I will keep here to question further; there may have been others concerned in the plot. Go!"

Annette cast a despairing look at Jane as she was led from the room, but the other could give her no reassurance nor encouragement. Their position seemed utterly without hope now.

"Good-by, Annette." That was all.

"May the good God be with us both, madame," whispered the French girl as the door was closing behind her.

"So," said Kavandavanda when the others had left, "you were going to run off into the jungle with Ogdli and be his mate? He was going to break his vow because of you!"

The shadow of a sneer curled the girl's lip. "Perhaps Ogdli thought so," she said.

"But you were going with him," Kavandavanda insisted.

"As far as the jungle," replied Jane; "then I should have found some means to escape him; or, failing that, I should have killed him."

"Why?" demanded the high priest. "Have you, too, taken a vow?"

"Yes—a vow of fidelity."

He leaned toward her eagerly. "But you could break it—for love; or, if not for love, for a price."

She shook her head. "Not for anything."

"I could break mine. I had thought that I never could, but since I have seen you—" He paused; and then, peremptorily, "if I, Kavandavanda, am willing to break mine, you can break yours. The price you will receive is one for which any woman might be willing to sell her soul—eternal youth, eternal beauty." Again he paused as though to permit the magnitude of his offer to impress itself upon her.

But again she shook her head. "No, it is out of the question."

"You spurn Kavandavanda?" His cruel mouth imparted some of its cruelty to his eyes. "Remember that I have the power to destroy you, or to take you without giving anything in return; but I am generous. And do you know why?"

"I cannot imagine."

"Because I love you. I have never known love before. No living creature has ever affected me as do you. I will keep you here forever; I will make you high priestess; I will keep you young through the ages; I will keep you beautiful. You and I will live forever. We will reach out. With my power to rejuvenate mankind, we shall have the world at our feet. We shall be deities—I, a god; you, a goddess. Look." He turned to a cabinet built into the wall of the apartment. It was grotesquely carved and painted—human figures, mostly of women; grinning skulls, leopards, snakes, and weird symbolic designs composed the decorations. From his loin-cloth he took a great key, hand wrought, and unlocked the cabinet.

"Look," he said again. "Come here and look."

Jane crossed the room and stood beside him at the cabinet. Within it were a number of boxes and jars. One large box, carved and painted similarly to the outside of the cabinet, Kavandavanda took in his hands.

"You see this?" he asked. "Look inside." He raised the lid revealing a quantity of black pellets about the size of peas. "Do you know what these are?" he demanded.

"I have no idea."

"These will give eternal youth and beauty to a thousand people. You are free to use them if you say the word. One taken each time that the moon comes full will give you what all mankind has craved since man first trod this earth." He seized her arm and tried to draw her to him.

With an exclamation of repugnance she sought to pull away, but he held her firmly; then she struck him heavily across the face. Surprised, he relaxed his grasp; and the girl tore herself away and ran from the room. Into the antechamber she ran, seeking to gain the corridor.

With a cry of rage, Kavandavanda pursued her; and just at the doorway leading into the corridor he overtook her. He seized her roughly, tangling his fingers in her hair; and though she fought to extricate herself, he dragged her slowly back toward the inner apartment.

30

"The Dead Men Fly!"

TARZAN and Brown had talked late into the night in an attempt to formulate a feasible plan whereby they might gain entrance to the village of the Kavuru, with the result that the ape-man had finally suggested a mad scheme as the only possible solution of their problem.

Brown shrugged and grinned. "We could sure get in that way, of course, though it all depends. But how we goin' to get out again?"

"Our problem now," replied Tarzan, "is to get in. We shall not have the problem of getting out until later. Perhaps we shall not come out. It really is not necessary that you come in with me if——"

"Skip it," interrupted Brown. "Annette's in there. That's enough for me to know. When do we start?"

"We can't do much until just before dawn. You need rest. Lie down. I'll wake you in time."

Tarzan slept, too—a little way from the others on the edge of the clearing where he had a view of the village. He slept in a low crotch a few feet above the ground; and he slept well, yet he slept lightly, as was his wont. The habitual noises of the jungle did not disturb him; but as the time approached when he must awaken Brown, he himself came suddenly awake, conscious of something unusual that disturbed the monotonous harmony of the forest.

Alert and watchful, he rose silently to his feet, listening. Every faculty, crystal sharp, was attuned to the faint note of discord that had aroused him. What was it?

Swiftly he moved through the trees, for now his sensitive nose had identified the author of the stealthy sound that his ears had detected—a Kavuru.

Presently the ape-man saw the dim figure of a man walking through the forest. He was walking rapidly, almost at a trot; and he was breathing heavily, as one who had been running. Tarzan paused above him for an instant and then dropped upon his shoulders, bearing him to the ground.

The man was powerful; and he fought viciously to escape, but he was wax in the hands of the Lord of the Jungle. The ape-man could have killed him; but the instant that he had realized that a Kavuru might fall into his hands, he had planned upon taking him alive, feeling that he might turn him to some good account.

Presently he succeeded in binding the fellow's wrists behind him; then he stood him upon his feet. For the first time, his captive looked him in the face. It was still dark, but not so dark that the Kavuru could not recognize the fact that his captor was not one of his own kind. He breathed a sigh of relief.

"Who are you?" he demanded. "Why did you capture me? You are not going to take me back to Kavandavanda? No, of course not—you are not a Kavuru."

Tarzan did not know why the man should object to being taken to Kavandavanda. He did not even know who Kavandavanda was, nor where; but he saw an opening, and he took advantage of it.

"If you answer my questions," he said, "I will not take you back to Kavandavanda, nor will I harm you. Who are you?"

"I am Ogdli."

"And you just came from the village?"

"Yes."

181

"You do not want to go back there?"

"No. Kavandavanda would kill me."

"Is Kavandavanda such a mighty warrior that you are afraid of him?"

"It is not that, but he is very powerful. He is high priest of the priests of Kavuru."

By simple questions Tarzan had learned from the answers Ogdli made enough to give him the lead that he desired to glean further information from his prisoner.

"What did Kavandavanda want of the two white girls that were taken to him?" he demanded.

"At first he would have killed them," replied Ogdli, willingly, for now he thought that he saw an opportunity to win mercy from this strange giant who was evidently interested in the two girls; "but," he continued, "he suddenly came to desire one of them for a mate. I tried to befriend them. I was leading them out of the village by a secret passage when we were set upon by several warriors. They recaptured the girls, and I barely escaped with my life."

"So the girls are still alive?"

"Yes; they were a few minutes ago."

"Are they in any immediate danger?"

"No one can say what Kavandavanda will do. I think they are in no immediate danger, for I am sure that Kavandavanda will take one of them for a mate. Perhaps he already has."

"Where is this secret passage? Lead me to it. Wait until I get my friends." He led Ogdli to where the others slept, and aroused them.

"I can show you where the passage is," explained Ogdli, "but you cannot enter the temple through it. The doors at either end open only in one direction, toward the forest, for those who do not know their secret; and only Kavandavanda knows that. One may easily pass out of the temple, but it is impossible to return."

Tarzan questioned Ogdli for several minutes; then he turned to Brown. "Annette and Lady Greystoke are in the temple," he explained. "The temple is in a small canyon behind the village. If we gained access to the village we would still have a battle on our hands to reach the temple. This fellow has told me where I can expect to find the prisoners in the temple; he has also given me other valuable information that may be useful if we succeed in getting to Lady Greystoke and Annette. I believe that he has spoken the truth. He says, further, that one of the women is in grave danger at the moment—I think it is Lady Greystoke, from his description;

so there is no time to be lost." Then he turned to Muviro. "Hold this man until Brown and I return. If we do not return before dark, you may know that we have failed; then you should return to your own country. Do, then, what you will with this prisoner. Give Brown and me the weapons that you took from the bodies of the fliers. They are of no more use to you, as you have exhausted the ammunition. Brown thinks we may find more in the ship. Come, Brown."

The two men moved silently out into the clearing, the ape-man in the lead. He bent his steps toward the ship, Brown treading close upon his heels. Neither spoke; their plans had been too well formulated to require speech.

When they came to the ship, Brown immediately crawled into the forward cockpit. He was there for several minutes; then he entered the rear cockpit. While he was thus engaged, Tarzan was busy over the bodies of the slain aviators.

When Brown had completed his examination of the interior of the cockpits, he descended to the ground and opened the baggage compartment; then he joined the ape-man.

"Plenty of ammunition," he said, and handed Tarzan a full box of cartridges. "That's about all you can manage— you ain't got no pockets. I've stuffed my pockets full—must weigh a ton."

"How about petrol?" asked Tarzan.

"Not much more'n a hatful," replied the American.

"Will it do?"

"Yep, if it don't take too long to get warmed up. Got the chutes?"

Tarzan handed Brown a parachute that he had taken from the body of one of the fliers; the other he adjusted to his own body. They spoke no more. Tarzan climbed into the forward cockpit, Brown into the other.

"Here's hoping," prayed Brown under his breath as he opened the valve of the air starter. The answering whir of the propeller brought a satisfied smile to his lips; then the ignition caught and the engine roared.

They had waited for dawn, and dawn was breaking as Brown taxied across the rough plain down wind for the take-off. He picked his way among boulders, choosing the best lane that he could find; but he saw that it was going to be a hazardous undertaking at best.

When he reached the limit of the best going, he brought the nose of the ship around into the wind, set the brakes, and opened the throttle wide for a moment. The motor was hitting beautifully.

"Sweet," muttered the American; then he throttled down to idling speed and shouted ahead to Tarzan, "If you know any prayers, buddy, you'd better say 'em—all of 'em. We're off!"

Tarzan glanced back, his white teeth gleaming in one of his rare smiles. There was a rush of wind as Brown gave the ship full throttle. It was a perilous take-off, swerving to miss boulders as the ship picked up speed. The tail rose. The ship bumped over the rough ground, tipped drunkenly as one wheel struck a small rock. A low boulder loomed suddenly ahead. It would be impossible to swerve enough to miss it without cracking up. Brown pulled the stick back and held his breath. The ship rose a foot or two from the ground. Brown saw that it was not going to clear the boulder. He could see but a single hope, a slim one; but he seized it instantly. He pushed the stick forward, the wheels struck the ground with a jarring bump, the ship bounced into the air as the stick helped to pull her up just enough to clear the boulder.

She had flying speed by now and continued to rise slowly. It had been a close call; and although the morning air was chill, Brown was wet with perspiration as he climbed in a wide spiral above the forest.

The village of the Kavuru lay below snuggled against the foot of the high escarpment that backed it, but it was not the village in which the two men were interested—it was the box canyon behind it where lay the temple of Kavandavanda of which Ogdli had told them.

Higher and higher rose the graceful plane, watched from the edge of the forest by Muviro, Balando, Tibbs, and Ogdli; and now, awakened by the drone of the motor, by Kavuru warriors congregated in the main street of the village.

"The dead men fly!" whispered a warrior in awed tones, for he thought that the ship was being flown by the two who had brought it down and who had fallen before the attack of the villagers.

The thought, once voiced, took root in the minds of the Kavuru and terrified them.

They saw the ship turn and fly toward the village, and their fear mounted.

"They come for vengeance," said one.

"If we go into our huts they cannot see us," suggested another.

That was enough. Instantly the street was deserted, as the Kavuru hid from the vengeance of the dead.

Above the lofty escarpment and the towering cliffs Brown

guided the ship. Below them lay the little valley and the temple of Kavandavanda, plainly visible in the light of the new day.

The pilot cut his motor and shouted to Tarzan. "Not a chance to land there," he said.

Tarzan nodded. "Get more elevation, and tell me when."

Brown opened the throttle and commenced to climb in a great circle. He watched the altimeter. Before they had left the ground he had known the direction of the wind and estimated its force. At two thousand feet he levelled off and circled the rim of the canyon to a point above the cliffs on the windward side.

He cut his motor for an instant and shouted to the apeman. "Stand by!"

Tarzan slipped the catch of his safety belt. Brown brought the ship into position again. "Jump!" he shouted as he brought the ship sharply into a momentary stall.

Tarzan swung onto the lower wing and jumped. An instant later Brown followed him.

31

The Wages of Sin

KAVANDAVANDA'S soft, youthful appearance belied his strength. Jane was no match for him, and though she fought every foot of the way, fought like a young tigress, he dragged her back into his inner apartment.

"I ought to kill you, you she devil," he growled, as he threw her roughly upon the couch; "but I won't. I'll keep you; I'll tame you—and I'll start now." He came toward her, leering.

Just then a pounding sounded on the outer door of the antechamber; and a voice rose in terror, calling "Kavandavanda! Kavandavanda! Save us! Save us!"

The high priest wheeled angrily. "Who dares disturb Kavandavanda?" he demanded. "Get you gone!"

But instead of going, those at the door flung it open and pressed into the antechamber to the very door of the inner room. There were both slaves and warriors in the party. Their very presence there would have told the high priest that something was amiss even without the evidence of their frightened faces.

Now, indeed, was he impressed. "What brings you here?" he demanded.

"The dead men fly; they fly above the village and the temple. They have come seeking vengeance."

"You talk like fools and cowards," grumbled Kavandavanda. "Dead men do not fly."

"But they do fly," insisted a warrior. "The two that we killed yesterday are flying again this instant above the village and the temple. Come out, Kavandavanda, and cast a spell upon them, sending them away."

"I will go and look," said the high priest. "Ydeni, bring this girl along. If I leave her out of my sight, she will find some means to escape."

"She shall not escape me," said Ydeni; and, seizing Jane by the wrist, he dragged her after the high priest, the warriors, and the slaves into the courtyard of the temple.

The moment that they emerged from the building Jane heard plainly the drone of a ship's motor far above them. Looking up, she saw a biplane circling the canyon.

With fascinated eyes the Kavuru were watching it—with fascinated, frightened eyes. Jane, too, was fascinated. She thought that the ship was searching for a landing place; and she prayed that the pilot might not attempt a landing here, for she knew that whoever was in the ship would meet instant death at the hands of the savage Kavuru.

Then she saw a figure leap from the plane. A gasp of terror rose from the Kavuru. The first figure was followed by a second.

"They come!" cried a warrior. "Save us, Kavandavanda, from the vengeance of the dead."

The billowing white chutes opened above the falling figures, checking their speed.

"They have spread their wings," shrieked a slave. "Like the vulture, they will swoop down upon us."

Jane's eyes followed the ship. As the second man jumped, it nosed down, then levelled off by itself, shot across the little canyon, came around in a steep bank, and went into a tail spin almost directly above them.

Brown had opened the throttle wide at the instant that he jumped, for he and Tarzan had planned this very thing, hoping that the ship would crash near enough to the temple to cause a diversion that would enable them to reach the ground before warriors could gather below to receive them on the tips of sharp spears. But they had not anticipated the reality, the fear that gripped the Kavuru at sight of them and the ship.

As they floated gently toward earth, a light wind carried them in the direction of the temple. They saw the crowd gathered in the courtyard looking up at them. They saw the ship diving with wide open throttle at terrific speed. They saw the crowd melt and vanish into the interior of the temple an instant before the plane crashed in the courtyard and burst into flame.

Tarzan touched the ground first and had thrown off the parachute harness by the time Brown was down. A moment later the two men started for the temple at a run.

There was no one to block their way. Even the guards at the outer gate had fled in terror. As they entered the courtyard, a few frightened leopards raced past them. The plane was burning fiercely against the temple wall a hundred feet away.

Tarzan, followed closely by Brown, ran for the main entrance to the building. Even here there was none to dispute their right to enter the sacred precincts.

At a distance they heard the sound of a babel of voices; and, guided by his keen ears, the ape-man hastened along corridors in the direction of these sounds.

In the great throne room of Kavandavanda all the warriors and slaves of the temple were gathered. The high priest, trembling on his throne, was a picture of terror. The girls of the temple, those poor creatures who were awaiting death to give eternal life and youth to the Kavuru, were crouched at one side of the dais, wide-eyed and terrified.

A warrior pushed forward toward the throne. An angry scowl darkened his painted face, made doubly hideous by the ivory skewer that passed through the septum of his nose. Many human teeth lay upon his breast, marks of his prowess as a hunter of girls. He pointed a finger at Kavandavanda.

"Your sins are being visited upon us," he bellowed. "You would have broken your vow. We who prevented Ogdli from taking the white girl last night know this. She bewitched him. She bewitched you. It is she who has brought the dead men upon us. Destroy her. Destroy her now with your own hands that we may be saved."

"Kill her! Kill her!" shrieked a hundred hoarse voices.

"Kill her! Kill her!" shrilled the fat, oily black slaves in their high falsettos.

A couple of warriors seized Jane where she stood among the cowering girls and dragged her to the dais. They raised her roughly and threw her upon it.

Still trembling, Kavandavanda seized her by the hair and dragged her to her knees. From his loin-cloth he drew a long, crude dagger. As he raised it above the heart of the girl a pistol barked from the doorway of the throne room; and Kavandavanda, high priest of the Kavuru, seized his chest and, with a piercing scream, collapsed beside the girl he would have killed.

Jane's eyes shot toward the doorway. "Tarzan!" she cried. "Tarzan of the Apes."

A hundred pairs of other eyes saw him, too—saw him and Brown advancing fearlessly into the room. A warrior raised his spear against them; and this time Brown's gun spoke, and the fellow dropped in his tracks.

Then Tarzan spoke, spoke to them in their own tongue. "We have come for our women," he said. "Let them come away with us in peace, or many will die. You saw how we came. You know we are not as other men. Do not make us angry."

As he spoke, he continued to advance. The Kavuru, hesitating to attack, fearful of these strange creatures that flew down from the sky, that had been dead and were alive again, fell back.

Suddenly Brown saw Annette among the other girls beside the dais. He leaped forward, and the warriors fell aside and let him pass. A great emotion choked the words from his throat as he took the girl in his arms.

The ape-man leaped to the side of his mate. "Come," he said. "We must get out of here before they have time to gather their wits." Then he turned to the girls huddled below. "Is Buira, the daughter of Muviro, here?" he asked.

A young black girl ran forward. "The Big Bwana!" she cried. "At last I am saved."

"Come quickly," commanded the ape-man, "and bring any of the other girls with you who wish to escape."

There was not one who did not wish to leave, and Tarzan and Brown herded them from the throne room and toward the temple entrance; but they had not gone far when they were met by rolling clouds of smoke and heard the crackling of flames ahead.

"The temple is afire!" cried Annette.

"I guess we're in for it," growled Brown. "It caught from the ship. Looks like we're trapped. Does anyone else know a way out?"

"Yes," said Jane. "There is a secret passage leading from the temple to the forest. I know where the entrance is. Come this way." She turned back and they retraced their steps toward the throne room.

Soon they commenced to meet warriors and slaves. These slunk away into side corridors and apartments. Presently they reached the apartments of Kavandavanda. Jane was struck by a sudden thought.

She turned to Brown. "We all risked our lives," she said, "and two of us died in a mad search for the secret of eternal youth. It is in this room. Do you care to take the few seconds it will require to get it?"

"Do I?" exclaimed Brown. "And how! Lead me to it."

In the inner room of the high priest's apartments, Jane pointed out the cabinet. "There is a box in there that contains what you wish, but the key is on the body of Kavandavanda," she explained.

"I got a key right here," said Brown; and, drawing his pistol, he fired a shot into the lock that shattered it; then he opened the cabinet.

"There," said Jane, pointing out the box that contained the pellets.

Brown seized it, and they continued on in search of the tunnel's entrance. But presently Jane paused, hesitant. "I am afraid we have come too far," she said. "I thought I knew just where the tunnel was, but now I am all confused."

"We must find some way out of the temple," said Tarzan. "The fire is spreading rapidly, following closely behind us."

Smoke was already rolling down upon them in stifling volume. They could hear the ominous roaring of the flames, the crash of falling timbers as portions of the roof fell in, the shouts and screams of the inmates of the temple.

A warrior, choking and half blinded, stumbled into view from the dense smoke that filled the corridor along which they had come. Before the man could gather his faculties, Tarzan seized him.

"Lead us out of here," he commanded. "That is the price of your life."

When the fellow was able to open his eyes he looked at his captor. "Tarzan of the Apes!" he exclaimed.

"Ydeni," said the ape-man. "I did not recognize you at first."

"And you wish me to lead you out of the temple? You who have slain Kavandavanda, our high priest?"

"Yes," replied Tarzan.

"If I show you the way through the village you will all

be killed. The warriors of Kavuru are recovering from their first fright. They will never let you pass. I could lead you that way and let you be killed; but once you saved my life. Now, I shall give you yours. Follow me."

He led the party a short distance down a side corridor and turned into a gloomy apartment. Crossing it, he pushed open a door beyond which was utter darkness.

"This tunnel leads out into the forest," he said. "Go your way, Tarzan of the Apes, nor return again to the village of the Kavuru."

*　　　*　　　*

Three weeks later a party of six was gathered before a roaring fire in the living room of Tarzan's bungalow far from the savage village of the Kavuru. The Lord of the Jungle was there, and his mate; Brown and Annette sat upon a lion's skin before the hearth, holding hands; Tibbs sat decorously on the edge of a chair in the background. He had not yet become accustomed to sitting on terms of equality with titled personages. Little Nkima, with far greater poise, perched upon the shoulder of a viscount.

"What are we goin' to do with this box of pills?" demanded Brown.

"Whatever you wish," said Jane. "You were willing to risk your life to get them. If I recall correctly, I think you said something to the effect that if you had them back in civilization they would make you 'lousy' with money. Keep them."

"No," replied the American. "We all risked our lives, and anyway you were the one that really got them. The more I think of it, the less I like my scheme. Most everybody lives too long anyway for the good of the world—most of 'em ought to have died young. Suppose Congress got hold of 'em? —just think of that! Not on your life.

"I'll tell you what we'll do. We'll divide them. There will be five of us that will live forever."

"And be beautiful always," added Annette.

"If you will pardon my saying so, Miss," observed Tibbs with an apologetic cough, "I should rawther dislike thinking of pressing trousers for so many years; and as for being beautiful—my word! I'd never get a job. Who ever heard of a beautiful valet?"

"Well, we'll divide 'em anyway," insisted Brown. "You don't have to take 'em, but be sure you don't sell none of 'em to no cab driver princes. Here, I'll divide 'em into five equal parts."

"Aren't you forgetting Nkima?" asked Jane, smiling.

"That's right," said Brown. "We'll make it six parts. He's sure a lot more use in the world than most people."